SHINING TARGET

DAVID ELLIOTT

DEDICATION

To Gabrielle, who makes every day, and especially the nights, "Happily-Ever-After."

ACKNOWLEDGMENTS

Thank you Todd Goldberg, Christine Sneed, Lynn Hightower, Robert M. Eversz, Taia Perry and Cynthia Martinez. My additional gratitude goes to every classmate and friend who read all or portions of this work, for all of your critiques and encouragement.

CHAPTER 1

The day my "happily-ever-after" ended began like a lot of other days - with a giant African-American trying to kick the crap out of me.

His name was Will McCoy. He attacked me relentlessly with a thickly muscled body dark as basalt, and a fighting style that earned him the nickname of "The Bull." Throwing his tight hooks to the body, interspersed with roundhouse kicks aimed at my thighs and knees, he was trying to lower my guard so that he could drop me with an overhand right.

Though we now sparred in a custom gym built next to my new home in the Hollywood hills, The Bull still took the same pleasure from trying to punish me now, as he did in a Colombian jungle camp when I first assumed command of his A-Team in the 7th Special Forces Group.

"As your Operations Sergeant," he'd told me that first morning he woke me before dawn, "it's my job to make sure the Captain's fit enough to keep from getting us killed - Sir."

I'm a little taller than Will and a lot lighter. My jabs peppered his head and I slipped to the side of his charges, countering with combinations of punches and kicks that weren't as effective as I would have liked them to be; I felt tired, a step slower than usual.

The Bull's blows made crisp thwacking sounds as they started to land more often. We were encased in headgear, padded gloves, shin and foot protection, but that only dulled the pain of a good shot.

I tried not to show relief when the buzzer signaled the end to our third, three-minute round.

"Two more to go." The Bull grinned.

"Just remember what happened to George Foreman when he got cocky with Ali," I said, gulping air as we paced around the ring waiting for the buzzer to end the rest period.

"That wasn't so bad after three weeks of tequila, greasy enchiladas, and four hours sleep," The Bull said. "You're just feeling the stress let down after worrying about shit twenty-four seven, boss man."

My name is Richard Braddock. I own Star Shield Security Group; The Bull is my Chief Operations Officer. We'd flown back just the night before from Mexico, where we'd been providing protection for Lauren Hunter while she was on location filming a movie currently titled *Forced Conclusions*. In addition to guarding against the physical dangers any celebrity is at risk of in a third-world country, we'd been working around the clock keeping the paparazzi from stealing photos Lauren didn't want them to take. A lot of the big name shutter-scum flew down in search of the unflattering bikini shot or worse. They were buying the local kids cameras, and promising them a year's wages for a good shot. The young caballeros were climbing fifty-foot palm trees, digging tunnels under the walls of the hotel, inventing new ways every day to make the five-man team I was leading earn our money.

That morning though, with Lauren finishing her movie in town and there no identified threats existing, she was only assigned one guard, Dale Irvin, just to insure no one bothered her on the way to and from Paragon studios, where she would be insulated from any annoyances requiring a larger team. The Bull and I were looking forward to some overdue R & R, before the awards season ramped up and demanded all our attention.

Just after the buzzer started our fourth round, the gym door burst open and my wife, Victoria, blew in wearing a terrycloth robe with a towel wrapped in a makeshift turban on her head. She had to shout to be heard over the *Public Enemy*, which we'd been blasting as the soundtrack for our sparring session.

"Did someone forget to take their cell phone off vibrate? Your office just called the house in a panic trying to find you."

I looked over at my iPhone, which had danced itself off the table.

"Morning Vic," Bull said.

She blew him a kiss, and then turned to me, "Though I think you look really hot all savage and sweaty like that, don't forget we need to meet the realtor at 8:00."

She smacked my butt, padded out the door, and ran gracefully over the flagstone walkway to our house. The Bull turned down the music while I took off my boxing gloves and dialed the office to find out what was so urgent.

After listening to my side of the conversation for a minute, The Bull turned off the buzzer that timed our rounds.

"What's going on?" he asked, when I hung up.

"Lauren Hunter didn't show up for her six a.m. make-up call. Producer's coming unglued. Dale Irvin checked out an Escalade from the office around zero-four-thirty to pick her up in, but we've heard nothing from him since."

"Did she get picked up?"

"Her security cameras show them getting in the Escalade shortly after five and driving out the gate. No one's called her house yet, because they don't want to cause a panic."

"What about the GPS on the Escalade, or their phones?"

"No hits on either one," I said, starting to remove my fighting gear.

The Paparazzi, or "rats," as we like to call them, will pay big money for the code to a navigation system or a phone number that could be tracked by GPS, if it's linked to a hot star. Everything is for sale in Hollywood. If one of our people is trying to shake a pack of those so-called journalists they'll shut down anything that might be broadcasting a compromised signal.

There were plenty of times when our clients would to go off the radar, so that there wouldn't be a record of where they were going or what they were doing. But the assigned guard was supposed to text a message to dispatch before they went silent.

"Maybe he signaled in but was out of range?" The Bull said. Velcro screeched as he removed his padding also. "Service in Malibu is sketchy."

"Why would he go silent though? No rat is going to get up before noon to get a shot of her being driven to work."

4

The Bull shrugged. "What if she was bringing Mika with her?"

"Maybe," I said.

Babysitting movie stars, rich foreigners, and high-dollar executives, has made us a lot of money. Lauren Hunter is one of our biggest single sources of income because she doesn't want her audience to know she's gay. If a successful leading lady or man comes out, it could cut their box office by at least 30%. Along with all the other privacy issues that celebrities hire us to protect, our job-one with Lauren was to ensure that no rat could ever gather any evidence to verify the rumors. I started working for her as a free-lance operator when she first became famous, and have protected her secret for over ten years. Her referrals created the operation we run now, with over fifty people on the payroll.

"Dispatch is monitoring the scanners, in case they had an accident," I said. "But so far there's nothing from the CHP, Sheriff, or LAPD, involving an Escalade. Dispatch even got Mike Crawford out of bed to drive to Malibu, and check the canyon between her house and PCH, to see if maybe they ran off the side of the road."

"I'll bet he was happy about that," The Bull said.

Mike Crawford was a retired Military Police NCO, who filled out his pension doing sub-contract work for us. He was fond of saying that the best part of being retired was sleeping through morning reveille.

My next call was to Barry Sheldon, the producer of the movie our missing client was working on.

He answered the phone with, "Who's this?"

"Braddock."

"Nice of you to finally call," Sheldon said. "Where the hell is my actress?"

"We're doing everything to get a situation report from her bodyguard," I said.

"Meanwhile, I have an entire film crew standing around here waiting for her, and it's costing me thirty thousand dollars an hour. Which won't be so funny when I deduct it from your fees."

Producers scream at me regularly. It was true, Paragon studios were writing the checks for our services, but only because of a clause in Lauren's contract to pay us as part of her compensation.

If Lauren Hunter had instructed her guard, Dale Irvin, not to take her to work, the studio couldn't hold me responsible. Our employees are only authorized to disobey clients if the request places someone in physical jeopardy. Lauren Hunter was still the boss, even though the studio was footing the bill on her behalf. Part of my job was taking the heat for our client's misbehavior.

"I want her real home and cell numbers." Sheldon continued shouting, "Not the ones that go to a machine she never listens to."

"Why? You think she'd pick up?"

"I want to make sure your guy didn't oversleep."

"Believe me, she'd be calling you if he had," I said. "You've got all the numbers she wants you to have."

"Maybe I'll have our attorney talk to you, smartass. Getting her to work on time is part of the security we're paying for."

"Her wellbeing is what she's hired me for, and whenever we give you guys a direct number it leaks out of your office in thirty minutes."

"I've never leaked anything, so don't 'you guys' me," Sheldon said. "I'm holding you personally responsible."

"Got that. I'll call you when our man checks in."

"It'd better be soon," Sheldon said, before the line went dead.

"Not a happy camper?" The Bull said.

He'd placed our gloves and pads in their spots on a drying rack, so we walked outside into the dewy morning air, where the view of Los Angeles waking up was a misty spectacle spread out before us.

"Lauren probably decided she just couldn't go to work without first having an herbal latte that they only make at a special place in Ojai," The Bull said. I followed him towards his Land Rover parked in my driveway. "She ordered Dale to go silent because she didn't want to hear any flack about it until she gets to the studio."

I shook my head. "So much for a day off."

"Hey man, just let me handle it? I know you and Vic have plans."

"Oh, and Bonnie won't blow a gasket if you have to work today?"

"All I was going to do was build a skateboard ramp for the boys, and she's sure they're going to crack their heads open with that shit, so the longer that goes undone, the happier she'll be. It won't be a problem for me to drop into the office and put out the fires." He pushed me towards my house. "You go spend time with your wife, I'll call you when it's all sorted out. Then you can call Barry Sheldon and do the ass kissing, which is all you're good for anyway."

I waved gratefully as he drove off the property. Our house sat on the ridge separating the Los Angeles basin from the San Fernando Valley. In the distance I could see the morning haze covering downtown LA with a sepia diffusion, which made the taller buildings look as though they were jagged rock pinnacles, jutting out of an uninviting mystical sea.

CHAPTER 2

Before heading into the house I stared at the city for a moment, trying to convince myself that my friend was right and this was just another case of a temperamental actress exerting her power. Except Lauren was older now, not the wild child anymore, she was deathly afraid of her star being doused by one of the talented ingénues that flooded into Hollywood every day. I knew she was tired and cranky from the traveling, from the long shooting hours, and the hounding of the paparazzi. She was also testier than usual, because her girlfriend Mika left Mexico a week early. They'd gotten into a snarling spitting argument because Lauren refused to give in to Mika's begging for her to come out, so they didn't have to continually sneak around pretending Mika was just her personal assistant.

When we were flying home on Paragon's G5 the day before, I'd reviewed Lauren's guard schedule with her, explaining that I was going to take the next week off to spend time with my wife. She'd said, "I remember when I had you all to myself Richard, now I'm just another pretty face you need to take care of. It's not fair, if I have to work, you should too." I'd taken her mock petulance as a joke, though often, nasty truths are masked with humor. Lauren was more than a client; she was also a close friend who I'd spent less time with since meeting my wife. It was possible Lauren was acting out because she was feeling abandoned.

What I hadn't confided to Lauren was that I was having troubles of my own.

Victoria performed as a featured dancer for the Joffrey Ballet, until she tore her Achilles tendon. Not just a little bit, but entirely off the bone, landing from a leap during the finale of Prokofiev's Romeo and Juliet.

I thought it would devastate her, but she just tossed it off, saying, "To everything there is a season."

But it wasn't that simple. Until that time, our relationship consisted of infrequent rendezvous in crazy and often exotic places. We only met occasionally in our LA condo, whenever there were a few hours or days when our schedules permitted us some brief time together. We would talk about the mundane pleasures of one day settling down together, like normal people fantasize about going to Tahiti.

As soon as she could hobble around on crutches she focused all her energy into "making us a nest," as she called it. She found us a house on a promontory of the Coldwater Canyon that had been tied up in a probate battle for years, with nobody living in it except mice, owls, and the occasional homeless person. She supervised the remodel and new construction with all of the passion and precision that made her so amazing to watch on stage.

We'd moved in six months ago, and ever since, I'd developed the feeling that somehow I was losing her. The reality of playing house and waiting for me to come home seemed to be driving Victoria slowly crazy. She'd become listless, moody, she stopped seeing her friends and our sex-life fell into a downward spiral. I suggested she start teaching, or choreographing, getting back into the dance world somehow, but she would only say that she wasn't ready.

Then, while I was in Mexico, Victoria told me she'd decided to open her own dance studio. She started researching properties and business plans. She asked me if I could take this week off, so we could enjoy a little road trip to the wine country and have some time together before she launched into the project.

The exuberant woman I came home to the night before, who was so excited she couldn't wait until the morning when she could show me the studio she'd found, reminded me of the woman I'd fallen for. She seemed more eager to get our clothes off than I was, and we made love like it was something we were just inventing.

I was supposed to accompany Victoria to sign the lease for her studio, and then after lunch we were going to head up the coast to a bed and breakfast in Los Olivos, the first stop of our vacation. Anticipating an evening of rare, delicious food, and Victoria in a four-poster bed, encouraged me to forget about what was going on with Lauren and let The Bull deal with the situation.

Victoria was in her dressing room blow-drying her hair. I stripped out of my sweaty clothes and showered quickly.

I dressed in Ralph Lauren jeans and a white oxford shirt. My phone rang when I was pulling a black blazer off the hanger. I expected it to be The Bull, reporting that Dale had called in with a sit-rep, but the screen showed Barry Sheldon's number.

"Well we know where your client is, do you?" Sheldon said.

"No." I felt queasy.

"Be in Rikki Wymen's office in forty-five minutes," Sheldon said.

"Barry, you're kidding me, what's going on?" Rikki Wymen was the head of Paragon Studios.

"You'll find out in forty-five minutes."

"Come on, that's bullshit."

"Maybe you should've given me the numbers I wanted, huh pal?" he said before the line went dead.

I removed my Kar .40 caliber automatic and holster from the gun safe, checked the clip filled with hollow points, checked the chambered round, and then placed it in the holster that clipped on my belt, resting the weapon in the center of my back.

I knocked on Victoria's dressing room door, and heard, "Come in sweetie." Her bathroom was upholstered and appointed in various shades of peach. She was sitting poised at the built-in vanity table applying makeup. Her blonde hair was plaited into an intricate French braid, back straight and smooth as porcelain, while her delicate hands deftly whisked her cheek with a brush, causing her compact, alabaster breasts, to dance jauntily with their reflection in the mirror.

"Hey babe," she said smiling.

I took a breath. "Sweetheart, I can't go with you right away, I'm going to have to meet you at your new studio."

I might as well have hit her with a sledgehammer.

"What's going on?"

"I don't know. Rikki Wyman just called me to her office."

"Can't Bull go?"

I explained who Rikki Wyman was. "Honey, in all the years I've been doing this, I've never been summoned by a studio head before. If I send someone else it would be an insult."

"Then I guess you can't do that."

"Lauren didn't show up for work this morning, they have a handle on her - we don't, and they're pissed."

She looked at herself in the mirror and nodded as if she were answering a question. "Should I cancel our reservations for tonight?"

"No. I probably just have to go down there, grovel, kiss the ring and make some fee concessions. As soon as I'm done I'll shoot over to your new place."

She stood up. I expected an explosion, but instead she offered a smile of disappointment.

"I know you wouldn't go if you didn't have to. I just wish you didn't have to." Then she swept past me, leaving me alone with her scent from Hermés.

I followed into her dressing closet, thirty feet of hanging garments, racks of shoes, drawers, and full-length mirrors. She stood at the opposite end in front of a fluted glass window; sliding her beautifully muscular legs into a pair of silk and lace tap pants. With half her frame eclipsed in shadow from the morning sun, I felt like I was inside a Helmut Newton photograph.

I wanted to grab her, crush her to me, and haul her back from across the chasm that I felt rupturing between us. Instead I said, "Honey, we will be out of here tonight, I promise. And I'm dying to see your new studio, I just need a couple of hours, okay?"

"Just call me when you're done," she said. "Maybe I'll take the realtor out to breakfast." I could see her struggling to hide her hurt and disappointment, as she walked over to me, and briefly touched my lips with hers.

Then I did pull her close, but her protectively tense muscles didn't yield to my embrace.

CHAPTER 3

Coldwater Canyon Drive is the main artery that winds through the Hollywood Hills, providing access from my house to the Los Angeles basin or the San Fernando Valley. Normally, I enjoyed the drive down into LA on this winding boulevard, bordered by sumptuous homes and planted with lavish greenery. In many places Oak and Willow trees, old by local standards, lined the parkway on either side, making the area feel more like other parts of the country, before a twist in the road would change the scenery to a row of giant palms and high-end architecture iconic to Beverly Hills. That morning I was only concerned with accelerating my restored 1968 Shelby GT 500 Mustang whenever possible, passing whomever I could, and running freshly red lights. I ignored the middle fingers flashed in my direction and the dirty looks the glossy black car received. I knew I was driving like a jerk.

I called The Bull, who was just getting to the office, and told him about Sheldon's call.

"If she's at Paragon, why hasn't Dale answered his phone, or called in?" he said. "It doesn't make sense."

"Somehow we've screwed the pooch here. Could Dale have flaked on us somehow? Did anyone see him this morning? Was he drunk or something? Find out. And let's make sure we didn't miss a call from Lauren or Mika, if he didn't show."

"Did you check your cell?" he asked me, "Could Lauren be one of the calls you missed when we were working out?"

I scrolled through my missed calls as best I could, while I tore through the morning traffic on Sunset Boulevard, but there weren't any numbers from the morning other than our office and Barry Sheldon. "If Dale didn't show, perhaps she just called the studio and had them send a driver. She'd be ripping mad, and might throw us to the wolves. Just in case though, pull her file, check the fan-mail review, comb through her watch-list, see if there's any indication of a threat or a nuisance that we could have missed."

The Bull assured me that he'd already alerted Marianna Ruiz, the head of our investigations department, to request she do just that. I hung up, and concentrated on driving.

It normally takes forty-five minutes to make it from my house to the studio in Hollywood during rush hour. I roared up to the giant arches that formed the entrance to Paragon twenty-seven minutes after leaving my driveway. Because of our many clients working in the film industry, I had an access badge for each of the major studios that buzzed me past the security gate.

To navigate from parking to the Administration Building, one has to take a circuitous route through the back lot, which even on a good day is a surreal experience. Actors made up as aliens in green, red, and purple rubber suits, with insect-like prosthetic heads, stood outside one soundstage casually smoking cigarettes. Electric carts of various shapes and sizes, each customized to carry wardrobe, lighting equipment, or pieces of scenery, zoomed back and forth. I passed crewmembers lounging on the lift gate of a semi trailer next to blood-spattered stunt dummies, and a guy painting the sprinkles on an eight-foot tall Styrofoam doughnut. Everywhere people walked at a brisk pace, talking rapidly to each other, or into cell phones and radios.

Rikki Wymen's office was perched on the top floor of the Executive Building. The elevator opened into a vast reception area that contained desks for Rikki's three assistants, one who greeted me with the admonishment of, "She's waiting for you."

He hustled me into a large Art Deco room, painted in lavender with cream trim. A wall of windows overlooked the entire lot. Paintings, which appeared to be originals of Gustaf Klimpt, adorned the walls, but they were probably reproductions painted by a scenic artist for one of Paragon's films. Several Oscar statuettes were placed casually around the room on the coffee tables and in the bookcases.

Barry Sheldon sat on a beige calfskin couch. His hawkish face was dominated by a sharp nose and dark mustache; it was framed by straight black hair showing streaks of gray. He wore jeans, a striped button-down shirt, and loafers with no socks. His left leg jiggled up and down nervously at an impressive rate, while he regarded me like something distasteful he'd found in the cream cheese of his bagel.

A striking African-American woman, with tight cropped hair, steel framed glasses, and dressed in a light gray business suit, sat at attention in one of the black lacquered guest chairs. A thin leather portfolio lay closed in her lap. The glistening of perspiration on the tiny hairs above her lip and at her temples was the only indication that she might be under stress.

Rikki Wyman lounged behind a chrome and onyx desk the size of a dining room table, wearing a white Versace suit with a navy blue silk blouse. Her brunette hair fell just below her shoulders on each side of an aquiline face. "Well, you're a handsome bastard aren't you," she said.

I'd heard she used her sexuality in whatever way would throw you off guard. "That's quite a compliment coming from such a beautiful woman," I countered.

"Yeah, well I'm up to my ass in charming men darling, why don't you know where your client is?"

Before I could craft an answer, Rikki said, "Barry," and waved her hand.

Sheldon pulled himself off the couch, and walked over to me with a couple of sheets of paper. He thrust them into my hands.

They were email printouts. The first page read:

From: <86521@brkndrms.com.>

To: Barry Sheldon <Barry_Sheldon@paragonpix.com >

Sent: Tuesday, January 15, 2009 7:13 AM

Subject: Re: Missing property

Mr. Sheldon,

Miss Hunter will not be showing up for work today. Please see attached photograph.

Retrieving her can be a quick and painless business transaction. Consolidate ten million dollars in one account, and prepare it for wire transfer. We'll give you 24 hours to accomplish this before we provide you with further instructions.

Should you consider contacting law enforcement of any kind, we'll know, and the price of the exchange will increase to 50 million dollars. It will become a much riskier affair for all parties involved, and we will make sure the media is informed.

We're sure you don't want to be known as the man who risked Lauren Hunter's safe return over a mere ten million.

The second page was a picture of Lauren Hunter gagged and handcuffed in front of a black background, with the front page of this morning's *Los Angeles Times* taped to her chest. Someone was standing behind her, but the only part of the person visible were a pair of meaty hands and forearms, taut with the effort of holding her still in the chair.

I noted the vein in Lauren's neck bulging the way it did when she was angered. But the most piercing part of the image was the expression in her eyes.

Lauren was a woman who irritated me constantly, often acting like an overly indulged child, who on several occasions treated me, or people I cared about, so badly that I'd thought of spanking her. But she was also someone I loved deeply, in the confusing, frustrating, yet visceral way that is usually reserved for family members. Despite all her antics, she always did the right thing when it really mattered. She also trusted me with the things that only loved ones should share.

I could see that in the moment the photograph was taken, she was probably feeling similar to when her brother and his friends held her down and raped her, in the damp musty leaves of a forest, years ago.

Missing from the image was any sign of her guard, Dale Irvin; a bear of a man who's first son was only three months old. I thought - *If he were alive, he would have been in the picture - unless those were his hands holding her down...*

"Is this the only communication you've received?" I said.

"Yes," Rikki Wymen answered. "And what I want to know, is why her high priced bodyguard didn't prevent it?"

I looked down at the piece of paper in my hand. "This message was posted at 7:13 A.M., which means that in less than two hours her captors abducted two people and a car, without attracting attention, then secured them well enough to photograph Lauren and send this message. I doubt this is from a crazed fan with a box-cutter. It seems like the work of professionals who knew the target was protected and created a sufficient tactic to subdue him."

"But isn't he supposed to be prepared for something like this?" Rikki said.

"Even the best people make mistakes," I said. "Otherwise, wouldn't every movie you made be a success?"

That forced a smirk out of her.

"Have you done anything about this?" I said, referring to the ransom note.

"We're getting the money together." Rikki waved her hand at the African American woman, "This is Tawny Campbell from legal."

"Mr. Braddock, I'm sure you'll appreciate that we're all open to liability however we proceed," the attorney said, with the hint of a West Indies accent. "If we don't inform the authorities and Miss Hunter is harmed or killed, a case could be made for negligence.

On the other hand, if we do inform law enforcement a similar argument could be made, because the note specifically warns against it."

"Either way, it's a nightmare," Rikki said. "Sit down," she commanded me. "I was looking at your company's brochure, your bio says you had hostage rescue experience in the military."

"That's true," I said, remaining standing.

"So, I'm sure you will want to attempt to rescue Ms. Hunter?"

"Well," I glanced at the attorney, "the FBI have the most experience, manpower and technology, when it comes to handling kidnappings." I wasn't sure where she was trying to lead me, but I was certain that I needed to be careful about anything I said.

"And suppose the kidnappers find out?" Rikki raised her eyebrows. "Then we've pissed them off. Who knows what they'll do to Lauren, and it could end up costing me five times as much." She caught herself fidgeting with her hair and stopped. "I mean, what're the chances of rescuing Lauren from these assholes anyway? Does that ever happen in real life?"

"I doubt the FBI would try to rescue her," I said. "But the chances of catching the kidnappers later would increase."

"So maybe we should pay the ten million, and call the FBI when we get her back?" Rikki leaned forward, placing her arms on the desk.

"That's a good plan if she's returned," I said.

"Why wouldn't they give her back if we pay the ransom?" Sheldon said.

"Unless you can gain some leverage, control the hostage exchange, very often kidnappers will continue to milk an account until it's dry. Also, she's a liability," I said. "She'll have microscopic forensic evidence on her. She might be able to identify them. Or, the ransom may be a ruse for how they actually want to exploit her."

"Do you mean sexually?" Sheldon asked.

"I was thinking more of a social or political agenda," I said.

"We relied upon your company to keep her safe," Sheldon moved to the side of Rikki's desk. "Would it be wise for us to contact the FBI on your recommendation when Lauren's captors have specifically warned against it?"

"I haven't made a recommendation."

The attorney leaned forward. "How much would it increase Lauren's chances for survival if we brought in the FBI?"

"I don't know," I said.

Rikki made a steeple of her fingers, and stared at me over them. Her plastic surgeon was extremely talented, but her hands betrayed the work that had preserved her face. "You see Mr. Braddock, whether they knew it or not, the people who did this have put us in a very bad position," she said. "Mr. Sheldon informs me that he can't finish his movie without Ms. Hunter. And as you may know, we've invested so much in the project already, that to scrap it now might put the entire studio in jeopardy, not to mention all of our futures."

"We were thinking you would have a vested concern in keeping this quiet also," the attorney said. "I'm sure Star Shield Group doesn't want to be known as the company that allowed Lauren Hunter to be kidnapped…"

I looked Rikki in the eyes. "So what's the deal?"

The attorney opened her portfolio, and handed me a letter printed on the studio's letterhead. "We are requesting that you cease and desist from any activity that would interfere with the safe return of Miss Hunter, including but not limited to, contacting any form of law enforcement, or any other action by you, your company, or any associate, which might be inferred as prejudicial."

I rolled the copy of the ransom note and the letter into a tube. "Okay, I'll have my attorney review this."

"You don't strike me as a stupid man Mr. Braddock. If things go smoothly we can handle this quietly with your insurance company," Rikki said. "We're preparing a story that Miss Hunter is unhappy with the final scenes of the picture and is holding out for re-writes. We hope you will support that story, and encourage Miss Hunter's friends and family to do the same, for her benefit."

"You're very thorough," I said.

"I hope you find that instructive." Rikki narrowed her eyes.

There were several things I considered replying with, but refrained.

"Of course we'll also have to restrict all access by you, or your company, to the studio and any of its employees, until this matter is resolved," the beautiful attorney said, adding a hopeful smile.

"Of course."

"And could we please have that copy of the correspondence from Ms. Hunter's captors?" she added politely.

"No," I said on my way to the door. "I'd like to keep it."

CHAPTER 4

Two uniformed studio security guards were waiting for me in the reception area outside Rikki Wymen's office. One was a fit Asian with a shaved head in his mid-thirties. The other was a white guy in his twenties who looked like he was doing security because he hadn't made the cut as an NFL lineman. He was trying to act casual, but his baton was gripped in his right hand tightly.

"Sir, we need to ask you for your ID badge, and escort you to your car," the Asian said.

They were both braced for a confrontation, but relaxed a little when I smiled.

"I know guys, you're just doing your job," I said, digging in my wallet, producing the plastic badge.

As we waited for the elevator, I heard one of Rikki's assistants say into his headset, "I have Security for you Ms. Wyman."

Several moments afterward, a soft chime announced the arrival of the elevator. At the same time, the Asian guard's radio squawked, "Dispatch to Seventeen."

He acknowledged the call as we stepped into the car, and the big guy hit the lobby button.

The dispatcher's voice on the radio blared in the small space while the doors closed. "The gentleman you're escorting has a document that is Paragon property. We need him to surrender that before he leaves."

I felt the big guy tense up again on my right, and he maneuvered his baton a little more forward. The Asian said, "Roger that," and looked at me with questioning eyes.

"They probably mean this," I said, showing them the attorney's letter and the ransom email, which were rolled into a tube. "Here," I thrust the role in front of the Asian, and released it.

As the tube unraveled and the papers slid from my hand towards the floor, the two guards leaned forward instinctually to catch them. I bent my knees, like I too was going after the fluttering pages, but then I twisted to my left, and sprung up, driving the fist of my right hand into the Asian's solar plexus with all the power of my legs behind the punch. He crumpled in that special way the body does when it's nerve ganglia are traumatized while I spun back towards the big man.

There wasn't any room in the cramped space for him to swing his baton, so he grabbed a hunk of my jacket with his left hand. Like most men who intimidate with their size he volunteered position, allowing me to windmill my right arm over his left, where I could get enough leverage for an arm-bar that exerted reverse pressure on his elbow; giving him the choice between getting pressed into the wall of the elevator cab, or having his arm snapped in half.

"Drop the baton," I commanded - releasing pressure on the elbow for a second -before driving the point of my kneecap into the tendons behind his left knee joint. His leg gave way, he let out an involuntary cry, the baton clattered to the floor of the cab, and I increased the pressure on his elbow to get better control of his thick wrist so I could drive his head down to the floor in the corner of the elevator. Once I had him in full control position, I was able to free my right hand and unsnap the flap of the handcuff pouch, clipped to the back of his belt. I removed the bracelets, and ordered him to let me cuff his right hand while I maintained pressure to the left elbow.

The elevator door opened, as I was closing the second handcuff on the left wrist of the big guard. The Asian was still struggling to draw air into his lungs, so it only took me a few more moments to secure him in his handcuffs, take their radios, and pick up the papers I'd dropped.

A young man, who looked fresh out of college, was waiting in the lobby for the elevator holding a cardboard banker's box. He watched me with a confused look on his face. I pressed the elevator button back to the top floor, and as the doors closed on the two manacled security men, I told him he would have to take the next car.

I was sorry to have tangled with those two guys. If they hadn't been instructed to retrieve the ransom email, I probably would have gone peaceably, but I needed the information on that paper. I used a computer contractor who could have hacked it out of Barry Sheldon's email account, but I didn't want him to waste the time that could be applied towards finding out where the message originated. There was also someone I wanted to see on the lot before I left, which probably conflicted with the guard's idea of escorting me to my car.

The fact that I was very angry might have had something to do with their misfortunes also.

I was angry at whomever had abducted Lauren.

I was angry at whomever had provided the abductors inside information, because I didn't believe it was a coincidence that she was snatched at the exact moment when she and the studio were most vulnerable.

I was angry with myself, because I hadn't been able to see an attack coming or prevent it.

And I was angry with those smug Paragon executives, who seemed more concerned with their liability than anything else.

The FBI had the National Criminal Information Center, which was the best central database of criminal activity. They had a computer tech unit with access to super computers that could analyze huge amounts of data, searching the web for the computer that sent the ransom email. They had hostage negotiation and rescue specialists. They had as many weapons as an aircraft carrier, and were just as quick and easy to maneuver. Also, the Feds were filled with too many hotshots who would see this as a ticket to a Directorship, and the Bureau leaked like a sieve. Federal agents had to follow procedure and obey the law; Lauren didn't have time for that. Until I found out who was ratting us out, I wasn't going to risk pissing off the kidnappers by involving the Feds. Neither was I going to be hampered by procedure or worry about breaking the law if it would help Lauren.

I made my way through the labyrinth of sound stages and support buildings comprising the Paragon backlot, using the guard's radio to monitor and elude anyone that looked like security. I tried my wife's cell phone, but only reached her voice mail. I didn't tell her that our vacation was going to have to wait, I just asked her to call me.

Then I called The Bull. I brought him up to speed and told him to start assembling a reaction team. "Only the core group," I said, "Get with Marianna to help you move shifts around, but this has to be only the inner circle. We have to look at the possibility that we got sold out by one of our own."

"Man, I can't believe that," The Bull said.

"Me either, but we'd be stupid to ignore the possibility."

"True that."

"I've got to see someone here, then afterwards I need to get out to Lauren's house to deal with her people. Have Marianna rent me a chopper. They can pick me up on the roof of the office at ten hundred hours. I'll meet with the team at eleven-thirty."

"I'll make it happen," he said.

When I reached the base camp of *Forced Conclusions*, the complex of trucks and trailers that housed all the people, equipment, and services needed to shoot a movie, I found a young Production Assistant. I asked her to call on the radio to get the location of Jeff Goodwin, the First Assistant Director.

She guided me to the mouth of Stage 14, where the huge "elephant doors" stood wide open. Inside the cavernous building people were engaged in organized chaos. Loud, beeping warning signals, blared from mobile basket lifts, which contained men hanging bright green screen material from floor to ceiling around the perimeter of the shooting area. The shell of a helicopter was hanging suspended from a crane, over a giant steel gimbal mechanism, which had hoses running like octopus tentacles away from it in every direction. Painters applied vinyl letters to the tail of the chopper. Special Effects technicians shouted over the din at one another while they prepared to connect the chopper to the gimbal contraption that would rock it in simulation of flight. Along the run of green curtain, ten-kilowatt lights were being lifted to the beams and catwalks sixty feet above the stage floor, known as the "grid" or the "perms."

Jeff Goodwin, the plump disheveled First Assistant Director known as "Goody," stood with two other men, who I recognized as the Production Designer and the Special Effects Supervisor.

Goody saw me approaching and hailed me with, "Your girl is killing us man!"

"It's not your big ass that's going to be up on that screen forty feet wide for every critic in the world to take their shot at," I responded.

"I could suffer that pain for twelve million," the Production Designer said, not taking his eyes off the painters working on the helicopter.

"She just wants to make sure someone else will be willing to pay her rate again," I said.

"So that she'll pay your rate, right?" the FX guy said.

"If you see stupid stamped on my forehead, let me know," I said.

The Production Designer started shouting at the painter, "You're not following the layout, it's getting crooked."

"They keep moving it," the painter complained, nodding in the direction of the Special Effects technicians.

The two department heads started to argue over who had priority.

"Can we step outside?" I asked Goody.

I became familiar with most of the department heads when I was on the set with Lauren filming in Mexico. But I dealt with Goody on a daily basis, since he was the man in charge of the production's schedule and needs regarding Lauren. In addition, I got a phone call one Sunday morning at 3:00 a.m., after Goody had partaken of more goods and services at the local brothel than he had cash to pay for. He couldn't use his credit or debit card, because his wife took care of all the bills. I paid off the club owner, and allowed Goody to pay me back over time out of his cash per diem. I'd like to think it was because I'm a great guy, but I knew what I was buying.

We walked outside where we could talk without shouting over the din, or be overheard.

"So what's really going on?" Goody said.

I quickly told him the chain of events.

"Rikki's just looking to make you the scapegoat," he mused.

"Either that, or she's already called the FBI and they told her to ditch me."

"What?"

"Do you know someone from Legal named Kinsey Larsen?"

"I don't deal with those people too often. Why would the FBI want her to fire you?"

"I'm a suspect, my people are suspect, and maybe the Feds don't want their involvement leaked? Just because you're paranoid, doesn't mean someone's not out to get you."

Goody laughed.

"I need you to let me know if there are any new people snooping around."

"Will do," Goody said.

"Also, get it out there that I've been let go. But be subtle. If there's a mole in the production, I want them to get that information."

My IPhone buzzed, and I saw that it was Mike Crawford. I said, "I've got to take this."

Goody said, "Go," and I answered the phone.

"Boss, Marianna Ruiz dispatched me to check out the canyon road between PCH and the client's house."

"Yes?" I said.

"There were some skid marks on the gravel shoulder, but no other sign of a wreck. I kept nosing around and found two shell casings with no oxidation on them about 30 feet up the road from those skid marks. Have you made contact with the client?"

"No Mike, what caliber?" I asked.

"Forty, Smith and Wesson auto."

It was a NATO round that was the standard issue for Star Shield side arms. "Anything else?"

"Looks like several vehicles were on the shoulder in the last twenty four hours, but I'm no forensics guy."

"Can you canvas the area? If there was shooting someone must have heard it."

"This is a part of the canyon where there aren't any houses near-by and I found the casings at the apex of a curve, so that you can only see it from a few hundred yards in either direction. The perfect spot for an ambush…"

"Okay," I said. "Go back to the Hunter house. Stay by the gate and let me know if any press shows up. Word's going to hit the street that something's up and there'll probably be some parasites headed that way. If anyone tries to leave the house delay them, and then call me. I'm on my way, but it'll take a while."

When I hung up, Goody said, "What was that?"

"It wasn't good news," I grabbed Goody's arm, "I need you to help me get these bastards."

"What can I do?"

"I want you to keep your eyes and ears open for a mole in the company. Think back, try and find out from your staff if there was anyone who seemed more curious about Lauren's movements and security than they should've been."

"Christ, it could be anyone who gets the call sheet."

"That's why I need you to pay attention," I said. "I need you to be my inside man. Keep an eye on anyone who's got an axe to grind with Lauren or the studio, with Barry, or the movie. I need to know who might be in drug or financial trouble."

"You just described everyone I know," Goody said.

I laughed.

"Well, I always wanted to be a detective." He smiled.

"Also, tell Tom's people to keep their heads up without telling them why. Lauren might not have been the only target."

Tom Grayson was the picture's male star. He always traveled with a four-man security detail supplied by one of my biggest competitors, Blackthorn Security. When your name was practically a franchise, and you were making twenty million a picture with points on the gross box office, the studio was less stingy with their perks than with an actress like Lauren, who they were only paying twelve million.

We shook hands, and then I ran to my car.

CHAPER 5

The sun in Los Angeles radiates a stark unforgiving light refracted only by carbon emissions once it burns through any moisture that's accumulated in the air overnight. It reveals the smudge collected on the drab stucco boxes, which comprise the majority of the city's buildings. It makes the palm trees appear dusty and pathetic, protruding like frizzy split ends fraying out of the city's coiffure. It exposes every imperfection of the skin, every stain on one's clothing, every artifice used to create the illusion that the city is an oasis where its citizens are glamorous without effort. Like most of Hollywood's icons at that hour of the morning, Melrose Avenue looked unhealthy and hung over. As I pushed the Mustang westward towards the Star Shield offices at 9200 Sunset Boulevard, the paint on its boutiques, which appeared alluring and exotic in the shadows of the night, seemed overdone and desperate without the aid of diffusion.

I called Victoria's mobile number again; it took me to voicemail. I said, "I know you're mad. You have every right to be, but please,

I need to talk to you." Then I called the wizard, Leslie Kaminoff, who had turned his childhood hobby of invading computer systems for fun into an extremely lucrative business and brought him up to speed, then lined up other resources for the rest of the drive to my office.

Charles Luckman's glass and steel tower, which contained the tenth-floor offices of Star Shield Security Group, is the last high-rise structure on the Sunset Strip before the boulevard becomes a parkway that snakes its way through the manicured lawns and mansions of Beverly Hills. I chose the location because the building felt like a watchtower between two levels of society. From my office windows I can see into the hills riddled with castles of the modern day nobility and into the slums of South Central. I find the virtues and the vices of both worlds equally fascinating.

Marianna Ruiz was waiting for me by the elevator, near my reserved space in the subterranean parking lot. Her horned-rim glasses and the conservative cut of her dark hair, contrasted with her lime green dress, and the cobalt blue pumps that accentuated her dark skinned bare legs. She handed me a stack of folders.

"Those are the files on Dale and the people on Lauren's watch list we haven't ruled out, as well as the questionable correspondence she received in the last month. I've got a forensics contractor headed to Malibu to investigate the area where Crawford found the shell casing, and the team you requested will be here at eleven-thirty."

I'd balked when The Bull lobbied to have her run the investigation division, but agreed to interview her. She asked to postpone the meeting for two weeks. The Bull fought my impatience, insisting that we wait, even though I was ready to hire a man from Pinkerton's with a proven track record. When the two weeks elapsed, Marianna walked into my office and presented us with a dossier containing private details of Star Shield's staff and clients that were highly confidential. When I asked how she'd obtained the information, she replied, "You'll have to hire me to find out."

I scanned the list of Lauren's unaccounted-for nuisances, and felt an icy trickle down my spine when I saw the name of Vincent Ito. "Why is Ito on this list? He's locked up."

"He's missing from the prison system computer."

"What?"

"I've been speaking with the Sheriff's department and they assure me that he's being transferred; that it's just a matter of the info not being logged into the system yet."

"Or the maniac's escaped and they're covering up," I said.

Every high profile client has a list of crazy fans that are confused about the thin line between love and hate. If someone presented a danger, we would do a weekly verification of his or her activities.

Two years earlier, Vincent Ito escalated his ardor from letters and emails to several attempts at a personal visit with Ms. Hunter. The last time we apprehended him, he was trying to break into her house wearing two samurai swords, a backpack that contained rope, duct tape, sex toys, and a note of apology that explained why he was going to have to kill the movie star before committing seppuku, the Samurai ritual suicide.

"Only this doesn't feel like Ito," I said. "He wouldn't want to share her with a team. He'd want everyone to know that he was responsible, and I doubt she'd have her clothes on if he sent us a picture. Still, we need to find out where the hell he is. I also want the office, computers, and pbx system, swept for bugs."

"We had our weekly sweep two days ago," she said, but off my look added, "...and we'll sweep them again before you get back."

"Okay," I said, "What's happening in the press?"

"TMZ's reporting that 'Paragon's on the hunt for Hunter, after a no-show at work this morning over a contract dispute."

"Great." I said.

"Mika called since you left Paragon wanting to know what's going on." Mika was Lauren's lover.

"What did you tell her?"

"I told her I'd get in contact with Dale and call her back," Marianna said.

"I spoke to her on my way here, and gave her a line of shit." I said. "Hopefully she can keep from hitting the panic button before I get out there."

"She sounded more annoyed than worried," Marianna said.

"What about Peter?"

"Are you kidding? He's probably not even awake yet."

Peter Hill was a comedic actor who'd starred in a hit TV series for a while, followed by a few film performances of tepid success. He and Lauren were legally married; they appeared together at public events to boost the image that they were a straight couple, and Peter lived in a wing of Lauren's home. But they lived separate lives when not acting as each other's beard.

"How about Dale's wife?" I asked, "Does she know anything about what's going on?"

Marianna adjusted her glasses. "I called her under the pretext of needing some administrative information, and she asked why I didn't just call Dale. I told her that his client's being difficult, and he won't be making any personal calls until his shift is over. She seemed okay with that."

"Do we have someone that can stay with her?"

"I'm working on that. What's the story going to be?" Marianna said.

"The truth. I'll try and break it myself. There's someone I've made an appointment to see in West Hollywood after the team meeting and I can stop by her house first."

The elevator doors opened. We climbed the stairs to the roof where a Bell Jet Ranger contracted from Celebrity Air at Santa Monica Airport sat on the helipad with its rotors turning.

"Thank you," I shouted over the roar of the rotors, holding up the file.

"One more thing," she handed me a printout from Google Maps, "This is the area that Mike Crawford found the shell casings." A black arrow indicated a point on Trancas Canyon Road. "I thought you might want to look at it from the air."

I gave her the thumbs up. She shooed me towards the helicopter.

I buckled in to the right seat of the aircraft and pointed out the location of Lauren Hunter's estate on the pilot's sectional chart.

The swimming pools and expansive roofs of Beverly Hills dropped away beneath me as I thought of the look of fear and fury that Lauren expressed in the photo from her abductors. I examined the files Marianna compiled looking for something we'd missed, feeling the weight of how badly we'd let her down.

As Rikki Wymen pointed out, I did have hostage rescue experience, which meant that I knew what a dicey prospect any ransom situation could be. Officially, the Operational Detachment I commanded in the Green Berets, commonly known as an A-team, were responsible for advising the Columbian military as part of the war on drugs. Unofficially we battled the anti-government guerillas, known as the FARC, who regularly used kidnapping as a strategic or fund-raising tactic. It was often our mission to obtain intelligence about, and rescue if possible, kidnapped Americans who worked for the many American oil and mineral companies investing heavily in that country. We'd reunited several men with their families, but there were also a few ghosts who woke me in the middle of the night to ask me why I hadn't saved them.

When the helicopter reached cruising altitude I reflexively looked in the direction of my home, but the pilot banked and pulled us away to the west before I could be sure which of the rooftops belonged to our house.

The anticipatory excitement I'd felt earlier from the wonderful night of reunion I'd spent with Victoria, was now replaced by a vacuum of sadness and trepidation. I knew as little about why I was losing my wife emotionally, as I did about how Lauren, Dale, and their vehicle, disappeared.

As we flew over the 405 Freeway's river of cars, snaking through the Sepulveda pass, I made the effort to ask myself the questions that would put me in the mind of my enemy. If I were going to capture Lauren for ransom, where would I hide? How would I make the money exchange? What would my escape plan be? There were still so many variables that the possibilities were legion. Why

Lauren? Was it someone that had a vendetta against her, against Paragon, against me? She was a big star, though not the biggest; but then Jodie Foster had only been a minor celebrity when a twisted fan, trying to win her favor, shot a President.

I searched my mind for any indication of who might be working this from inside my company. If Dale were an accomplice, leaving spent shells at the abduction sight would be a good way of deflecting attention from him. Everyone made mistakes; the casings were either the first of the kidnapper's to be discovered, or an effective ruse.

We needed to find the connection quickly.

The pilot said, "We're five miles out."

After a moment of orienting myself I pointed out Lauren's home. "Make a big circle," I said.

Trancas Canyon was the only twisting artery weaving through the mountains up to Lauren's house from Pacific Coast Highway. Higher up, past the entry to Lauren's, the road branched off into several dead ends that led to other sprawling estates. I looked at the sharp corner of the road that Marianna had marked on the map. If I were going to plan an attack on that road the indicated position offered the greatest tactical advantage.

We veered in towards Lauren's home, which was laid out like a Mediterranean villa sprawling across a knoll away from the main canyon road. I showed the pilot the large rotunda at the front entrance offering enough open area to land the helicopter.

I could see Mike Crawford's car parked just around the corner from the front gate.

Thankfully, I didn't see any news vans or paparazzi crawling through the brush.

After the chopper touched down and I was exiting the aircraft, Lauren's lover Mika burst through the front door of the house. She wore a white tank top with no bra, dark blue yoga tights, and white running shoes. The long ringlets of her hair were pulled back and held with a big pink plastic clip. "What the hell is going on Richard?" she said. "I've been trying to call you."

I moved to her, and over the screaming of the helicopter turbines powering down, said, "Lauren's been kidnapped."

"What?" she said.

"I'm sorry, Mika."

"When did you find this out?"

"Barry Sheldon got a ransom note early this morning."

"But you said everything was fine?"

"I wanted to tell you personally."

"Son of a bitch, son of a bitch," Mika repeated several times clutching her arms to herself as if she would explode. "My God, you're kidding right?" she said, her eyes starting to glisten.

I reached out to touch her, but she shook it off and flooded me with a torrent of questions. "Why? When? How did they do it? Where the hell was Dale? Why didn't he do anything?"

Before she was finished, the front door opened again, and Lauren's husband, Peter Hill, stepped out. "What's going on?" he asked.

"They've fucking taken Lauren," Mika shouted.

"What?" Peter asked. He was tall thin and handsome, but he had a bad case of "bed-head." He was dressed only in a yellow Ralph Lauren robe and blue corduroy slippers.

"They've fucking taken Lauren," Mika said again, over the diminishing noise of the chopper. "She's been kidnapped."

"Really?" Peter said, looking at me.

I nodded my head.

"Oh my God." The coffee cup he was holding slipped from his hand, shattering on the flagstone, splashing his bare legs with the hot liquid. "Shit, shit, shit..." he said, dancing on his scalded legs.

"What do they want?" Mika asked.

"A lot of money," I said.

"Well how much?" she said. "We'll give it to them."

"The studio is getting the money together," I said.

"And you fucking trust them?"

"Could you liquidate ten million dollars by tomorrow morning?" I said.

"You lied to me," her eyes were blazing.

"Mika..."

"Don't you fucking lie to me again!" She started punching at me in frustration. "I've been sitting around here all morning trusting you."

I let her strike me. She was a strong woman, her small fists hurt where she pounded my arms and chest.

"We'd just made up," she said.

"I know." The blows getting less intense as she tired.

Mika stopped hitting and looked up, her eyes burned into me, black streaks of mascara creating dark parenthesis on her mocha colored cheeks. "Don't you lie to me again, you understand?"

"Mika," I returned her gaze, "I couldn't tell you over the phone."

She looked at the helicopter, sitting in the driveway of her home, as if seeing it for the first time. "What now?"

Peter was still trying to wipe spilt coffee from his legs with the hem of his robe.

I said, "Why don't we go inside?"

"What do the police say?" Mika said, leading us into a parlor to the left of the main entry.

"Well Mika," I said, "that's another reason I wanted to wait until I spoke to you in person, because we have to be very careful about involving the authorities."

We sat on the two matching, overstuffed yellow couches adorned with red silk pillows, which faced each other between a fireplace and a bay window. The room was painted a jade color, trimmed with a soft yellow. Sad and lonely looking women from previous centuries gazed down upon us from original works in gilt frames, painted by masters I didn't know. It was quite elegant, but not to my taste.

"What?" she said, her eyes wide, "Why?"

I explained the details of the ransom note, and the possibility of a mole who might reveal police involvement. I didn't tell them about the shell casings Mike Crawford found, or their implications, but did say that a superior force had prepared a well-planned ambush and most likely overwhelmed Dale.

Mika got up and paced the room. "I can't believe this is happening. What do we do? What's going to get her back safely?"

"Mika, Peter, did either of you have someone here who wasn't logged, while we were still in Mexico?"

She stopped pacing, and said, "What?" slamming her hands onto her hips.

"We're going to review the tapes."

"You're going to put this on us?" Her eyes darted towards Peter, who was studiously inspecting a fingernail.

"The only way I can help Lauren is to find out who did this and why." I stood up, and strode towards the part of the house that held a closet containing a digital recorder that stored 30 days worth of time-lapse images, from each of the security cameras. "I have to look at every possibility, and I know you guys were having problems."

"Wait," Mika said.

I stopped, turning to her expectantly.

"I was fed up with the pretending, you have no idea what it's like."

"Mika, that's none of my business. I just need to know who was here. Could they have gotten access to Lauren's schedule, or anything else that could be a problem?"

"I wasn't the only one," she said.

"Meowch," Peter said to Mika.

"Look guys," I said. "I just need to know who it was, how long they were here, how to contact them, and if they had time to get into mischief when you weren't with them."

"I don't know if I still have her number, it was just a thing, you know?" Mika said. "Unless she did shit while I was asleep. I told her I was house-sitting."

"Where'd you meet her?"

"The Palms," Mika said, barely audible.

I knew the place. It was one of the only gay bars in West Hollywood that catered exclusively to women. If you didn't know what you were looking for, you wouldn't stumble in by mistake. It catered to a rougher crowd, that didn't wear a lot of lipstick. I said, "I need to check her out."

"This is crazy," Mika said.

"Did she approach you? Or did you start it up?"

I thought Mika might start hitting me again, but then she said, "I'll see if I have her number," and left the room.

"Peter?" I turned to Lauren's husband.

"I didn't have anyone here that's not on your list already, I just didn't log them because…" he waved his hands dismissively.

"What about the gambling tables, are you in any trouble there?"

"Nothing that would get anyone kidnapped."

"How much?" I said.

Peter mumbled something.

"What?"

"Around a hundred?" Peter said, picking at the arm of his robe.

"Thousand? We just cleared up that other thing."

He just shrugged. "They haven't even gotten nasty yet. I'll cover it, I've got work coming."

I walked to where I could stand directly in front of the actor. "Did anyone offer to make it go away?"

"No. God, don't get all storm trooper on me. What, you think I'd sell Lauren out? Fuck you."

"Peter, you have a problem. People with problems hurt their friends - whether they want to or not."

"Fuck off," Peter said, "Don't blame me because you didn't do your job."

I wanted to slap him. "If I find out that any of this happened because you shit the bed, you're done."

"Get away from me," he said, putting on a show of being injured.

"You are not to leave this house, make a phone call, or send an email that breathes a word of this. You hear me? Where did you lose the money?"

He murmured the names of the men holding his markers. I also obtained the names of the visitors that Peter entertained who weren't in the log. When I was finished taking notes I called Mike Crawford, telling him to come to the house. I went to the control panel that opened the front gate. I then downloaded the security camera images for the previous thirty days into a flash drive.

Crawford knocked on the front door, just as Mika was slumping back down the stairs. He greeted me with a nod of his head. He was six foot-two inches tall and weighed about two fifty. His hair was still clipped in a military flat top that had all turned white, but his facial hair retained much of its original dark color, making him look like a polar bear with a mustache.

Crawford looked around at the sweeping circular staircase of white marble with its finely filigreed wrought iron railing, the bouquets of giant fresh flowers in five-foot Cloisonné vases, the ancient tapestries, and framed pencil sketches by renaissance artists adorning the Venetian marbled walls. "Wow," he said.

I introduced Mika to Crawford. She handed me a piece of paper with a woman's name written on it, and a telephone number. "Will Lauren have to know?" She emitted the odor of someone who'd just thrown up.

"I'll only do what I have to with this," I said, folding the paper into the pocket of my shirt.

I herded them back into the parlor. Peter still sulked on the couch where I'd left him.

"Soon," I said, "the press is going to want to know what's going on. If anyone gets through to either one of you, refuse any comment. Should you feel you have to say something to friends or family, repeat the story the studio is putting out, that Lauren is requesting some script revisions."

Mika nodded slightly and Peter didn't move.

"I'm going to have Mike stay here with you. Do either of you have any appointments?"

"Just a manicure," Mika said.

Peter made a visible show of reigning himself in before he spoke, "I have to record a children's story for Books on Tape next week. But other than that, I was just going to do some shopping and visit some friends in Palm Springs this weekend."

I knew what that meant, and my disapproval showed on my face.

"Look, I'll do whatever you tell me to, if it'll help." Peter said. "I don't have to go anywhere."

"Thank you. We'll get things back to normal as quickly as we can." I said. Two birds splashed and sang in the garden fountain that could be seen through one of the windows.

"I just can't believe this is happening," Mika said again. She sat down cross-legged on the Persian carpet, with her fingers laced through the back of her hair.

"Make a list of anyone who you think might have done this," I told her. "Take your time. Don't exclude any possibility, no matter how ludicrous it may seem. If there is anyone who you've seen in the last few weeks that's given you the creeps, or just seemed odd to you, caught your attention in any way, do your best to describe them."

Peter and Mika nodded their heads but made no move to do anything.

"Whatever you do, don't talk about this on a cell phone, near a window, or outside, where someone could catch you with a directional mike or read your lips. If there's any question you have, any concern, don't hesitate to call me."

"Do you really think we'll get her back?" Mika asked.

I took her shoulders in my hands and looked her in the eyes, "I'm going to do everything I can."

She nodded, and I headed out to the helicopter.

CHAPTER 6

Marianna Ruiz was waiting for me when the helicopter landed on the roof of our office building. In the elevator down, I handed her the flash drive containing the thirty-day memory from the security system, and a handwritten sheet of paper containing my notes from the visit to Lauren's house. I said, "Let's get all that checked out ASAP." At reception, I asked our girl to have one of the interns make me a sandwich and a cup of coffee before hurrying down the hall.

We pushed through the conference room doors, encountering the Star Shield colleagues who I'd served with in the military, or who had distinguished themselves as trustworthy beyond the role of employee. Some were formally dressed in the suits they wore on duty, while others were clothed casually, depending on what they'd been doing when they received the call from The Bull or Marianna for this emergency meeting. They were bantering with each other in the combative humor of those who constantly push all the limits.

"Okay sewing circle's over, listen up," I moved behind the chair at the head of the conference table. "Thank you all for getting here so quickly, I know that some of you were on personal time." I nodded to Will McCoy; "Hopefully The Bull's briefed you on the facts that we know." I took a moment to look at each person in the room. These were not just employees, but friends who I'd spent more time with than my family. "We've been ambushed by someone who knows what he or she is doing. Lauren and Dale could be in serious danger. If we don't find out who targeted us, and retrieve our client intact, we all may be out of a job. The studio has made it very clear that we're the scapegoat. I was booted off the lot and can only assume that all our privileges there have been revoked."

The room was silent. Then The Bull's deep and melodic voice rumbled. "Looks like the only way out of this is to not let them get away with it."

"Of course, The Bull's the first suspect we should look at, because I know he'd do just about anything to get away from his wife's 'honey-do' list," I said.

The group humored my joke with smiles and some agreement.

"Alright then," I said, "let's get started." I pulled back one of the wooden panels on the interior wall of the room, revealing a large screen. "Marianna, could you please give me a thirty mile radius of Malibu?"

She punched a few keys, made some movements on her track pad, and a map of the Southern California coastline materialized on the screen.

"Okay," I said. "Miss Hunter's car left her house around 05:15 this morning, headed for Paragon Studios." I pointed to the points on the map. "If it were your mission to abduct her, where would you do it?"

Bodies started to change position and fidget, as the gears started moving in the minds of the team.

A stocky man, with dark brown hair as thick as an otter's, a prominent Italian nose, and wearing a Pacifico Beer t-shirt, said, "If I were going to take control of the vehicle, I'd want to do it before they got to PCH, or onto the freeway." Phil Triano was the 18C – Engineering Sergeant, for The Bull and I in Columbia. After proving his ability to procure high-quality steaks for the unit, in a country where beef was often no better than shoe leather, he was rarely called anything but T-bone. "At that hour of the morning, Trancas Canyon would be an easy place to stage a traffic accident, road work, a downed tree, or some other ruse, which if you were in Indian country might seem suspicious, but on a Monday morning in Malibu might not be something we would want to pass by without giving it attention."

A tall tanned woman in her forties with dark curly hair pulled into a ponytail raised her hand. Natalie Williams put in twenty years with the LAPD, and now was in charge of coordinating large-scale events for Star Shield. "There's no doubt what you're saying is true T-bone, but if Dale took the 10 freeway he'd have to travel surface streets through the hood, where even if there are witnesses, they're not going to be calling 911 if they see an Escalade being jacked."

"Good point, Willie," Marianna said. Even though Natalie was known by the masculine shortening of her last name, and she was lean and tough, no one would ever mistake her for a man. "But we didn't receive any kind of a mayday from Dale, and if he were under attack he would have hit the panic button."

Each of our vehicles and all of our phones were programmed with a one-touch alert button that would contact dispatch with our immediate position.

"Unless he was head-shot while waiting at a stop-light," T-bone said.

The room was quiet for a moment while everyone contemplated the truth of that statement. We were all aware that if someone was willing to commit the felony of kidnapping for ransom, they probably weren't going to be deterred by the prospect of a murder penalty.

"There's also the possibility that Dale didn't call in because he sold out," I said.

"I just can't see it," The Bull said. "He just had a baby. I've never once gotten a bad vibe from him."

"None of us want that scenario to be what we're up against," I said. "But it's something we've got to consider. Or, it could be someone else in this organization that compromised us. So, even in our office, this has got to be a covert operation.

"What's our cover story boss?" Willie asked, "I was hoping I could just go out in the field and say, 'Hey. Can you help me find Lauren Hunter?'"

Chuckles emanated from around the room.

"Leslie?" I addressed a man who hadn't seemed to be paying attention, because he was focusing so intently on the screen of his notebook computer. Leslie Kaminoff was the bearded computer specialist, who looked more like a yogi than a cyber-nerd in his saffron clothing. "Do you have someone who can alter a photo of Lauren Hunter so that it still resembles her, but looks like a different person?"

The computer man nodded his head while typing on his keyboard. Leslie was the only man in the room not a Star Shield employee. Legally, he ran his own IT and computer graphics firm. He and his people also did contract work for us on a regular basis, and for the right price there wasn't anything in the digital ether he couldn't find.

"Good, we need that right away. Take a few years off her also," I said to Leslie, and then spoke to the group. "Present it as a missing persons investigation. Show this photo around. We'll call her… ahh… Lisa Harris. Lisa was at the beach yesterday afternoon and hasn't been seen since. Her parents are worried, they don't want to wait the required twenty-four hours to file a report with the police, so they hired us."

The group nodded and smiled. "Good one," T-bone said.

"Okay, pretty soon the press is going to pick up the scent, and come looking for the story with everything they've got. Any mission specific information needs to be encrypted. We need strict communication discipline everywhere outside this room. Everyone clear?"

The group gave their assent.

"Also," I said, "

Again I turned to Kaminoff, the computer consultant. "What do you have for me on the ransom note?"

The gaunt, bearded man looked up from his screen, and said, "Unfortunately not much. They've done a good job of hiding themselves. My guess is they're using source routing or transmitting from multiple units, because the domain keeps changing its IP address."

My expression prodded him to explain. "It's like they're calling from different payphones, and then destroying them afterwards."

"Okay," I said.

"I don't think you're dealing with just some casual hacker here." Kaminoff stroked his beard with his fingers. "This is a professional, who doesn't want to be discovered. It's going to take me time to find this one. Is it true we might get some help from the Feds?"

"I don't know yet," I looked at my watch. "We all should be aware that the Feds might be involved sub-rosa, looking at Star Shield as a suspect."

I let that information sink into the room before again speaking to Kaminoff. "Did Marianna give you the crew list from Lauren's movie?"

"Yes, but there too, password breaking all those email address-es is going to take time. Marianna's given me a number of key words and phrases to search, and we'll get the results back to you as soon as they're available…" The computer man queried me over the screen of his laptop with raised eyebrows. "As long as you know it's going to cost a shitload of money?"

"Whatever it takes." I said. "In the mean time, we need to start with the little physical evidence we possess."

Willie was one of our best investigators, I paired her up with Steve Kelvin, a guy I'd met when he was an officer with the 470th Military Intelligence Brigade. They were tasked with canvassing the Trancas Canyon area; working their way down from Lauren's property to the beach, looking for anyone who might have seen the Escalade, or anything suspicious.

I detailed a former detective with the Sheriff's department, Jack Gillis, on hunting down the woman that had the one-night stand with Lauren's lover, Mika.

The Bull, T-bone, and the other two men who'd served in our Green Beret team, Sparky and Kelly, I sent to canvas the area between the freeway and Paragon, followed by verifying the physical whereabouts of the people on Lauren's watch-list.

"Before you head out, I want two Escalades prepped with anything you think we might need; weapons, night-vision, radios, a full hostile territory kit; Bull take one, and Willie, you take the other. Also, make sure our two surveillance vans are gassed up, and that the camera batteries are charged. T-bone, Sparky, Kelly, I'd like you to use your motorcycles. Things are going to happen fast, as soon as we have more information. We're not going to stop until this plays out one-way, or the other. If you think you might need something, pack it. The second we get a lead, or they make a move, I want you to be ready to open a can of whoop-ass."

"Hoo-yah!" The team grunted the gung-ho response that had started with the Rangers, but was now an all-service affirmation of esprit de corps.

"Alright, hit the bricks," I said.

As the men and lone woman saluted, before exiting the room, Leslie Kaminoff said, "Don't forget to pick up the altered photo of Lauren before you leave. We'll be sending it to the printer in the copy room, when it's done in a few minutes."

Marianna Ruiz remained behind.

"Can you get accounting do a cost projection?" I said. "Tell them to liquefy whatever assets are necessary."

She nodded, and made notations on her laptop.

One of the office assistants knocked on the door, and then brought in my food and coffee.

"Oh, God, I'm starving," I said tearing into the sandwich. It tasted delicious; ham and Swiss cheese, slathered with mustard and mayonnaise, accented by crisp lettuce and some thinly sliced red onion, just the way I would have made it myself. I made a note to ask who the kid was. Either Marianna had schooled him well, or he had made an effort to be noticed.

I got up and walked over to the large windows overlooking Los Angeles, wrapped in its sepia haze. Before ripping another a hunk off the sandwich, I said, "What else do you have working?"

"I've got one investigator doing backgrounds on the film crew. She's starting a cross-reference list for several factors like criminal record, previous employment with the client, etc. I've got someone else going over the fan mail, researching visitors to Lauren's website, searching for a pattern or a warning."

Marianna's computer alerted her to an incoming email. She clicked on it, and said. "If you're not going to jump out that window, do you want to look at the picture Leslie's people did for us?"

Marianna put up the altered picture of Lauren on the conference screen. It was uncanny; all the important features remained the same, but the graphic artist had stretched here and there, moved an eyebrow, etc. so that it was a photograph of a woman who could easily be mistaken for Lauren Hunter, but was not the movie star.

"God it's amazing what they can do these days," I said. "Did you run a financial on Dale Irvin, see if he might have a reason to sell Lauren out?"

"This has all come so fast, I don't have enough people…"

"Okay," I held up my hand. "I know this has happened quickly, but maybe we need to hire some subcontractors? We'll need confidentiality agreements, copies of their insurance, the works, but get what you need. There'll be a lot more data coming. We can have them investigate it, without telling them what it's for.

"Do a full re-evaluation on Dale. Look at anyone we've hired in the last year that could've given us up. Give it to the outside people, and don't tell them what it's about."

She nodded gravely. Marianna was a beautiful woman in such a different way than my wife. She was short and sturdily built, with a prominent bust and muscular legs. Her skin was very dark, and when she shook your hand it was with a firm, confident grip. Her clothes were always colorful and alluring, just on the tasteful side of immodest. "Have you ever met Tony Cerda?" I asked her.

"No, but I know who he is," Marianna said.

Anthony Cerda was the Capo of a crime family that came out to Los Angeles when the studios were getting started. They moved in on the burgeoning labor unions, films in need of financing, the newly wealthy with bad habits, and desperate people willing to do anything to succeed.

"I have a grudgingly respectful relationship with Cerda," I said. When I was starting out, a star that commissioned me neglected to mention that it was the mob he needed protection from. Several of Cerda's soldiers went to the hospital before I was able to arrange a meeting that negotiated the resolution of this client's debts without further violence. "He likes pretty women. If I can arrange a meet this afternoon, I'd like you to come along."

"Why Mr. Braddock," Marianna said, "you're not thinking of pimping out our employees now are you?"

"Just trying to use the carrot instead of the stick."

"I'll be there." Marianna knew the value of her charms.

"Let me know if anything breaks," I said, getting up to leave.

"Richard?"

I stopped.

"Something I was thinking about… Why was the ransom note sent to Barry Sheldon, and not Rikki Wymen?"

"He's the Producer of the movie."

"Yes, but they obviously are aware that the money will be coming from Paragon. It wouldn't be that much harder to get Rikki Wymen's private e-mail address than that of Sheldon? Why go through him?"

"What are you getting at?"

"I just think we should be looking at him."

"As a suspect?"

"No, I'm not sure. It's just a feeling I have."

"Do we have someone to put on it, with everything else on the list?"

"I'll deal with it myself, I just wanted to get your reaction."

"I don't have a strong feeling about him. But if you've got a hunch, go for it. Just do the work on Dale first." I looked at my watch, "Did you get me a female to stay with Dale's wife?"

"Christina Caruthers."

"Have her meet me at Dale's house in thirty minutes," I said, on my way out the door. "I want to get a read on how his wife reacts to her husband's disappearance."

CHAPTER 7

In the subterranean parking garage of the Star Shield office building we rent a large room the employees called the Pit. It contains the personal lockers for the operatives; as well as weapons lockers, radio & cell phone charging stations, coffee and soda machines, a refrigerator, two card tables with chairs and a couple of worn couches.

When I came out of the elevator, on the way to my car, a black Escalade, and a black Suzuki GSX-R750 "rice-rocket" motorcycle, were parked next to the Pit. Bull McCoy was loading tactical vests and duffel bags filled with other assault gear into the Escalade.

T-bone was helping him. He said, "Hey skipper, seems like we're going to have some fun?"

"Yeah," I said, "it's crackin' me up."

"Don't worry boss, we'll make you smile before this is over…"

"Well, how 'bout we get this truck loaded first?" The Bull said. "Make sure the Tasers are charged and the ammo box is filled." He threw a hand the size of a bear paw on my shoulder and guided me towards the Mustang. "Well?" he said.

"Other than this, how you enjoying the parade Mrs. Kennedy?" I said.

"Paragon's going to hang us out to dry?"

"They're just covering their ass. If this goes to shit, it'll look like the right thing, and if it doesn't there's no downside for them."

"The Brass doing what they do best. Fucking déjà vu all over again," Bull said.

"Yeah, feels like it." I said. "Only this time we know we're being screwed going in."

We walked silently towards my car.

T-bone, The Bull, myself, Sparky and Kelly, were the only survivors from a hostage rescue mission gone bad in Columbia that led me to resign my commission from the military.

When we arrived at the Mustang, Bull smacked me on the back while I was getting in, and said, "We'll just keep fighting until they kill us, or we get out of here," quoting something I'd said on the day that changed our lives.

I started the engine, rolled down the window, and said, "Thanks big man," before roaring out of the parking structure.

After spending twenty minutes in the car on the phone, arranging meetings with people who made their livings from the less than heavenly part of the city of angels, I arrived on a tree-lined street in Mar Vista. It's a small community of post World War II development, close enough to the beach that every now and then you get a cool breeze off the water, but far enough away that a young couple might still find a small fixer-upper they can barely afford. Big Wheels, bikes, and basketball hoops populated almost every property.

I met Christina Caruthers at her silver Prius, parked in the middle of the block. We greeted, then I said, "Marianna brief you? You ready?"

Caruthers nodded her head. She was a solid woman almost my size, with curly blonde hair, and a very nice smile. Dressed in jeans, white canvas sneakers, and a floral print blouse, she looked more like a homemaker, than the Olympic Silver Medalist in Judo she was.

We walked to a light blue stucco bungalow, much like the other houses on the block. It distinguished itself however, by the attention paid to the landscaping. Dale Irvin's wife planted so many different varieties of flowering plants in their front yard that it looked more like an English country cottage than a California tract home.

We could see a white Volvo station wagon in the open garage, but there was no answer to the doorbell.

"Let's check around back," Christina said.

We walked down the driveway, which was bordered on either side by Morning Glory and Lantana. The rear of the property was also nicely manicured; surrounded by additional varieties of foliage. A stroller sat at the back of the yard, with a bundled baby snoozing peacefully.

I thought about saying something to announce our arrival, but didn't want to wake the baby. As we walked further into the yard, we could see Dale's wife, on her hands and knees in a vegetable garden, sectioned out on the land behind the garage.

"Mrs. Irvin?" I said quietly.

She jumped and let out a little gasp. "Oh, you scared me." Becky was not fat necessarily, just a well-fed girl from the mid-west who'd recently given birth. Her sandy hair was pulled back in a knot, but several strands had come loose, and hung across her face. She wore sweat pants and a light pink short-sleeved shirt. Her expression went from embarrassment to trepidation, as she recognized whom her callers were.

"Mr. Braddock," she said while trying to stand up, "what's happened to Dale?"

Her effort to stand up went awry, and she toppled into a sitting position in the dirt. Christina and I knelt on either side of her.

I put a hand on her arm and said, "We've lost contact with Dale."

"What does that mean? What does that mean?" she asked each of us.

I told her that Dale and Lauren had disappeared, that there was a ransom demand for Lauren.

"What did they say about Dale? Did they say anything about Dale?"

"No, Becky," I said. "But that doesn't mean anything. Lauren's where the money is." It wasn't exactly a lie.

"I have to get up," she said.

We helped her to her feet. She walked over to the stroller as if she were going to get the baby, but then veered off, and walked along the edge of the property, absently touching the plants with one hand while rubbing her face with the other. Christina followed at a respectful distance.

Becky Irvin circled three quarters of the yard before turning around and saying, "Dale wouldn't just let them take her would he?"

"I'm sure he did his best," I said.

Dale's wife nodded her head a couple of times, then turned and vomited violently.

I stayed with Becky Irvin for a little while longer; making placating statements that left me feeling cheap, because I'd hit her so hard with the truth.

However, as I drove away, I was relieved thinking that if she had anything to do with the caper, she was a better actress than Lauren.

Chapter 8

In the block that once housed the venerable Schwab's Drug Store, an open-air shopping mall has taken the landmark's place. It houses everything for the hip West Hollywooder; Art-house movie theaters, a Trader Joe's Market, the Crunch Gym, restaurants, exclusive clothing shops, and a Burke Williams Spa. Each of the businesses surrounded a central - first floor courtyard, which contained a pair of escalators that carry patrons to a second story promenade.

I sat on the upper level, in the balcony of the La Pecorea restaurant, at a brightly tiled table, next to the filigreed iron railing, protected from the afternoon sun by a canvas awning, the stripes of which matched the tiles on the tables with their random primary colors. I watched people mill about the central plaza of the shopping area looking hip and unaffected, while I caught up with messages from my investigators and skimmed the entertainment news sites on my IPhone, until the person I was waiting for, Holiday Landau, strode through.

Her professionally sculpted, porn-star body, moved with a haughty grace on stiletto heals. The only thing covering her torso was a buckskin mini-skirt and a Chanel top, which left her midriff bare.

As she click-clacked across the smooth, mosaic, terrazzo floor, four tourists in backpacks, shorts, and wearing socks with their sandals, stared openly, elbowing one another to not miss something that could never be seen where they came from.

Locals were less obvious, tracking her movement in the reflection off the glass of the stores, or masking their glances with a sip of their cappuccinos from the tables outside Buzz Coffee.

Mounting the escalator, Holiday tossed her mane of highlighted hair, and struck a pose for the short ride up. She was one of the most passable transsexuals I'd ever seen.

Holiday's father was a German politician, who'd shipped his son to the United States as a teenager, because "she" insisted on being an embarrassment to him. Holiday soon found that her tastes exceeded the allowance he'd allotted for her, so she went into business for herself. She currently ran a stable of courtesans that catered to unusual tastes, and she owned several "private" clubs. Every now and then, Holiday's people needed the type of help my company could provide, but more often, Star Shield's clients desired the services that Holiday catered to. Most importantly to me, Holiday was better than TMZ when it came to her knowledge of the current gossip.

When she came sashaying towards my table, I could read the lips of a Beverly Hills Botox victim, lunching a few tables away, saying to her equally artificial companion, "Oh, my, god could she dress any sluttier?"

I stood to pull out Holiday's chair. We kissed Parisian style. She smelled of Jasmine and sandalwood. Holiday seated herself so that everyone could see her long, bare legs.

She said, "To what do I owe the pleasure? You don't want to discuss an appointment do you?"

"Not today."

"Well, a girl can only hope. You know darling, if you ever do decide to swing my way, I'd make you a luscious introductory offer?"

"You'll be my first call, if I ever get that adventurous," I said.

The waiter arrived, placing a Kir Royal – Champagne mixed with Cassis - in front of Holiday.

She raised her lavender drink, "I'm flattered you remembered." After a sip she said, "You seem tense dear, what's the matter?"

"I need a favor."

She gave me an, "I'm all ears," look.

"I'm interested in some people you might know, or know about."

"What people?"

"I'll tell you in a moment, that's only half of my favor."

"What's the other half?"

"I can't tell you why I need it, or who I need it for."

"Richard!" she pouted.

"Holiday, in all the time we've known each other, have I ever asked you for anything like this?"

"No, because you are afraid of owing me something."

"That's not it, and you know it. Except for disclosure, you can name your terms."

"Be careful, older men are my weakness."

I said, "Thanks a lot."

"Who are these people?" she asked again.

"Anyone who might be up to no good at Paragon, or have a grudge against the studio, Barry Sheldon, Rikki Wymen, or me."

"Oh my god," Holiday interrupted. She leaned over conspiratorially, "Lauren Hunter's your client isn't she? Does this have to do with her being missing?"

I felt like I'd just been kicked in the stomach. I looked around to see if anyone had been listening. People at other tables were furtively staring, but none sat close enough to overhear. "She's not missing," I lied.

"That's not what I heard," she sing-songed.

I took a gulp out of my iced tea.

"Come on Richard, you can tell me. I talk to her make-up artist, André all the time. If she were going to hold out for script changes, he would have heard about it. Lesbian's are worse than old queens when they're not getting what they want."

Holiday leaned over the table. Though her cleavage was artificial, it was the best that money could buy. "These people you want to know about, are they trying to hurt her? Is that why she's hiding?"

"Holiday..."

She sat back, and sipped her champagne, letting me squirm for a moment. "Do you know why I know so much Richard?"

"Holiday..."

She flipped her hands out. "Because I have no secrets. But for some reason people think I'm trying to hide a big secret." Her hands flipped back inwards, the long fingers pointing to her lap.

"So people tell me their secrets. But you must know by now that I only tell the secrets that want to be told."

"We're not in the same business Holiday, my clients aren't coming to me so they can play with fire."

"You want me to help you, but you're not willing to respect me with your trust." Once again she drew from her cocktail.

"People's lives could be at stake."

"Oh, isn't that dramatic? Darling don't you think I know that you and your nasty boys could bury me out in the desert if I spoiled too much of your fun. I thought we were friends."

"We are. I just can't afford to be careless."

"Seems like you already have been."

There was nothing for me to say.

"Oh, stop looking so morose, it doesn't suit you, and it certainly won't help keep these straight girls jealous of me." She raised her glass to the well-groomed ladies, who had been looking our way sniping. "If you want my help, you'd better hurry, I have a facial in a few minutes."

I leaned over and whispered in her ear that Lauren had been kidnapped.

Holiday gasped, "No! Really? Well," she tossed her hair, "those bitches at Burke Williams can wait to poke at my nose."

Quietly I told her the details.

Holiday tossed her hair again, "I can't say that I'm sorry. Anyone in her position that doesn't out themselves, just makes it that much harder on the rest of us. But I never judge a dyke, until I've walked a mile in her ugly flat shoes." She laughed at herself briefly, "I'm sorry, I can see you're in no mood for humor. My first thought would be David Holt? I wouldn't put it past the little shit."

"I don't know him."

"The V.P. of Back-lot Operations? Or, I should say 'Ex'. He was in charge of all the equipment, all the crafts, anything unglamorous about the Studio. Well, since everything went across his desk for approval, he decided to set up a couple of phantom companies, which would sell or rent equipment to Paragon that didn't exist, or that he stole, and then charged back to the studio."

"And he got caught?" I said.

She nodded emphatically while lighting a cigarette, "But it went on for years. He owned a condo in the hills, all rigged with cameras. He'd treat the boys he was doing business with to all the drugs and sexual entertainment they wanted, while he was getting it all on tape. It made people less inclined to turn him in.

"I worked one of his parties. That was enough for me. His friends are trash; they're not looking for quality, just holes to come in. I heard a girl O.D.'d on his drugs, and instead of calling an ambulance, he dumped her in a cab."

"A girl he got from another service?"

"He was throwing parties every weekend. After a while no one wanted to work for him. He started pulling sleaze off the streets."

"So what happened?"

"Little Davey got greedy. He was over-billing, double-billing, and padding orders to all the movies and TV shows using the lot. Some of those shows are for other studios. An outside auditor got nosy and it unraveled like a cheap pair of nylons."

I nodded. "They didn't prosecute?"

"You know the studios darling. They just want you to steal more for them than from them. Who knows what a criminal investigation would turn up? Besides, he had a lot of those tapes…"

"Still, it's a long way from embezzlement, to what we're talking about," I said.

"Ooo, Ooo, Ooo," She bounced up and down in her chair. "OMG, I just thought of someone else. I can't believe I didn't think of him sooner."

I put my fingers to my lips in the 'shush' position, to calm her down.

Holiday leaned over the table, and whispered, "Kyle Pemberton."

The name sounded familiar, but I couldn't place it.

Off my quizzical look, she said soto-voce, "He's the guy who was sent to prison for sexually assaulting Denise Morton?"

"That was a while ago, wasn't it?"

Holiday counted on her manicured fingers, "Six-ish years ago." She was animated, with the eagerness of a child, bursting with a secret. "They were making that movie where Denise joins that macho Navy unit who doesn't allow women."

"The S.E.A.L. team?"

"I think so. Anyway they'd set up this boot camp thing, to get the actors in shape, and rehearse some of the fighting scenes, before filming started; this Kyle Pemberton ran it all. He was the show's – how do you call it – in charge of army things?"

"Military Advisor," I said. "I remember him. He handed out hats and T-shirts to actors he trained, that said, *Pemberton's Pit-Bulls*?"

"Ya, that's him. All the Hollywood tough boys wanted one."

"I think I was in Europe when all this happened, but didn't Bruce save her from this Pemberton guy or something?" Bruce Weller was a big action star that was married to Denise Morton back then.

"Yes," she said. "But Brucey got badly beaten up, and they had to shut down the movie he was working on."

"Right, right, yeah it's coming back to me. But how does this tie into my client?"

"It doesn't." Holiday rolled her eyes. "You asked me about Barry Sheldon, Rikki Wymen, and Paragon. It happened on their movie."

Holiday was taking her pleasure playing me along, so I didn't show my impatience. "Ah," I said, sensing there was more that she was dying to tell me.

She took another dramatic sip of her drink, and then leaned close to me conspiratorially. "I heard that Pemberton never should have gone to jail."

I too leaned in, with my eyebrows raised.

"Apparently," Holiday said, "Kyle had been working out Denise horizontally - after hours - at that boot camp, and Bruce attacked Pemberton when he caught them in the act."

"I still don't see how this is relevant to my current case."

"Okay. Okay," Holiday said, conciliatory now that she had me on the hook. "Bruce got badly beaten up. Yes? That's not so good for the pocketbook if you're an action star. So Denise said that Bruce rescued her from being sexually assaulted. Once the press got a hold of it, she couldn't change her story, and they arrested Pemberton."

She put her hands on my wrists, imploring me to wait until she was finished. Her hands were startlingly warm.

"I was told that Barry Sheldon knew Pemberton and Morton were having an affair, but Rikki Wymen forbid him from saying so in court. Bruce Weller and Denise Morton both had deals at Paragon, and she didn't want anything affecting their box office."

"I'd think Pemberton would want to go after Morton or Weller. They're the ones that lied, Sheldon just didn't speak up."

Holiday made a disparaging face. "I don't think you could get ten thousand dollars if you ransomed Morton and Weller together these days."

I took Holiday's hands in mine and squeezed them in appreciation. "It's definitely worth following up."

She started tickling my forearm seductively. "And there isn't anyone who's anyone that wouldn't want to see Rikki Wymen take a fall…"

"Hmn, yeah, I met her this morning for the first time."

"Really?"

"She's a handful."

"The only thing I can say about that Rikki Wymen, is I'd like to be her; of course twenty years younger. That bitch makes all the little boys get down on their knees."

"Really?" I asked.

Holiday laughed, because I'd taken her literally. "Honey, she's too busy being the Queen Bee to play around, and if she does, I haven't heard about it."

I questioned Holiday about the other high profile people on the picture. She had juicy tidbits about some of them, but nothing that would make them suspects. Except for Cece Harris, the Line Producer.

"That girl would eat kittens if it would help her career. Some of my clients dated her. They liked her for the same reason they like me, only mine doesn't have to be strapped on," Holiday said. "She's also had a problem with the nose candy..."

She looked at her watch, "Oh, I'm late, they get so upset." She took my hand, leaned over and whispered, "Now, don't you worry, I'm not going to say anything about our little secret, and I'll try to find out some real information for you."

I stood up with her. "I'm trusting you to be a good girl."

"I know, and that's what's so frustrating about you sweetie," she sidled up close to me, and ran her hand down my back, resting it on the cheek of my butt. "I keep hoping you'll trust me to be a bad girl." She kissed me lightly on the mouth, gave my derriere a squeeze, and sashayed off towards the day spa.

I wiped lipstick off my mouth with a napkin, and threw some money on the table. As I walked by the two women who'd glared at us the whole time, I smiled and tipped my head.

Their envy of Holiday was one of the only things I'd found amusing all day.

Chapter 9

I called Marianna at the office, and asked her to investigate the leads Holiday shared with me. I made my way out of West Hollywood, weaving the Mustang in and out of traffic, southbound on La Cienega Boulevard; from the corridor of exclusive boutiques, and the restaurant row that created the eastern border of Beverly Hills. I continued past Wilshire Boulevard, to the dreary strand of auto-body shops and liquor stores, then onto the long stretch without traffic lights that snaked through the oil fields of Baldwin Hills. Traffic was still light enough so that I sailed through the desolate chaparral and the bobbing heads of donkey-shaped petroleum-pumping rigs that were the only scenery of note. This wasteland separated the dubious glamour of the northern part of the city from the sprawling expanse of south central Los Angeles. There refineries, anonymous industrial parks, and urban blight, gained territory daily on the few manicured residential neighborhoods scattered throughout.

On the north edge of Inglewood, the community that bore the brunt of all the air traffic on final approach towards the six runways of Los Angeles International airport, I intercepted the 405 Freeway briefly before jumping onto the 105 eastbound and exiting at Vermont, where I dropped down into Compton.

The Mustang drew stares of admiration and avarice from the people shuffling along the sidewalks or lurking around the boarded up storefronts, laundromats, thrift, and liquor stores. The healthiest looking groups wore the distinctive uniforms consisting of vicious stares, t-shirts, baggy pants, baseball caps or do-rags, in the specific color combinations associated with gang sets. The uniforms changed every few blocks as the street population blended from African-American, to Latino, and back again. Occasionally women, some just wearing a large t-shirt and filthy cotton slippers, tried to catch my attention, with thumbs pointed towards their open mouths pantomiming oral sex, or by revealing their breasts, butts, or bushes. Boys flashed the hand signals for drugs. Everyone, even the working men and women littering the bus stops, carried themselves like shell-shock victims from the unrelenting toll of drugs, hatred, low pay, and airplane engines rattling the windows of the places they lived twenty-four hours a day.

Past 135th Street I turned into a side street that led me by old industrial buildings and dirty houses with brown grass.

Turning another corner brought me to a black cinder block building with a dirt yard out front. It was enclosed with chain-link fence topped with concertina wire. A few custom Harley's were parked in the protected lot. There was no sign, but anyone who knew of the place called it the Hog Barn.

I pulled the car into the driveway and got out. A crusty German shepherd pulled itself off the ground amid the bikes, and growled.

One blocky Hispanic, with a flat and pockmarked face, sat at an overturned cable spool playing dominos with a thinner, meaner looking cholo, in wrap-around shades. They both wore leather vests exhibiting the Mongols motorcycle club patches.

"I'm here to see the Fish," I said. "Don't fuck with the car."

"Don't know no Fish," the guy with the sunglasses said, he pulled on a Fu-Manchu beard.

"What's the heat doing with such a nice ride?" the other guy said. "You on the take Bro? Or you just joy riding in my tax dollars?"

"Big tax-payer are you?" I said, "I hope you're not filing as a comic."

I skirted the dog, which continued to growl. The two bikers looked like they might start barking too, but neither one moved. I opened the security door that led into the shop.

The interior was surprisingly clean and brightly illuminated. Several mechanics worked on Harley Davidsons in various states of customization. Newly painted frames and tanks hung in a spray booth gleaming with lacquer.

In the back, another huge Mexican guy stood behind the parts counter. He sported a shaved head creased by rolls of fat and was scrutinizing a copy of Butt Man magazine with such deliberation that he didn't look up, even when I stood right in front of him.

"Studying for an exam, Henry?" I said.

Snapping out of his reverie, the man flipped the magazine over, revealing a young lady with her own arm sunk into her anal cavity, past the wrist. "You believe that shit man?" Henry said.

"Yeah, and I'll bet she's a great cook. Fish downstairs?"

Obviously disappointed that I didn't share his appreciation for fine art, Henry grunted, while turning to the next page in the magazine. "Oh man you got to check this out," he said, even though I was already moving down the stairwell behind the parts shelves.

It is unusual for a building in Los Angeles to have a basement. However, Reyes Hernandez, known as El Rey de Pescado – The King of the Fish – or just Pescado if you were a friend - and The Fish if you were a gringo friend - had this basement specially built, with a vault to house his wares. It also had three different escape tunnels that led to adjacent houses.

At the bottom of the stairs, two Samoans sat in leather reclining chairs, watching the Charlie's Angels movie on a big screen TV. Each held an Uzi machine pistol pointed at me.

I held my arms up saying, "Small of the back as usual."

One of the men took my weapon, and verified my story with a thorough pat down, while the other kept the Uzi trained on me.

"Hit the fucking pause button bra," the one doing the frisking said, "I want to see this part." It was Cameron Diaz flirting with the UPS man.

"Good movie, huh?" I said.

The Samoan's only response was to painfully slap my crotch area to make sure there was no weapon or wire there.

When he was finished, the Samoan waved to a hidden camera, and pushed me towards one of the doors the two men were guarding. The heavy steel door opened automatically, making a deep thunking sound. I walked into a small room with mirrors on every wall. The door closed behind me before the mirror to my right opened.

The Fish sat in a huge leather chair behind a large black desk, talking on the phone. There were two chairs in front of the desk, and a bank of video screens to the left monitoring the shop and the streets around it. Otherwise, with the exception of a few doors, the room was enclosed with giant Lucite fish tanks, containing everything from sea horses to sharks. Even overhead sea life swam back and forth above a glass ceiling.

The Fish hung up the phone, and then walked around from behind the desk to give me a hug. He was a big man in his sixties, with a salt and pepper goatee and a rim of white hair surrounding his big, perfectly round, head. He wore loud surfer's shorts, a dark blue tank top, walked barefoot, and smelled like a combination of Ben-Gay and suntan oil. Even though he spent a good portion of each day in this labyrinth, he started each morning with a swim in the ocean, or surfing. "You must be here on business, because I know you're too busy to drag your ass down to the hood just to shoot the shit."

"Actually I just came by because I like having the Kulaui brothers feel me up. Do those guys ever do anything except watch television?"

"Yeah, they eat poi, and scare vatos off the beach while I'm in the water. You want something to drink? Let me show you some pictures of Darlene? How's the old man?"

I spent a few minutes looking at pictures of the Fish's new granddaughter, and talking about my father's recent prostate surgery.

The Fish earned his nickname as a member of the Navy's Underwater Demolition Team in Korea. He served with my father, and was instrumental in the forming of the Navy's modern day

S.E.A.L. teams. Unlike my dad, Vietnam disillusioned Fish. When he expressed his displeasure with the corruption of the U.S. Military it got him a dishonorable discharge. So the Fish chose to exploit that corruption and it made him rich. The Fish was an employment agency and a weapons broker for free lance mercenaries looking for jobs that couldn't advertise in the classifieds.

"I'll tell you," Fish said, "when the doctors want to stick a knife up my ass, I think I'm just going to put a gun in my mouth instead."

"I know the old man thought about it, but he still believes it's a sin."

"One sin more or one less, isn't going to make a hell of a lot of difference in any of our lives, if that shit matters." He went behind his desk, pulled out a bottle of Don Julio silver and a roll of Dixie cups. "But, your dad always did see himself as the righteous warrior."

I just nodded my head. That was a whole discussion I didn't want to have at the time.

"They broke the mold after making your father." He pushed a Dixie cup full of the clear liquid across the desk. The peppery smell and the soothing fire it promised were incredibly tempting.

"I better not," I said.

"Well this must be serious. What'd you get yourself into this time?"

I told him the specifics of the morning, as if I were de-briefing a mission. The Fish sipped his tequila from the paper cup. He asked to see the e-mail with the picture of Lauren. A few other times he stopped me to ask specific questions.

When I'd finished the Fish took a slow sip of his tequila. "So what're you doing here?" I noticed that the top of his head had turned from brown to a rusty red. It could have been the agave, or anger.

"This all feels like someone who might have our kind of connections, who might've done our kind of work. Maybe they needed some specialty items, or some crew?" I said.

Fish spent a moment sitting perfectly still. He was looking directly at me, but his eyes weren't focused on mine. "Cuño, how long do you think I'd stay alive if I couldn't be trusted to mind my own business? Even if I knew anything about these pendejos, now that you've come here, it wouldn't take much for a pissed off customer to find out where the information came from."

"I just hoped it'd be tougher for you to tell me no in person."

Fish smiled, "You're a smart boy. Just watch your fucking step with this shit. We're close, but if you pull something like this again, it could shoot you in the ass and blow up in your face."

"I wouldn't have come here if I wasn't in serious trouble."

Fish walked over and gave me another short hug, then pushed me toward the door I came in. "I know. But you got to leave now. I never know who's monitoring this place, or has got a fucking surveillance camera on it." He pushed a button on the desk and the door swung open. The sea animals in the aquariums surrounding it swirled agitatedly. "Quidado hijo."

I nodded as the door shut behind me.

I regained my weapon while exchanging more banter with the Samoans on the way out. I navigated the Mustang out into Compton's desolation, thinking about what just transpired.

If Fish didn't know anything he would have just said so. He would have offered to help in any way he could. What Fish just told me, was that there was some professional he'd done business with recently, who bought something, or hired someone, that could have been for this job.

Our meeting was all on security tape. If a client wanted to accuse Fish of betraying them, he could play the tape to show his lack of cooperation.

'Quidado hijo,' meant be careful my son. The Fish usually called me 'niño,' which meant boy, less of an endearment.

He'd said, "I never know who's monitoring this place, or has got a fucking surveillance camera on it." Fish would definitely know if someone were watching him. Nothing existed within two blocks of the Hog Barn without Fish being able to know what, or who, it was.

Was he trying to tell me that my opponent had sophisticated surveillance equipment? Video cameras?

He'd said, "…watch your step with this shit… it could shoot you in the ass and blow up in your face."

Was he saying that they had rocket-propelled grenades, or explosive booby traps, rigged with trip wires? I searched my memory for anything else the Fish had cryptically told me.

Chapter 10

The route to my next meeting at the Hollywood Park Racetrack carried me east into Inglewood, where its proud citizens were trying desperately to fight off the invasion of poverty that turned a community into a wasteland. Fresh coats of brightly colored paint adorned the businesses that were not boarded up, and the criminal element hadn't overrun the main thoroughfares, though there were definitely side streets where it wasn't wise to travel without an invitation or a gun.

Jack Warner built the thoroughbred racetrack back in the late nineteen thirties with the help of other film magnates like Darryl Zanuck, Sam Goldwyn, and a host of their stars, during a time when Inglewood was still mostly cattle ranches being prospected by oil speculators. Though the neighborhood around it has deteriorated from some of its original beauty, the colorfully landscaped raceway grounds and clubhouse pavilions, built around two infield lakes and interspersed with sumptuous palm groves, have remained an oasis of glamour and a memorial to the allure of fast money.

It was 15:45 p.m. and I'd scheduled the meeting at four o'clock with Anthony Cerda. He was not a man who would wait around if we were late.

Looking for Marianna's car I did a quick circuit of the racetrack parking lots before parking near the entrance to the horse barns. I opened the door and inhaled the aroma of manure and spilled beer that emanated from the paddocks and the parking lot. I started to call Marianna to get her ETA but then her yellow Corvette skittered into the parking lot and accelerated towards me before I could dial her number. She hopped out of her car, saying, "Hey, good news. Steve Kelvin text messaged me from Malibu with something interesting while I was driving down here."

I caught a pleasant waft of her perfume as she walked up. She gave me a big smile with freshly glossed lips. I steered her towards the entrance to the paddock area.

"Steve talked to a woman," she said, "who was out running this morning on Trancas Canyon Road. This witness saw a road construction crew that set up for work, but then they drove off in the space of an hour, around the time Lauren went missing."

"Okay," I said.

"This girl also thinks she saw one of the men who was driving the trucks this morning before, on foot, in the same area a few weeks ago, and he said he was scouting for a movie…"

"We've checked with the utilities right?"

Marianna said, "There's been no scheduled or emergency work in that area for the last two weeks."

"Vehicle thefts?"

"Nothing matching a utility truck in Southern California recently."

"Did you check Picture Vehicle Houses?"

"I'm sorry?"

"You know, where they rent cars and trucks to movie companies. They have all kinds of utility vans."

"I didn't think of it."

"Get someone on it."

Marianna called into the office, while I talked to the gate guard, and waited for our visitor passes to be processed.

She finished her call as I guided her through the gate, where the pavement was replaced with worn turf, which quickly gave way under one of Marianna's heels, throwing her off balance.

I grabbed her under the arm. She blushed and apologized.

"No, I'm sorry," I said. "Navigating in pumps is not a consideration I usually think of."

"It will keep me on my toes, no? I'll try not to topple into the horse droppings in front of Mr. Cerda."

I smiled. As she gingerly made her way, leaning on me a little, through the labyrinthine stable area, I was confident that she would be an asset at this meeting. As usual, she was immaculately put together. Well-toned muscles flexed the brown skin of her bare legs, the neckline of her lime green linen suit showed a tasteful, yet alluring, amount of cleavage.

In the few minutes it took us to maneuver towards the barn where we were meeting the Mafioso, I shared my interpretation of my meeting with the Fish.

When I finished she said, "I brought the information we gathered on those suspects Holiday suggested, I think you're going to be interested in what we dug up on Kyle Pemberton."

We turned a corner and one of Cerda's beefy bodyguards stopped us.

They asked us to surrender our weapons, along with anything electronic. After we unloaded they used hand-held metal detectors to ensure that neither of us was holding out. Then we were ushered into the row of horse stalls where Anthony Cerda was inspecting one of his thoroughbreds, running his hands over the mare and speaking with the horse's trainer in hushed tones.

Cerda sat in a custom built wheelchair, with off-road tires that made it easier for him to maneuver through the barn area. He was now a paraplegic as the result of an assassination attempt.

He wore a white sleeveless V-neck sweater over a black polo shirt. His arms were tan and muscular. His jet-black hair was cut short and tousled stylishly. When he spun the chair around to greet us, his blue eyes immediately met Marianna's, after which, a smile broke across his face.

"Well, good afternoon. Richard, you didn't tell me you'd be bringing a friend."

"Actually she's an associate. Ms. Ruiz is the head of our Investigations Department."

"Really?" he pushed the chair forward. "Am I being investigated?"

"Why, would you like to be?" Marianna held his gaze with a little smile.

"I'm sure it would be more enjoyable for me than dealing with those stunads at the D.A.'s office." He held out his hand.

"Anthony Cerda. Forgive me for not standing in the presence of a lady."

She said. "Forgiveness is only warranted when there has been an offense."

He started to smile, but then something crossed his face, he let go of her hand, and spun the chair back towards the horse. "I'm sure Mr. Braddock informed you of my situation. However, it's still pleasant to meet someone who handles it with style. Do you bet the ponies Ms. Ruiz?"

"They're beautiful animals. I like to watch them run."

"Well, you should put some money on this little darling. I don't think you'll be disappointed. Danish Manners in the fourth race."

"Win, place or show?"

While moving around to the other side of the horse's head, and turning back so that he could stroke it's flank and speak to his guests, Cerda said, "Playing the safe money takes all the fun out of it, don't you think?"

"I suppose you're right," Marianna said. "May I touch her nose? I just love the way they feel."

Cerda ignored the sour look on the trainer's face saying, "Certainly. It's a shame she's running today, otherwise you could feed her carrots."

Marianna carefully stepped over to the mare and stroked her gingerly. The horse snorted hot air, and bobbed her head up and down.

This time Cerda acknowledged the trainers consternation. "I think we had better let the young lady prepare for her race."

The group stood silent for a moment, watching the trainer lead the horse away, before Cerda spoke again. "I never really cared for racing much before my accident. Now I'm fascinated by it. I'm sure the psychology of that is painfully obvious. But still, here I am… So, what is it you really want?"

I stepped in, "Someone snatched one of my clients and they're trying to get Paragon to pay a lot of money to get her back. We're wondering if you heard anything about it?"

Cerda seemed amused. "No. No, I haven't."

I explained some of the details and said, "The way it's being handled, I thought it could be people you might know."

"It's a pretty smart con. If it wouldn't fuck up all the other things we've got going, I'd be tempted to try it myself. However it wouldn't be one of my people because they'd be shitting where I eat."

"That's what Mr. Braddock thought," Marianna interjected, "But perhaps it is one of your competitors? Or someone trying to make a name for themselves?"

"Richard, did you not inform the lovely young lady that the film industry provides us such an easy avenue for legitimizing the profits from our other sources of income, that only a complete idiot would do something to disrupt it?"

"I've been informed," Marianna straightened a line in her clothing, "But I've noticed that there is no shortage of idiots in any line of business."

"Well, you certainly have a point there," he said laughing. Then he reached out and touched her forearm in the same way he'd touched the horse earlier, lightly, with admiration. "It would have to be someone who's not connected, someone very stupid, or very desperate."

"How about movement on hot utility trucks?" I asked.

Cerda shook his head.

"Is there any idiot you can think of who might be stupid or desperate enough?" Marianna asked nicely.

Cerda laughed again and thought for a moment. "There's a guy named David Holt who might be both."

I shared a look with Marianna. "His name's come up from other sources today."

"So you know the scam he pulled at Paragon? If he'd involved us, I could've been wetting my beak and maybe kept it from blowing up. But now he's in serious trouble with the Russians."

"And he's having trouble with the Russians because…?"

"Because he's an idiot…" Cerda smiled appealingly. "He needed to do something with the money he was skimming, so he started investing in apartment buildings, and like every other knucklehead who got drunk on the housing boom, he overleveraged his capital. He didn't want a bank snooping around Paragon performing due diligence, so he borrowed from my Eastern European competitors. Now that he's lost his sources of income, they're foreclosing in their own special way."

Cerda smiled again, but this time it looked predatory. "Apartment buildings are good places to run hookers and drugs out of, and Holt has all those nicely established shell companies to provide a legitimate front for other business…"

"If there's any investigation, the paper trail points to him," Marianna said.

Cerda shrugged. "Or, there's always the witness protection program… Please send my regards, should you pay him a visit."

"If this solves our problem, I'll see it's worth your while," I said.

Cerda waived his hand. "Whoever it is, if they get away with this, it's just going to create problems for us all. I'm not doing you any favors, and I'm going to make damn sure this isn't someone I know." He looked at his watch.

"Mr. Cerda, if you could just give us a few more moments?" Marianna said, ignoring my warning glance. "I'm sure you must have access to artists in the documentation field. This crew is going to want to leave the country. You'd probably have better luck than we would finding where they've gotten their I.D.'s."

Cerda spun his chair a quarter turn and patted the back of Marianna's thigh. "You've got to do something more than just look pretty darling. I'm not the Private Eye, you are."

"How about a man named Kyle Pemberton, do you know anything about him?"

Cerda rolled his chair away, "Never heard of him," he said and continued going. Two of the four guards, closed in around the chair, and the other two invited us to take our guns, phones, and leave.

After we holstered up, and started back to our cars, I said, "Well, you certainly know how to wear out a welcome."

"At least I didn't pimp anyone out today."

"You were working it pretty hard without any help from me."

"Good thing this isn't 'hump the handicapped week'."

"You could do worse."

Marianna glared at me as she started walking back to the parking lot. "You owe me a new pair of shoes."

"So, what were you going to tell me about Kyle Pemberton?"

"He certainly has the experience to run a professional abduction."

I looked to her for elaboration.

"Before getting into the movie business Pemberton worked as an asset for hire, mostly in Africa. He left the Marine Corps with a Disciplinary Discharge, but he ran a Force Recon team in Desert Storm."

The Recon boys were as tough as they come. "Seems like maybe he wanted more of a war," I said.

"Maybe it's nothing." She brushed a strand of hair from her cheek. "He's been out of prison for seven months, and checked in with his parole officer last week. Still, I'd like to question him."

When we arrived at our cars, she removed two folders from her briefcase in the corvette, and handed them to me. I flipped through the downloads of news articles covering the Pemberton sexual assault story, and a few magazine stories profiling his work as a combat advisor to the movies, while Marianna knocked the mud and manure off her expensive pumps, and then slipped her feet back into them.

"Where's Pemberton right now?"

"Living in Woodland Hills since his release, but he doesn't answer his numbers, and he's not gone to work since that meeting with his P.O."

"Where was he working?"

"He's teaching Martial Arts at several places."

"Did you send someone to hunt him down?"

"I hired a subcontractor to do a physical locate."

I looked at the second file with research on David Holt while Marianna freshened her make-up. It contained his personal information and residence address, his real estate holdings, and a number of addresses linked to his businesses. He had no criminal file.

"All but one of those business addresses are private mail boxes," Marianna said. "But there's one that's brick and mortar out in Van Nuys. I sent someone to his home, and told them to sit on it until he shows."

"Good, I'll talk to The Bull, and see if one of his people can put eyes on this business address." I held up the files she'd given me. "This is great work in such a short time."

"That's why you pay me so well," she said.

"Hey, and thanks for in there." I pointed my head towards the stables. "I wouldn't be surprised if he called you."

"Maybe he'll be able to keep me in the style I've become accustomed to without having to bust my ass all the time. You'd be sorry then."

"It'd serve me right," I said, getting into my car.

Both sets of tires chirped, as our cars raced out of the parking lot.

CHAPTER 11

Around four o'clock in the afternoon the Los Angeles automotive circulatory system clogs like the arteries of a fat man eating a Pastrami sandwich. There was no fast way of getting anywhere unless you were airborne. I was tempted to have the chopper pick me up and get me to the office, but if I left the Mustang anywhere south of Slausen Avenue, it would be a chassis sitting on blocks by the time I got back to it, if it was there at all. I used the time on the phone getting situation reports from the office and everyone in the field.

The Bull's team had struck out on the canvassing they did along the surface streets from the freeway to Paragon. I didn't think it would pan out, but we had to do our due diligence. They had moved on to physically locating and verifying alibis of the crazies on Lauren's watch list. I briefed them on the information we'd gotten from Cerda. The Bull's team was already in the Valley, so he dispatched T-bone to go have a look at Holt's business address. He was on a motorcycle and could weave through even the worst traffic.

Kaminoff's supercomputers hadn't turned up any link to the kidnappers, but his hackers were getting wired into the email accounts of the *Forced Conclusions* production staff, and were running searches for anything suspicious. Investigators at my office were still wading through the backgrounds of anyone connected with the movie to see if there were cross-references with any of the suspects.

Marianna called to inform me that she'd gotten confirmation from the Dept. of Corrections that Vincent Ito, the fan who wanted to make love to Lauren with a samurai sword, was trying to escape from Corcoran State Prison, a maximum-security unit, so they'd transferred him to Pelican Bay, which was designated as a Super Max facility.

She also told me that Jack Gillis was having a hard time locating the woman who Lauren's lover had brought home from the bar. Jack had developed some leads though, and was pounding the pavement.

We were approaching the halfway point of the twenty-four hour window the kidnappers gave us until their next scheduled communication, and although we had done a huge amount of work I didn't feel we were getting close enough.

After I'd called everyone I could, and tried Victoria again with no connection, I sat stewing in traffic for a while before Marianna called again. She said, "We've got a lead on two trucks, painted to match LA Department of Water and Power, they were rented by Derosier's Picture Cars to a Broken Dreams Productions. I called the phone number for the production company - there's no answer, no voice mail. I had the office run some searches on the company, and they seem as legit as any independent production company; they've had a few blurbs in the trades talking about a low budget action-adventure they were trying to get off the ground. But it seems weird that they wouldn't answer their phone."

"Where are they located?"

"They've got an office in North Hollywood." She dictated the address on Riverside Drive, and I scribbled it down.

I said, "I'll call The Bull, and have him check it out."

We hung up, and while I was dialing, my phone rang showing T-bone's number. "Hey boss," he said. "I took a run at that Holt address you wanted me to check out, and it's a can of worms."

"How so?" I said.

"It's a group of buildings. The big one that fronts Woodman Place houses a strip club with a parking lot, but behind it there's a fenced in area sectioned off with some nice cars parked in it, a bunch of trailers, and a smaller building. Then separated by another fence, is this third building that backs up to a cement plant. It almost looks like a separate business, because it's got it's own parking lot and entrance, but I saw an Armenian looking guy walk from the middle building to the one in the back, and he had what looked like a chrome plated .45, shoved in his waistband."

"So what's your feeling?"

"That back building would be a good place to hide a hostage, if you had one."

I told T-bone to sit tight, called The Bull, and brought him up to speed. He agreed to send the rest of his team over to support T-bone, while he checked out the Broken Dreams Productions office himself.

My original plan was returning to the office, but with the development of an armed man, connected to a suspect who had been substantiated by two sources, I needed to get my tactical gear. Returning from Mexico the day before, I'd gone straight to my house from the airport, so all of my radios, surveillance gear and weapons, were still packed in their travel case that I'd dropped in my study. I also hoped that Victoria would be home, so that I could finally have a few minutes to explain what was going on in person.

When I wound up our driveway, I saw Victoria's Jaguar parked in the garage, confirming my suspicions that she purposely avoided speaking with me for the entire day.

I sat behind the wheel of the Mustang for a few moments. I'd been running on adrenaline and coffee all day. If I went into the house appearing as though I were just there to solve another problem, it would only exacerbate her feelings of diminished importance. I took deep breaths and tried to clear my mind of the urgent "to do" list revolving in my head.

Our garage enters into a mudroom, adjacent to the kitchen. I could hear John Coltrane's version of "My Favorite Things," playing from the living room. I took off my sport coat, hanging it on the back of a chair. I unclipped my gun from the back of my pants, and placed it in the pocket of the coat. Though I'd taught Victoria to shoot and she wasn't uncomfortable with weapons, going armed in the house was not one of my wife's favorite things...

In the living room I saw Victoria's head silhouetted above the couch, looking west. The sun was setting behind the surrounding hills, bathing the room in amber.

I sat on the love seat, at right angles to the sofa she occupied. A bottle of Pinot Noir stood on the coffee table. Victoria held an empty glass in her hand. She wore a camel colored full-length shift, her hair was tied back, and she sat with her knees pulled up under her chin.

The song finished, but instead of moving on to another track, it started in again from the beginning.

She said, "I just thought I'd listen to it a few more times."

"Okay."

"No, it's not okay Richard. It's not okay."

"Okay," I said again, and we sat listening to the music.

Finally she moved to pour herself more wine.

"I love sitting here watching the sunset," she said. "I love this house."

"Victoria…" I started, but she cut me off.

"No," she said. "No. I know you have some perfectly good reason. I just can't take it anymore. I just can't stand being alone this much."

"I know it's hard for you," I said, moving to sit next to her, but she shot to her feet, skittering away from me.

"No. Don't be charming. I'm not going to let you," she said placing the coffee table between us, her long body a cameo in the picture window.

"It's not your fault," she continued. "It's my fault. You haven't changed, I have."

"No, it is my fault," I said. "I know you've heard it before, but today I just had to be there."

"Oh, Richard that's not it."

"Well then what is?" I said, hearing the anger in my voice.

"I want a divorce," she said.

"What?"

"I'm getting older Richard. I'm not the woman you married."

"What the hell is that supposed to mean?"

"I'm not a girl anymore. I'm thirty-two. It's time for me to grow up. We've just been playing house in this marriage. We're not a family, we're like a couple of kids shacking up together."

"In a pretty nice shack," I said.

"Oh for Christ's sake, that's not the point, and you know it."

"Well then what is the point?"

"I want more than this Richard. I want more. I want a family. I want children. I want a divorce, so I can possibly make a life before I get too old."

"When did this happen?"

"I've been trying to tell you, but you just wouldn't listen."

"How? How could I not listen, when this is the first time in our entire lives you've said to me, 'I want to have children'?"

"There are more ways to communicate than talking. I've been throwing out hints for months. I'd say, 'Isn't that little boy cute?' and you'd just say, 'Yeah,' and go back to whatever you were doing."

"Oh, come on, that's not fair."

"Would it be fair for me to try and rope you into it? Would it be fair if I pressured you, so that you'd do it just to make me happy?"

"But I do want you to be happy."

"And I have been. I've been really happy, but if we try and stay together, one of us is going to end up resenting the other, and we'll never be truly happy again."

"So that's it? I don't have a choice in this?"

"Don't you see," she said moving to the back of the couch, so that half of her face became illuminated. "This is not something we can sit down and talk about, like where we're going to take our next vacation. You have to want it." She turned and faced the last of the sun as it disappeared over the mountain. She was fully lit and then slowly cast in shadow. "The problem is, that I can't stop looking at babies and wanting one."

"But I told you from the start I didn't want kids." I stood up, and walked away from her, towards the fireplace. "And you said you didn't want any either."

"I know, I know, I'm sorry," she said beginning to cry. "I told you it was my fault. I stood there in the studio, imagining what it would be like, to teach all those little kids how to dance, and it just made me realize how much I need to have one of my own now."

"Victoria, Jesus…" I said, turning back towards her, "Couldn't we…"

"I know," she said again, holding up a hand as if to ward me off. "I know this isn't the right time to talk about it. I know you have something bad happening. Maybe that's why I just had to say it tonight, because your defenses are down. I'm sorry."

"That's not what I was going to say." I kept moving after her. "Work can…, we can talk this out. I had no idea."

"I can't," she said backing away from me. "You'll be charming and sweet and understanding. You'll make me not want to lose you. " She moved into the kitchen. "And I don't. I don't want to lose you. That's why we can't talk about it, I just have to do it."

She grabbed her keys off the counter and ran out the garage door.

"Honey, come on..." I called after her, but by the time I was in the kitchen, I heard the Jaguar start. When I made it to the garage, the car was already backed into the driveway.

"Victoria. Wait, Goddamn it. You can't just fucking leave," I shouted.

I could see her hesitate for a moment. She looked at me, when I got closer to the car, with an expression of torment I'd never seen on her face before.

But then she turned her head and popped the clutch. The Jaguar's tires screeched as the car shot down the drive.

I almost caught up to her where she had to slow and turn onto the street, but she didn't event touch the brakes. Sparks flew from where the undercarriage slammed against the asphalt, her tires emitted the acrid odor of singed rubber, and then squealed again as she shifted into second, accelerating away from me.

I could have run back to my car and chased her. I could have easily gotten a fix on her GPS, but I didn't.

I walked back to the house thinking about all the things she'd said, about all the things we hadn't talked about. I didn't want to have children because I was afraid to. I'd been responsible for bad things. I'd been responsible for people dying who didn't deserve to be killed. I felt that if I dared to bring life of my own into the world I would be punished for it.

Coltrane was still wailing when I got back inside the house. I shut him up.

I went upstairs to change into a black polo shirt, and black jeans. I exchanged the cowboy boots for a pair of lace-up black boots with the soles of a tennis shoe. I replaced the blazer with a dark blue windbreaker.

I came down to my study, and spun the combination to the weapons vault. I removed what looked like a fat guitar case, specially made to carry my tactical equipment, and checked its contents.

Folded tightly inside, were my Kevlar flack vest, containing radio, headset, earplugs, extra battery, and clips of ammunition. Fit snugly into molded foam cutouts, was a Styer AUG assault-rifle, and its three interchangeable barrels. The molded gray composite body was lightweight, easily concealed under a windbreaker or coat, because the 42 round clip was mounted on the stock behind the trigger housing. It could fire single shot, fully automatic, or in three round bursts. The short and easily concealable 350 mm Carbine barrel could be quickly changed in the field to the 621 mm length, for long-range accuracy that rivaled most "sniper only" weapons.

Packed into the opposite side of the case was a Frachi SPAS shotgun with collapsible stock. This weapon could fire 8 shells automatically, or by pump action, thus enabling the use of non-lethal rounds or tear gas canisters by just changing the magazine.

So far, the only thing either weapon had been used for was eye-wash, shredding paper targets, and wowing clients.

Anyone who hasn't done it - thinks killing is cool.

But they're right too. It was so cool it was stone cold.

The chill from death made me so cool that I was more comfortable with these pieces of steel, plastic, and explosives than I was with a beautiful woman who wanted me to share the warmth of new life.

After re-locking the case, I grabbed a knapsack containing rope, climbing gear, first aid, a variety of grenades, and other goodies.

The weapons got locked in the trunk of the Mustang. Then I started the car and careened it through the winding streets down the hill towards the San Fernando Valley.

CHAPTER 12

There's a joke about Neil Armstrong placing a sign on the moon that said, "Los Angeles City Limits." LA seems to be an unending conglomeration of mini-cities, covering more area than the state of Rhode Island. Van Nuys, sits right in the middle of the San Fernando Valley, where manufacturing and aerospace companies paved over rich orchard land in the middle of the last century to build many large plants and factory compounds. Then, as those companies outsourced their work to other states and other countries where the labor was cheaper, or the tax loopholes were bigger, many of the plants were bulldozed to make way for bunkers of low-income housing and strip malls. The rest were subdivided into a nest of stone yards, auto dismantlers, cabinet shops, and movie equipment warehouses. Strip clubs, like the one allegedly connected to our suspect David Holt, were sprinkled throughout the maze of anonymous blue-collar businesses, catering to some of the men who worked in the neighborhood, but gaining the larger part of their clientele from white collar businessmen who enjoyed the camouflage the industrial district afforded them from their spouses, girlfriends, and business associates.

By the time I reached the blocks of stucco apartment buildings that line Sherman Way - the major east/west boulevard south of Holt's address - Bull's team had created a surveillance perimeter on the rooftops surrounding the Holt compound. He directed me to park the Mustang on Raymer Street, in front of the concrete plant that bordered the rear of Holt's property. Raymer was deserted, illuminated only by a few lights around the office of the cement works, which shone on the mixing trucks corralled behind a block wall that had broken glass protruding along its top. The rest of the expansive property contained mounds of different sands and gravels, the mixing tower, with its many conveyors and shoots, but nothing that would really be worth stealing, unless you were going to do it with a crane, a skip loader, and a dump truck. Hence, the only security was an oxidized, chain link fence.

I popped the trunk of the Mustang, threw on my climbing harness and tactical vest, slid the shoulder strap of the Styer AUG across my chest so that the assault weapon nestled under my arm, and donned the windbreaker, which was sized to hide everything unobtrusively beneath the jacket. The men had unwoven a strand of the chain link fence surrounding the concrete plant, creating a breach that a man could easily slip through. Using a flashlight with a red night lens, I walked along inside the fence bordering the edge of the property as it traveled along the backs of the industrial buildings, adjacent to the mixing yard. I waded through the tangle of weeds, stacks of broken pallets, cement sack remnants and plastic bags the fence caught on the wind until I came to a black climbing rope the team had left dangling down the back of a massive brick building.

After scrambling up the rope and climbing over a parapet surrounding the top of the structure, I could see the top of The Bull's hulking silhouette backlit in the dim radiance of artificial light spilling from somewhere below the left side of the building. I trod quietly across the crunchy surface of the deteriorating asphalt roof to The Bull's position, which looked into the rear of the Holt property. The parcel of land was a rectangle, bordered on one side by the building upon which we were perched. A cinderblock wall topped with barbed wire bordered the streets at the front and on the opposite side of the compound. The concrete plant was the only rear neighbor visible and created a dead end to the side street. On the large building at the front of Holt's property, I could see the colored lights of a neon sign advertising the Bare X-ellence Lounge, flashing above the entrance off the parking lot that T-bone had described to me on the phone. Several pick-up trucks and a few cars indicated a sparse early evening crowd.

Two eight-foot tall iron bar fences, running from one side of the property to the other, partitioned the middle third of the property from the front and the rear. An electric gate offered vehicle access to parking spaces for a dozen cars within the center enclosure, though only a silver Mercedes SUV and a maroon Lexus sat there now. A low flat building with a shed roof, two doors and one window, covered the side of the property next to the street, while the rest of the area was populated with six mobile office trailers; the kind you usually see at construction sites, except that there were different colored curtains covering the inside of the windows. The spaces between the trailers provided barely enough room for the metal steps leading to their entry doors.

A giant corrugated tin building, like a Quonset hut only bigger, covered the entire length of the fence bordering the concrete plant at the back of the property. It looked like half of a giant oil drum laid on its side, with two dormered entrances accessing the parking lot in front of it, and three dormered windows that showed the glow of interior light behind paper shades caked with grimy dust. On the cracked asphalt, between the Quonset building and the fence enclosing the trailers, two black Lincoln Town Cars were parked next to a black Lincoln Navigator, and an older model, Crew-Cab pickup truck. Another electric gate provided access to the side street for the vehicles, and there was a man-sized door in the iron fence, for travel to the front of the property that looked like it might have an electric lock on it also.

When I finished assessing the layout of the area, and hunched down next to The Bull against the rolled roofing of the parapet, he said, "You alright?"

"What do you mean?"

"You look like shit man. Like someone just kicked you in the balls."

I didn't address the irony of his statement. "When I went to get my gear, Vic told me she wants a divorce because now she wants to have kids."

"With everything that's going on?"

"She doesn't know, I haven't told her," I said.

"What the fuck?"

I held up my hand. "I didn't want to get into it with her, and I don't want to get into it with you now. What have we got here?"

Bull tilted his head at the Quonset building, "T-bone and Kelly are on the roof, and they've unscrewed the vent turbines and peeked inside. Sparky's taken a high position across the street." He pointed to the top of a stucco building on the other side of the dead end, but the moon hadn't shown itself yet, and though there were lights that spilled onto the ground from the corners of the buildings, the roofs were so dark, that I couldn't see any of our team members.

"Anyone show themselves since you've been here?"

"That Mercedes SUV pulled into the center lot, a heavy set guy with thinning dark hair got out, went into the smaller building, and then a few minutes later was escorted out to one of those trailers. T-bone says, the guy that showed the Mercedes driver to the trailer was the same guy he saw going back to the Quonset hut, but he had a jacket on this time, and I couldn't confirm that he was packing a weapon."

"What do you think, they've got a little get-up-and-go brothel set up there?"

"That's what it looks like," The Bull said. "They have any problem, get any law or city inspectors snooping around, they just hook that Crew Cab up to those trailers, and move them till the storm's over."

Lately there had been a crackdown on a lot of the massage parlors and acupuncture clinics fronting for whorehouses throughout the city. Human rights groups started revealing to the public and the press that the women working in them were often illegal immigrants, forced to work off a travel debt by unscrupulous traffickers, who lured them to the US with bogus promises of legitimate jobs. The panderers took the women's passports, and forced them into the sex trade, threatening to hurt their families back home if they escaped, rebelled, or refused to provide certain services.

"Build a better mouse trap, they'll build a better mouse," I said. Then I switched on the radio secured in my tactical vest, worked in the earpiece, and pressed the mike button. "T-bone, what've you got over there?"

"Hey boss," T-bone whispered over the radio. "There's at least five men in the building, and a room at the back of the space that's been recently constructed, which would be good for containing a hostage out of sight."

"What are the men doing?"

"Mostly smoking cigarettes and bullshitting it looks like, playing games and watching TV. Then every once in a while, a noise comes out of the back area, and the men either just shout at it or get up to pound on the door, and shout something in their language that seems like 'Shut up' with some elaboration or commentary."

"Copy," I said into the radio. Then privately I asked The Bull, "Did you have the office run the plates on all the vehicles?"

"The plates on the Town Cars and the Navigator are registered to one of Holt's companies, none of the others belong to anyone on our radar. Sparky went into the club for a little while, but didn't see anyone matching Holt's description."

"What about utility trucks?"

"Nothing."

"What do you think?"

He shrugged. "If we had time, I'd say just watch and see what's going on."

"If we had time, you and I wouldn't be on this roof," I said. Then over the radio for the rest of the team, "I'm on the move to T-bone's position."

"Roger that," crackled in my earpiece, from each of the men.

A grappling hook secured a rope to the edge of the parapet, and I carefully slid down the ten feet to the top of the Quonset's metal roof, then moved quietly in the dark to the first of the two vent turbines, spaced so that they divided the building in thirds. The crown shaped fan was set aside carefully at the apex of the curved roof, a few feet from where the vent tube poked through. The vent was a round cylinder, made of aluminum sheet metal, with a dusty screen attached to the bottom of it. I looked down it briefly, but could only discern a clutter of what looked like lighting equipment used in the film business, so I made my way to the second tube, that was closer to the side street, where T-bone and Kelly crouched in the darkness.

We greeted each other silently and I looked down into the tube. They had clipped away the screen, and pushed it open. By leaning over, and sticking my head and shoulders into the tube, I could get a better view of the cavernous space. I had to pull my head out, and re-position around the tube several times in order to get the full view of the area below.

Workbenches were placed in a fairly organized fashion within the space, and there were a number of metal shelf units, that contained plastic bins with parts, cables, and other items, related to the pieces of lighting equipment. The bins were stacked in sections according to their kind over most of the remaining floor area. Some of the equipment was marked with a green paint that I'd seen marking the equipment used at Paragon studios, and I wondered if these were perhaps a collection of pieces that Holt had pilfered from the studio during his tenure there.

Towards the street side of the building the equipment had been carelessly pushed aside. A couple of mismatched leather couches, which were torn in spots, faced a big screen TV. Two bare, badly stained mattresses lay on the floor a short distance from the couches. A small refrigerator was plugged into the wall, next to another table, closer to the entry door, the top of which was littered with pizza boxes, Chinese take-out containers, and empty Bud light cans. An overflowing trashcan of the same detritus stood next to the table. Two men who had the size to be bouncers from the strip club sat on one of the couches, watching the television that was blaring a sitcom with sub-titles in some Cyrillic language, while another three men with sharp features, dark hair, and solid colored dress clothes, sat at a wooden table playing dominos. Leaning against the arm of the sofa nearest to the table of domino players, were an AR-15 rifle and a pump shotgun. One of the domino players, displaying two bare arms sleeved in tattoos, wore a shoulder holster, enclosing a large plated revolver with rubber grips.

I scooted around so that I could see the other end of the building. At the back stood the partition that T-bone had described. A wall constructed of new-looking plywood rose from floor to ceiling, making a separate room out of the last quarter of the Quonset hut. It contained only one door, held closed by a large bolt slid through a hasp.

"They haven't gone in there while I've been here," T-bone said. "Just the shouting."

"And you say the noise is like an animal?"

"It's like this high pitched moan or wail, like a lonesome dog."

"Maybe that area's for dog fights. The Russians are into that shit."

"It also could be a woman crying, but I didn't want to read too much into it."

"When was the last time you heard it?"

"About twenty minutes ago."

"And these guys have just been sitting here the whole time, no one's come or gone?"

"Not even to the shitter."

Among the equipment strewn around the building I'd also seen several rolls of black fabric called Duvetyn, used for many purposes in the film business, but mainly for blocking light. The photo of Lauren had been taken against a black background, and some of the men looked meaty enough to own the thick forearms that held her shoulders in the photograph.

I looked at my watch. We could either find out what was in that room, or sit there with our thumbs up our butts all night waiting for something to happen. "Bull," I whispered into the radio mike, "get your big ass over here. I've got a job for you." While he was making his way to my position, I laid out my plan over the radio.

I told Sparky to get down from his roof across the street. His job was going to be to create a diversion on my signal.

The Bull was going to lower me down through the ventilation tube that was closest to the plywood enclosure, once Sparky got the attention of the men inside the building. Kelly was to hold T-bone's legs, so that he could hang upside down through the front ventilation shaft and shoot, if necessary.

"What are you going to do if Lauren's in there?" The Bull said.

"I'm going to call you on the radio, and tell you to call in the cavalry, while I stay with her and shoot anyone who comes through that door not wearing LAPD blue."

"And if she's not?"

"Then you're going to haul me out of there and we're going to find out where she really is."

The Bull gave me one of his looks that said he thought I was crazy, but he'd known me long enough by then not to try and talk me out of something I'd decided on, unless he had a much better idea.

When everyone was ready I gave Sparky the signal, and shortly we heard the rumble from the pipes on his Suzuki before seeing his bike weaving down the side street as if its rider were looking for an address. He stopped the bike in front of the Quonset building and got off while leaving the motor running. He banged on the loading door that faced the street. Hearing the first set of loud bangs, I climbed through the vent tube in the roof to a point where I could ease my weight from my arms onto the figure eight ring on my climbing harness. The Bull held my weight, belayed on the rope, and I sat suspended thirty feet above the concrete, watching as the group of men talked about what to do about the banging on the door.

At first they seemed to agree to ignore it, but Sparky was persistent. Eventually, the man with the tattoos and the shoulder holster carrying the chrome .357, went over to answer the door, saying, "Who is it?" in heavily accented English.

The other men looked after their comrade, each seeming to lean forward expectantly for an answer.

As soon as I heard Sparky's voice launching into an explanation about how he was new in town, was lost, and late for his debut as the male lead of Alice in Anal Land, I started to slide silently down the rope behind the backs of Sparky's rapt audience. I touched down softly and released tension on the rope, The Bull pulling it up into the vent shaft, as soon as he felt the absence of my weight.

I swung the Styer AUG up into a covering fire position and took a quick look behind me for obstacles. Then I moved cautiously through the warehouse, up to the door of the plywood enclosure.

I removed the bolt that kept the hasp closed, and eased through the door into a completely dark room, pulling the door closed behind me. A putrid odor assaulted my nostrils. As I clicked on the soft red beam of my flashlight, what it revealed at first confused me, then filled me with loathing and anger.

CHAPTER 13

I swept the room, with the compact red beam of my flashlight, trying not to gag from the smell of shit, piss, sex, vomit and blood, as the dim light exposed a little playpen of sickness.

Sheets of plastic were hung against the walls and covered the floor. In the far corner was a small fetid shower stall, one toilet, a sink, and a claw-foot bathtub, which looked like it had been dropped over there as an afterthought and wasn't connected to any plumbing. A garden hose was attached to the water supply below the sink, and had a pistol grip spray nozzle on the end of it.

Two of the plywood tables, like the ones in the outside room, stood at odd angles, with chains bolted around the perimeter of their tops, handcuffs and other restraints hanging from the chain. One table's legs were sawed off, so that it was only about two feet off the ground. An assortment of mismatched chairs, tables, and two sofas, were thrown around the room, dark stains embedding the fabrics and leatherette. Sex toys littered the floor and the furniture; giant dildos, speculums, whips, and other things I didn't want to learn the purpose of.

A number of large plastic and wire animal carriers were lined against the back wall and halfway down the side of the room nearest the door. A few were empty, with their doors ajar. Behind the steel mesh doors of the rest, the beam of my flashlight found the faces of young girls and a few boys, some with bruises, some recoiling as the light fell across them, all with matted hair, sharing the expressions of terror mixed with resignation, resentment, and a glimmer of hope that this time it won't be their turn.

Several voices pleaded in Spanish, others in languages I didn't recognize, and from the darkness of a cage I hadn't shone the light on yet, I heard a flat voice say in English, "Please, I'm ready to do whatever you want if I can just get out of here."

"Lauren?" I whispered.

"I'll be Lauren if you want me to be," the girl who spoke in English said.

After a quick examination of each cage I realized with some relief that my friend, my client, wasn't in any one of them. Only a collection of immigrants and runaways who were scooped up by the demons that prey on the thousands of children who arrive in LA each year, with nothing to protect them but their dreams of a better life.

"Shhh," I said. "I'm going to get you out of here."

If we called 911, the rest of the night would be spent tangled up with the police answering questions I didn't want to be asked. Some of the foreign girls were starting to make more noise, despite my efforts to quiet them.

"I've got a room full of kids that need our help down here," I said into the radio. Briefly describing the scene. "What's the situation on the other side of my door?"

"The Russians are getting angry because Sparky won't go away."

"Bull and Sparky, cover us from anyone who joins the party. T-bone in position?"

"He's good," The Bull answered for him, since T-bone was hanging upside down through the forward vent hole, and Kelly was belaying his legs. "What's the plan?"

"Take these fuckers down and get the hell out of here, I'll let you know the details later. I'm coming out hot."

I flipped the Styer's safety off, and kicked the door so that it slammed open with a bang. The two bouncer looking guys were still on the couches. One of the domino players was still at the table, while the second one was on his way to join the tattooed guy with the shoulder holster, who was at the front of the building arguing through the closed loading door with Sparky. "Hands in the air. Now," I shouted, using my command voice.

The two bouncers turned in my direction, the guy at the table moved for the AR15, the unarmed domino player started to raise his arms, and tattoo boy went for his .357.

"Don't," I said, but tattoos drew the pistol and was aiming it towards me - until I put three bullets in his chest.

At the same time, T-bone lit up the arm of the sofa where the AR15 and the shotgun rested with a short burst from his Styer. The domino player who was reaching for the weapon fell backwards from the explosion of wood, upholstery, stuffing, and bullets.

The other domino player dropped his hands and made a run for the door, but I squeezed three bullets into the doorjamb ahead of him, causing him to stop abruptly, and practically dislocate his shoulders getting his hands in the air again.

T-bone shouted, "Stay down asshole." But one of the bouncers let out a beastly yell as he climbed over the back of the sofa and charged me.

T-bone couldn't swivel around to get him.

I was really tempted to shoot the ugly charging face, but I'd never shot an unarmed man before and didn't want to start, so as he got close I thrust the barrel of the Styer into his throat, creating a very surprised and painful look on his face, as he slammed into me.

We crashed to the ground and I heard T-bone's weapon fire again. He was shouting, "Now don't fucking move," as I untangled myself from the behemoth, who was rolling around on the concrete floor clutching his crushed larynx, learning how to breathe in a whole new way.

The other bouncer and the two domino players now stood with their hands in the air, amid the cloud of dust and cordite created by T-bone's warning shots in their vicinity.

I advanced with my weapon pointing from one to the other, "Who's got the keys to the Navigator?"

They looked at each other, not wanting to be the one who spoke first, so when I got to the bouncer who was the closest to me, I cracked him in the nose with the butt of the Styer. He let out a cry like a wounded seal, and bellowed in his guttural language at the guy standing by the table, who, when I pointed the weapon at his face, reached into his pocket and produced a ring of keys.

"T-bone, get down here. See if you can find the switch for the gate to the parking lot."

Kelly hauled him back up to the roof, and then provided cover so that The Bull could let T-bone down on the rope.

"Company's coming," The Bull's voice announced over the radio. The crack of weapons reported three times from the roof, as I herded the Russians into the room where the captives were stashed, and T-bone hunted for the switch. At gunpoint, I made the men handcuff each other to the S & M table, and then I smacked them each on the head with the butt of my Styer to give them something to think about besides getting free.

I checked on my tattooed victim, careful not to step in the pool of blood, and didn't find any pulse.

T-bone hadn't found any way to open the gate, so I told him to forget about it, and start getting the girls out of their cages.

"What do we have outside?" I asked over the radio.

"One guy poked his head out of the building in the middle and a couple of guys came out of the strip club after the gunfire, they went back in and came out armed. We encouraged them to stay inside, but they're probably calling for reinforcements by now."

"I'm coming out," I transmitted, and stepped out into the amber haze of the artificial light of the parking lot. I found the keys for the Navigator, ripped them off the ring, and backed the vehicle up to the door of the Quonset building that was nearest the room full of prisoners. I opened the back doors and folded the back seat down, creating one large cargo area. The kids were going to have to put up with a little more discomfort, all jammed in the back before we got them to safety.

I yelled at T-bone to load them in, and then I sprinted over to one of the Town Cars. I fumbled through the key ring until I found the keys that worked. I fired up the engine, jammed the shift lever into reverse, and squealed the tires, as I whipped the big luxury car around one-hundred-and-eighty degrees, so that it's trunk was facing the iron gate. Then I floored it. The impact bent some of the bars, but the gate did more damage to the car. I drove forward, and then made another assault on the gate with the rear of the car, this time aiming closer to the side where the gate was latched. The second effort proved successful in knocking the gate free of the latch, bending it off its track a little. I continued ramming the gate in this manner, until I'd bent it into the street enough, so that the Navigator would be able to squeeze through. I drove the Town Car back into the parking lot, and left it there running, with its rear bumper and trunk pushed almost into the back seat.

"Bull, are you ready to make a quick exit?" I said over the radio.

"Don't worry about us Captain, we're ready to bail out the back."

T-bone was having trouble getting some of the foreign women to cram themselves into the Navigator willingly, so I said to the girl who spoke English, "Please help us, we don't have much time?"

"Who are you?" she said.

"We're here to help you, I swear, just get these girls in here or we're going to get shot."

"I help," a rail thin Mexican with long dark hair said. I would have thought he was a girl if he wasn't naked.

I thanked him and we corralled the remaining victims into the back of the Navigator, all of them creating a racket in their native tongues.

"Hurry up boss," The Bull's voice crackled in my radio earpiece, "I can see SUV's two blocks away, hauling ass towards us."

"You drive," I told T-bone, and he jumped behind the wheel. I hopped on the passenger's side running board, next to the rear door, and held on to the roof rack with my left hand, the Styer cradled in my right. I flipped the control switch to 'automatic' and shouted, "Let's go."

The Navigator moved sluggishly, carrying so many bodies as it moved towards the gate. I could see the SUV's Bull warned of screeching to a halt and blocking off the exit of the dead end street.

"Ram them!" I shouted at T-bone as he maneuvered the ponderous Navigator through the gate, and started his turn up the street. I could see the dome lights of the SUV's pop on as men jumped out of them. Then, both of the vehicle's glass exploded, in concurrence with the Brrrrrrap sound of 9 x 19 Parabellum cartridges being fired in bursts of 680 rounds per minute, from The Bull's, Kelly's, and my weapons. Whether our adversaries were hit or sought cover, they disappeared quickly, and long enough for T-bone to cover the distance between us, gaining as much speed as he could without us receiving any fire. I released the Styer to hang from its strap, grabbed the luggage rack with both hands, and crunched my legs and torso up as high as I could moments before the Navigator impacted the spot where the two vehicles met in the center of the road nose to nose.

There was a huge bang, followed by the sound of deforming metal, and the kids screaming from inside the car. I was almost ripped free of my hold by the sudden deceleration, but the behemoth Navigator had enough momentum and fortitude to push the other two smaller SUV's out of the way, so that we continued to trundle down the street with a severely crumpled hood, steam spewing from the grill, and smoke emitting from where the front tires were rubbing on the crumpled sheet metal of the fenders.

I shouted directions through the window to T-bone, getting us back to the front of the concrete plant. He stopped in front of the Mustang, and I said, "Does that thing have navigation?"

T-bone gave me the thumbs up signal, and I shouted "Nearest hospital."

Again I got the thumbs up, and he punched at the dashboard while I pulled off my windbreaker and unstrapped from the Styer. I threw the assault rifle in the foot well of the passenger seat, and fired up the Mustang.

"Bull?" I said into the radio microphone.

In my earpiece I heard rustling from the big man keying his mike while running and his voice was broken by the cadence of a sprint saying, "We're on our way."

T-bone looked at me questioningly, and I held up my hand. When I was able to see the figures of Kelly and The Bull, running full out, through the trash, along the fence of the concrete plant - and didn't see anyone in pursuit - I gave T-bone the hand signal to go.

We obeyed all the traffic laws, on the five-minute ride to Valley Presbyterian Hospital. I had T-bone pull over on one of the side streets, so that I could unscrew the license plates from my vehicle, in case there were any security cameras at the hospital. When we pulled up to the Emergency entrance I crashed into the admitting area and grabbed the triage nurse who looked like she was the least likely to be concerned with protocol, and said, "I have victims outside that need your help." She protested, but allowed me to drag her out to the Navigator.

"These kids have been kidnapped and tortured," I told her. "We can't stay. You have to help them and call social services." I pulled open the rear door of the Navigator, revealing the pile of naked, wailing victims. "It's your turn to do the right thing," I said.

T-bone was already in the passenger seat of the Mustang, and as we pulled away, the nurse was standing at the entry door to the Emergency Room shouting orders to people inside.

CHAPTER 14

The team reconvened in the parking lot of a Walmart at the corner of Roscoe and Van Nuys Boulevards. I think we all felt surreal, standing on the asphalt while couples pushing strollers argued with each other as they walked by, on their way to buy Pampers or whatever household item drew them to shop at 8:30 p.m. that night.

We grappled and high-fived each other, filled with the emotions that flow after you've killed and escaped death, emotions that would never be talked about. "Men," I said, "Normally, what we just did would call for a few shots and a number of beers, but tonight we've got to shake it off and keep our focus on the mission."

"Bullshit," The Bull said. He dropped the tailgate of his Escalade, and sitting nestled amid the weapons and equipment the men had shoved into the cargo compartment earlier that day, two six-packs of Heineken rested under a bag of ice. "I ain't doing shit until I've had at least one beer," he said. "Fuck me you crazy bastard, we just shot the shit out of the Russian mob. Lauren can wait thirty minutes while the pee I dribbled down my pants dries up."

We all laughed, and no one, least of all myself, turned down the frosty cold green and silver can he handed us. For a few minutes we rehashed our victory, like men all across the country who had just won a softball game, or who's kids had just won a hockey tournament. Despite the fact that tomorrow might see the derailment of our dreams because of circumstances we'd failed to control, for that brief few moments, we knew that we'd pulled together to do something extraordinary, and that no one other than the five of us would know what it was like. Hopefully, no one would know we'd ever been there.

However; unlike other men that night who could go to sleep in a beery glow of self-congratulation, our euphoria soon wore off and we saw in each other's eyes the knowledge that despite our brief success, the fact was that we had just spent the last couple of hours diverted from our mission, and that it was time to get back to work. We smacked each other and shook hands, talked about who needed to do what next, and then we each turned to our cars, SUV's or motorcycles, sober despite the alcohol, and maybe even a little more daunted by what lay before us.

When I got back to the car I checked my phone. During the action I'd ignored any incoming calls, and there were a couple of messages from Marianna Ruiz marked "urgent".

She answered my call with, "Are you all done playing cowboys and Indians?"

"I know you're just jealous, because you're stuck in the office," I said. "What's so urgent?"

"We got a call from Kaminoff. His people found emails. They were sent to addresses with the same server threads as the kidnapper's ransom demand email. I didn't want to move on it until you approved it. They're from a personal account of Cece Harris, the Unit Production Manager of Lauren's movie."

"I know who she is. She's almost as big a pain in the ass as you are."

"Yeah, but she's no way as guapa as I am, and she wouldn't put up with your stupid-ass jokes."

"Maybe, but why would she get involved in this mess? She makes over a quarter mil a year."

"I don't know. Maybe it's just a coincidence. But the emails are encrypted with some type of code. Kaminoff's people have software that can get through the encryption, but it takes time, and they have to do it one by one. He wouldn't give me a time frame on the code."

"Why is she writing encrypted messages to anyone?" I said.

I heard the clicking of a keyboard before Marianna said, "We ran a background on her and she was a wild girl when she was young. Drug charges, prostitution, but all dismissed. Maybe cause Daddy paid for good lawyers and rehabs."

"I don't think you can get a job in Hollywood unless you have a drug record," I said.

"She also worked on a number of movies with Barry Sheldon. Maybe she wants to torpedo him and take his job. Two of those movies also show Kyle Pemberton on the crew list."

"Where are we at with Pemberton?"

"Nowhere on him, but his parole officer told me about a possible girlfriend in Studio City."

"Anyone talk to this girlfriend yet?"

"No. But she's home, we tested the number. Just thought you might want someone to go in person."

"Do you know where Harris is?"

"She's still at Paragon, as far as we can tell. I was hoping that we could put T-bone or Sparky on her tail."

"Alright," I said. "Get them over there. I'll call my inside guy on the movie and see if I can get anything else on Cece. And give me the address of Pemberton's girlfriend in Studio City."

"I'll text it to you."

I asked her if there was anything else.

She gave me a rundown of the crew list cross checking. There were a number of people who would warrant a look if we had anything hard to tie to them, but nothing hot. She also told me that they still hadn't located the woman who had picked up Lauren's lover Mika, but there were some good leads developed that were being tracked down.

"Hey Ruiz?" I said.

"Yes Boss?" she said dragging it out like she was Charro or something.

"Good work."

"Thank you Boss."

She hung up.

I fired up the Mustang and headed towards Studio City. Traffic was never good in Los Angeles, but at least the crush of workers returning home was over, so I hoped it wouldn't take that long.

I clicked on the hands-free, and called Goody's cell phone number.

"Hey. Perfect timing," he answered. "I just got out of a meeting."

"How's it going? Are you in a place where you can talk?"

"Yeah, I'm in my office. Everybody's freaking out, trying to figure out how to keep shooting without Lauren. Your name was mentioned once or twice in not too nice a way."

"Really?"

"Yeah someone asked if you might be any help in getting Lauren to come in before the script re-writes were finished. Sheldon said that we, "weren't getting any help from that asshole." Meaning you. He also said Lauren might be back day after tomorrow, any truth to that?"

"Wishful thinking maybe. Was Cece Harris in that meeting?"

"Oh yeah," Goody said.

I was zigzagging the Mustang through cars Eastbound on Roscoe Boulevard. "How was she?"

"Other than being the bitch on wheels she usually is?"

"Yeah, I'm looking for anything that's different than normal."

"Okay, well she's still as nasty as ever."

"Do you know if anyone would have use of her email accounts other than her?"

"The Production Supervisor, Bob Nilgore. He's the muscle-builder dude with a face like a toad."

"Yeah, I remember him," I said. "I just can't figure out why she'd get mixed up in something like this."

"Well, you know," Goody's voice got low and conspiratorial, "there's been some rumors that she's up for a big job at the Mouse

House. There's no secret they have their eye on acquiring Paragon, and if this movie goes down it could give them the leverage they need. God knows there's no love lost between Cece and Lauren, or Cece and Rikki Wymen either, but I have a hard time seeing her involved in a kidnapping."

"Do you know if she's left the studio yet?" I said.

"I think she's still here, we're all going to be headed home pretty soon."

"Anything else?"

"I don't know, ever since we talked this morning I've been looking at everybody differently. At this point in the movie though, everyone's tired and cranky. I tell you, the only person who acts like they don't have an axe to grind is that Nilgore guy we were talking about. Usually he mopes around here - and who wouldn't working for Cece - but today he was humming at the craft service table. Maybe he got laid or something."

"Alright, well that's something. What time is call in the morning?"

"We're coming in at seven a.m. We've still got helicopter stuff we can shoot without Lauren."

I thanked him and we hung up.

I called Marianna, and asked her to have Kelly pick up Nilgore too.

"It's going to be tough for Kelly to keep the tail by himself."

Maintaining surveillance on someone in Los Angeles traffic was tough enough with two people, and often impossible with only one. "Understood," I said. "Cece Harris is the priority, stay doubled up on her, and Kelly will just have to do his best to hang onto Nilgore."

When we hung up, I was almost at the home of Pemberton's alleged girlfriend. The San Fernando Valley could change in a matter of blocks from industrial parks, to tree-lined streets with multi-million dollar homes on large plots of property, then back to blocks of blighted apartment bunkers that smelled of fried food, cigarettes, and dirty diapers. I checked the address Marianna sent me, and turned onto Otseggo Street.

Pemberton's alleged girlfriend was named Kathy Sullivan. She lived in a compound of eight duplex condominiums, which were built in the last five years. Two "Unit For Sale" signs stood sentry, in front of the complex. It was a security building where you had to get buzzed into the entry if you didn't have a key.

I pulled over in front of a hydrant down the street, and reviewed the file on Kyle Pemberton that Marianna gave me at the racetrack. When a car pulled up to the target building's garage entrance, I put the Mustang in gear and pulled behind, then followed him through the automatic gate. I parked the Mustang in an empty space, hoping it belonged to a vacancy, and jumped out just in time to follow the tenant through the door into the building.

He gave me a look, but I said, "Hey, how's it going?" and took the stairs ahead of him two at a time, not looking back.

Being a white middle class male, there's not too many places where people are going to stop you from coming in if you act like you've got every right to be there.

Kathy Sullivan's door was in the upper, back, part of the building. I could hear someone practicing scales rapidly on a piano. I knocked loudly.

The scales continued, but a woman in her forties opened the door. She was attractive, in an 'I do yoga' fashion. She didn't say anything, just looked at me expectantly through the partially opened door, protected by one of those little security chains it would have taken me two seconds to kick through.

"Is Kyle here?" I asked.

"Who are you?"

"I just want to talk to him for a minute," I said.

"How'd you get in without getting buzzed up?"

"A pizza guy was ahead of me, I followed him in," I lied, thrusting a business card through the crack in the door. "I just want to know where I can find him."

"That makes two of us," she said looking at my card. "What, did my ex send you?"

The piano scales stopped.

"No, it's nothing like that," I said. "I just want to ask him some questions."

A girl about nine or ten appeared in the foyer. "Everything okay, mom?"

The woman looked at me, and then again, at my card. "Yeah, go finish your practicing," she said.

The girl looked me over.

I gave her my best 'Good Guy' smile.

It must have passed the test because she shuffled off down the hall.

"Well, Mr. Security Consultant, he's not here. I haven't seen him in over a week."

"That's what they told us at his work too. Do you have any idea where he might be?"

"Why do you want him?" she asked.

This was the Bullshit test. If I failed it, the drive here would be for nothing. "We have a client who's in some trouble," I said, "and we think Kyle may have something to do with that trouble."

Kathy Sullivan gave me a hard once over, but she opened the door a little to do it. "He doesn't live here," she said. "He just stayed here... We went out a couple of times."

I nodded. "You don't seem like the type to date someone fresh out on parole?"

"I met him in a health food store," she said. "He's very polite." The door opening got smaller.

"From the information I have, he may not have belonged in jail at all. And he has quite a military record."

"Well, I once heard," she said, "when the Devil comes calling, he won't be wearing horns and a tail..."

I laughed appreciatively.

"He didn't say anything about going anywhere, he just stopped showing up, stopped returning my phone calls." She started closing the door, then stopped. "Are you looking into any other girlfriends?"

"You're the only one on our radar."

"But you wouldn't tell me the truth about that anyway would you?"

"Probably not," I said. "But it's good when I don't have to lie."

She hovered there ready to shut me out. Sometimes questioning a witness is like fishing; you don't want to jerk on the hook before they've tried to swallow the bait.

"What kind of trouble is your client in?" she asked.

I took a breath, and looked away for a moment. "Someone is missing. Kyle's name came up, and he hasn't checked in with his parole officer. I've been hired to check him out."

"Does this person have a lot of money?" she asked.

"Yeah."

She drummed her fingernails on the doorframe. The piano was silent. She looked at her watch, "Hey Cheryl, you've got five more minutes," she yelled. The piano started plinking out something that might have been Bach, but I'm no expert.

She laughed, shrugged, and said, "Sorry." It made her look pretty.

"It's good you're keeping after her," I said. "If my Mom had stayed on me about the cello, I might be playing in some concert somewhere, instead of bothering nice women on their doorsteps."

Kathy shook her head. "He was ashamed of not having any money. You probably know he was a big shot in the film business for a while. He said that every penny he had went to his lawyers." She shrugged again. "It didn't bother me, but it bothered him."

"Are you saying that he might have done something drastic to get money?"

She waved her hand and made a face. "The last time I saw him, we went to Disneyland. He took Cheryl and me. We stayed at the hotel down there and he spent a lot on dinner for all of us; wine, drinks, dessert, everything... this from a guy who'd been scraping together money to buy whole-wheat Ramen noodles. But, he said that a deal he'd been working on was coming through, and he wanted to celebrate with us. Then I never heard from him again."

"Just like that?"

She shook her head. "I didn't want to file a missing persons, 'cause I didn't want to get him in trouble."

"Maybe his deal didn't work out, and he's embarrassed," I said. "I'll let you know if I find him."

She laughed, but without a trace of humor. "Yeah, well you know how you play things back in your mind? That was the farewell. You'd think by now I'd start to recognize when a guy says, 'Thanks for the memories,' without having to say it."

"What did he say exactly about this deal?" I asked.

"That he didn't want to jinx it by talking about it." She chewed her lip for a minute and then said, "Did you talk to his friend Joe?"

"Joe?" I said, searching for more to go with it.

"I can't remember his last name, we double dated a couple of times. I've tried him, but he's not returning my phone calls either."

"Do you think I could get that number, and an address if you've got it."

"I've got his number somewhere," she said.

"I'd appreciate it."

I thought she was going to say something else, but then held up her hand, and disappeared into the apartment, closing the door.

I stood there listening to her daughter struggle through whatever she was playing. I'd never touched a cello in my life.

After what seemed like a long time, the woman opened the door again. She thrust a scrap of paper at me.

"That's Joe's number, it's all I've got. I just hope your client isn't one of the people who fucked him over. He was nice to us.

I wouldn't have known he was an ex-con if he hadn't told me." She shrugged. "I don't know anyone whose life turned out the way they'd hoped."

She looked at me pointedly holding up my card. "I want you to call me and let me know what you find out," she said shutting the door. This time I knew it wasn't opening again.

Chapter 15

After leaving Kathy Sullivan's I pointed the Mustang towards the office and got on the phone. For years I hated having to drive a car with an automatic transmission for work, because I always needed one hand for the phone and one for the wheel. The perfection of Bluetooth technology now enabled me to use the Mustang, with its manual transmission that allowed me to chirp up through the gears, or use the engine to brake through the turns by downshifting while conducting business.

The Bull went back to the production offices for the movie that had rented two trucks painted as knock offs of LA utility company vehicles, and used his lock pick set to let himself in.

"It was only a small office," he said, "like something that would hold only four to six people, but it was cleaned out, and I mean cleaned out. Too clean; there wasn't even a paperclip left in any of the desks, or toilet paper in the bathroom, but I did get lucky."

"Yeah?"

"Trash hadn't been picked up. I rooted through their dumpster and found two trash bags full of miscellaneous shit, with their address on junk mail, and two bags full of shredded documents that I think are theirs. I called Marianna, and she's bringing in some temps, to play jigsaw puzzle with the shreddings."

I looked at my watch. It was nine-thirty. "I doubt they'll be able to pull anything useful before the morning."

"So we shouldn't try?" he said.

I called him an asshole, and dialed Marianna. I gave her the number for Pemberton's friend "Joe," from Kathy Sullivan. She searched it on the computer and it came up as belonging to a pre-paid cell phone company.

"Well that sucks as far as tracking him down," I said, "but it's making me like this guy Pemberton as our #1, more and more. Cross-reference him for Joes, Jacks, Pauls whatever. Let's look at anyone we can find that's been close to him, and shake the trees. Don't you know someone in the Sheriff's Department that's for sale? I want to know his cellmates if you can."

"If she's not on duty, it's going to cost a bundle," Marianna said.

"I'm not going to have anything left if we don't figure this out, so let them name their price. We need that info. ASAP."

While she was busy with that, T-bone called to report that they'd picked up Cece Harris when she left Paragon.

"We couldn't have kept up with her if Sparky wasn't on his bike," he said. "She's got a Porsche, and that bitch can drive it. I thought for sure we'd hooked a live one, but now we're sitting out-side Kate Mantellini's restaurant, and it looks like she was just late for a dinner date."

Kate Mantellini's was a diner for rich people, located on the edge of Beverly Hills. It was open late and you could get everything from caviar to onion rings. The name gave me a pang of sadness, because it was a ritual stop for Victoria and I when one of us was picking the other up from the airport.

"Who's she with?" I asked.

"Some older guy with silver hair. He was waiting for her when she got there, so I've only seen him through the window."

"Have they ordered yet?"

"No."

"What's going on with her Production Supervisor? I can't remember his name."

"Bob Nilgore?" T-bone said. "Kelly has his tail. He went to a gym called Muscle Mechanics in West Hollywood, it just looks likes he's working out."

"These people are doing pretty normal shit for priority subjects. But they're all we've got at the moment. Stay on them, and let me know the second they move."

I called Marianna to have her search for Cece Harris's home address. It took me several tries because I was navigating the Mustang through Laurel Canyon, another twisting artery that weds the San Fernando Valley to Hollywood through the hills, where the down hill curves on the Los Angeles side are cut so deeply into the canyon that cell service is intermittent.

Once I reached her, I only had to wait thirty seconds for Marianna to give me Cece's home address in Westwood. I could have a quick look-see before Cece finished her dinner. I was hoping that she might have a computer at home that would be carrying the key to her email code.

"Tell Kaminoff's people that I might be calling in for emergency adult supervision if she does have a PC there," I said, and we hung up.

Laurel Canyon dumped me out onto the Sunset Strip, which was clogged with tourists and kids, but once I passed our offices at the 9200 building, I was able to open up the Mustang and slide her smoothly through the S-curves that started near the border between Beverly Hills and Bel-Air.

At Lamont Drive, I down-shifted using the engine to brake the car through the turn, then entered the maze of residential streets comprising Westwood east of the UCLA campus until I was gliding by Cece Harris's Spanish-style home. A light showed through drawn curtains on the second floor. If Harris headed back this way the surveillance team would alert me immediately. The light could be on a timer, but it could also be a housekeeper or other live-in help.

Circling the block I didn't find a service alley that would enable me to access the home inconspicuously, so I parked down the street and sat observing for a short while, waiting to see if there was any activity and getting a feel for the block. There were a number of cars and a couple of motorcycles parked on the street, but nothing that seemed out of the ordinary or occupied.

The front yard of Harris's property rose at a sharp angle to meet a two story house that looked like it could be Zorro's country home, with lots of heavy stucco, Spanish tiles, dark paneled doors and heavy exposed timbers. It was an odd house for a single woman.

After taking a last look for late-night dog walkers, I quietly exited the car, crossed the street, and then scrambled over the six-foot fence on the right side of the house. As I crept along the side of the house a small dog in the neighboring home began barking incessantly.

A large pool dominated the back yard. It was surrounded with a terraced stone patio. I ducked beneath a long wooden table covered by an umbrella situated in the middle of the patio. The dog next door kept up its racket until the neighbor's backyard light came on. The dog's owner peeked out cradling a small terrier in his arms.

I sat motionless in my dark tactical clothing, hoping that the neighborhood hadn't suffered recent break-ins, so the dog's commotion would be attributed to raccoons or skunks, not burglars. While waiting for the neighbor to go back inside with his dog, I studied the back of Cece's house.

The far end held a Dutch style door, probably leading to the kitchen, which seemed at odds with the design. The rest of the arched windows and a big pair of French doors all fit the Mission-style architecture.

The neighbor was speaking to the dog in soothing baby-talk. A slight breeze carried through the back yard, causing a movement in my peripheral vision. It was a small piece of curtain ruffling out of an opening, created by one of the French doors standing slightly ajar.

It was convenient that I wouldn't have to pick the lock and possibly get the dog going again, but Cece Harris didn't seem like the type of person to leave a door open so the cat could come and go.

When the neighbor took his dog back inside I crept towards the open door, staying low and drawing my weapon. I used the barrel of the pistol to nudge the door open just the slightest bit more so that I could listen for several moments, but I heard nothing.

I'm not keen on bursting armed into a private residence and having a freaked out relative, friend, or housekeeper calling the police or having a heart attack, but something didn't feel right.

I pushed the curtains aside. In the light spilling from an open doorway on the other side of the room I could make out several bookshelves, a few framed paintings, a fireplace, and comfortable looking furniture. There was a dining area to the right, through a wide archway.

I moved across the room, swept the muzzle of my weapon into the hallway in front of me, before I sensed movement at my back.

I tried to bring the gun around only it was too late. The attacker covered the distance from his hiding place in the shadows of the dining room with an athletic leap, smashing into me with a perfectly executed sidekick.

I was able to get my right arm up against my side, where it caught most of the blow and kept my ribs from being broken, but the attacker's full weight followed through the kick. It sent me hard against a wall filled with small picture frames and decorations. His momentum prevented me from getting any leverage as we crashed to the floor, after which he immediately started raining blows down on my head.

As we flailed on the floor, thoughts flashed through my mind like explosions. I knew this guy was a pro. He was wearing night-vision goggles. He hadn't shot me, which meant he didn't have a gun, or didn't want to use one.

His punches, targeting my temples, eyes and nose, were doing a good job of hurting me, while he used the rest of his body to prevent me from shooting him.

So I let go of the gun. It clattered on the hardwood floor.

I felt the relief in my assailant's body, and took the opportunity to swipe upwards at the night-vision goggles. The contact was glancing; but enough to dislodge their position, temporarily blinding him, and allowing me to get back in the fight.

The attacker had to use one hand to get his night-vision back, but he groped for my eyes with his other one, trying for a gouge. I shook my head vigorously to avoid the searching fingers, while grabbing the sleeve of the arm groping my face, and drove my right forearm into the elbow. A satisfying crunch and a cry of pain followed.

Without hesitation the attacker drove downwards with his good elbow into my face. The strike broke my nose and possibly my left cheekbone. The pain made me grunt.

I felt him rise up, and expected another blow to come crashing down. Serious fear pumped adrenalin into my bloodstream, and I threw everything into an effort to buck him off, while striking again for the elbow I had injured.

He wasn't attempting another elbow strike though; he was trying to get his feet under him. This time he brought his right knee down into my abdomen, while at the same time wrenching his injured arm free.

The body blow hurt badly. I tried to re-grapple with him, but I'd lost strength. He broke free, stood up, and then stepped back. I pursued, wanting to get my body between him and my weapon, lying on the floor. A vicious kick came. I deflected the blow with my forearms.

He grabbed a lamp from the table next to the couch, swinging the heavy base down, connecting with my right shoulder and back;

keeping me on my hands and knees. Then he reversed his swing, bringing the lamp up and letting it go like a softball pitch, trying to catch me in the face.

Again I blocked the lamp, but it knocked me backward.

The attacker bolted, slamming out the open door into the night.

I scrambled around on the floor slick with my blood, until I found my weapon, and then took off in pursuit.

The dog next door was barking full alert when I rushed along the side of the house. The neighbor's light switched on again. As I vaulted the fence and clambered down the steep slope of the front yard, I could see my fugitive sprinting up the street where it curved to the left.

I scuttled down the steep front lawn to the street and ran after him. He was straddling a motorcycle on the far side of the road. The bike's engine roared to life and its tires smoked propelling him away seconds before I could close the gap.

It was too dark to get the license number. I watched the rear light of the bike disappear around a corner, feeling my nose and eye throbbing with pain.

One of the neighbors would be on the phone with private security or the police, so I ran to the Mustang, and tore away with the lights off.

Chapter 16

I drove into the commercial section of Westwood, a tangle of streets containing shops, bars, and restaurants, which catered to UCLA. I found a liquor store. The attendant behind the counter didn't bat an eyelash when I walked up with two bags of frozen peas, a container of Advil, and asked for a bottle of Tequila, looking like I'd just gone a couple of rounds with Mike Tyson. I guess working the late shift in LA, there's not much that's going to shock you after a while.

As soon as I got my change, I pressed one of the bags of icy peas to my face and shoved the other under my shirt, onto the shoulder that absorbed the most punishment in the fight.

I crossed the street to where I'd parked the Mustang in a red zone. I got in and reclined the seat. I needed to call Marianna at the office to get a handle on what everyone was doing, but wasn't feeling up to it just yet. The icy bag of peas felt soothing on my throbbing face. I poured out a handful of capsules from the Advil bottle, and washed them down with a few nasty swallows of Cuervo Gold.

While I waited for the liquor to make its way through my system, the weight of the day's events seemed to press me into the leather seat, crushing me with questions.

The cold from the icy bag of peas began burning my skin, and I thought of the axiom we learned in boot camp: *pain is just weakness leaving the body.* A few more swallows of Tequila brought on the comforting warmth, but also loosened the door behind which my doubts knocked.

I wondered where the mistakes were made that left Lauren so vulnerable.

I thought about the things Victoria confronted me with. I wondered how willingly I'd ignored her attempts to help me see that her desires were changing, and that she now felt compelled towards motherhood.

When I met Victoria, we were perfect for each other. We were each able to compartmentalize our pain, train our bodies, and suppress our emotions in order to excel. We could unleash our passion with each other and find a willing partner. Even after we were married, we each had our own lives that we combined occasionally under the same roof. Domesticity was a fantasy that we shared until her accident. Except like most fantasies, normal home life lost a great deal of its luster for me once it became a reality.

There was also the fact that it scared me, because I felt I didn't deserve to be happy.

I looked at the bottle of Tequila in my hand, bringing it to my mouth for another swallow, greedy for its anesthesia, but instead it seemed to intensify the feeling that my past was finally demanding retribution, and with those feelings came the flood of memories and images from Colombia, eleven years ago; the smell of a fire that had changed my life, which would forever leave me wondering what the ultimate cost might be…

Guerillas in Columbia known as the Fuerzas Armadas Revolucionarias or *"FARC"* had kidnapped an Occidental Petroleum engineer who held both Colombian and American citizenship. My team was tasked with locating where the rebels were holding him and providing a rescue assessment. With the use of satellite and drone infrared imagery, we were able monitor the guerilla's larger bases of operation in the marshy ranch land and dense jungle mountains surrounding Arauca, the main city that serviced the oil sands being exploited by Occidental. It was just a matter of getting helicopter support to drop us in for a closer look at each camp until we found the one where the engineer was being held.

I didn't join the military as some hayseed off the farm in Nebraska, my father's bitterness over his two tours in Vietnam inculcated me with wariness of the American mission abroad, but I'd enlisted and volunteered to lead one of America's elite fighting units because I felt that I could make a difference, and that if I wasn't part of the solution, I was part of the problem…

I was willing to suffer the bites from mosquitoes, leeches, and other animals, that could find the smallest piece of exposed flesh, the excruciating rashes where pack straps rubbed for too long against Anglo-Saxon skin navigating through the undergrowth of the kapok tree jungles. I enjoyed MREs, and creeping unnoticed within feet of the wood fires where the sturdy women with oval faces, almond eyes, and dark plaited hair, cooked guinea pigs and corn empanadas for their stoic Arawak Indian men, who made up the majority of the FARC forces in that region. I was willing, because I felt that I was doing the right thing.

I saw Columbia like our own Wild West; we often referred to our enemy as the Comanche. Whenever a civilization was brought into the industrialized world, a struggle of transition ensued resulting in casualties. The oil and mineral dollars Occidental was investing could create a first world economy in the region, and the benefit to be derived by the local's overall rise in standard of living, outweighed the cost of the few villages, farms, and ranches, that would be disenfranchised. That's how we were briefed, and that's what I bought.

After several close inspections of rebel strongholds, we found the group that was holding our engineer in the dense jungle forests south of Cuivas. After two days of observation, we also determined that in the hour before sunset, when the men of the camp played soccer, we could extract the hostage with a minimum of risk or bloodshed. When I forwarded that assessment, I was asked to provide a probability of success, which I evaluated as ninety percent, great odds in that business, but security at this camp was undisciplined, complacent, and the men seemed poorly trained.

We'd been authorized to engage on other missions to rescue Americans where the risk was greater, but my orders came back to maintain forward observation without engagement. What I didn't know at the time - while my men and I spent days sequestered in the one-hundred-eighteen degree jungle being eaten by bugs, watching one strike opportunity after another pass - was that because the hostage was also a Colombian citizen, Battalion Command was being ordered to coordinate the rescue with the National Army of Colombia, so that there would be some good press clippings to send back to Washington. Finally, I was ordered to synchronize the rescue operation with Capitán Morales of the GAULA – Groupos de Acción Unificada por la Libertad Personal – a unit of the Colombian National Army that dealt with kidnapped nationals, who's men would be dropped in and make their way to our position the following day. Hours after I received those orders, fifteen additional squared-away fighters arrived at the FARC camp, took command, and quickly tightened up all the holes in camp security. That evening none of the men played soccer.

When I reported the situational changes, and the obvious breach in operational security that coincided with the GAULA's involvement, I was told to advise Capitán Morales, and that he would make the 'go/no-go' decision.

We heard Morale's squad moving through the jungle half an hour before they arrived. I sent T-bone and Sparky out to meet the force, and guide them in. Morales was a handsome young man with an aristocratic bearing that I disliked immediately, but I provided him with a sit-rep, advising him of the changes in my assessment of the mission's risk.

"You are worried about a few farmers with guns? I thought you Green Berets were supposed to be bad asses?" Morales said. "We'll show you how we deal with these campesinos."

I should have taken him out right then, but instead I was a good soldier and spent the afternoon haggling with Morales, until it was agreed that my unit would secure the hostage, and Morales' men would neutralize any reaction by the FARC soldiers and protect our rear while we extracted to a clearing about a quarter mile to the south, large enough for an evacuation zone, which we'd prepared while waiting for orders. Whereas previously we could have snatched the hostage during the soccer game when he was only guarded by one man, and probably been out of there without a shot being fired, we now had to take out the four men who were on close guard of the engineer and several others, without being noticed.

The guerrilla encampment was a farm that the FARC commandeered, consisting of a large mud-brick and tarpaper main house that sheltered the group's leaders. It also housed the women who cooked and did all of the chores that kept the camp going, as well as providing sex on demand while each cared for several small children. The bachelors slept in the animal sheds or out in the open under improvised clumps of mosquito netting. Our engineer was enclosed in a fortified goat pen of pointed stakes, which had a camouflage tarp pulled taut over the top. Until the day before, there'd been a lone sentry stationed at the gate of the goat pen, who slept a good part of the time; whereas now, an additional three of the new, disciplined soldiers, were placed in a triangle around the pen, each within sight of the other. Between the engineer's cell and the closest encroachment of the jungle, about a hundred feet of cleared ground needed to be crossed, so the possibility of sneaking up on the guards unseen was slim.

During the day, sentries had been doubled up around the perimeter of the compound. Two of the new FARC soldiers were positioned in a jeep with an M60 machine gun mounted with a swivel base that commanded a field of fire over most of the open area in the camp. The new soldiers ordered supper cooked an hour earlier, so that the evening meal would be over before dark. I wanted to ask Morales which one of his men was providing the FARC leader with our plans from his cell phone, but refrained.

As darkness fell, we crept into our positions, and I was happy to see that Morales' men were more disciplined with their bush craft, now that they were in range of the FARC's weapons.

Eight of my men assembled their composite crossbows - silent, but highly accurate and lethal weapons at less than a hundred yards. They clicked their radios when they had the engineer's guards in their sights. With each target covered by two shooters, there was a good probability that each guerilla could be killed silently, or at least prevented from killing the hostage if a full on assault were necessary. The other four in our team, T-bone, Sparky, The Bull and myself, slid within feet of the closest perimeter sentries. I confirmed with Morales that his men were in place and then gave the 'go' signal.

We didn't make any more noise than a sudden rush of wind. The titanium bolts flying from the crossbows each found their mark in the rebel's necks and skulls, dropping each of the guards with no more noise than a man clearing his throat. My other team members and I sprung from the overgrowth, and were choking out our targets, as the crossbow shooters divided into teams of two who broke the weapons down, confirmed the deaths of the guards with KA-Bar knives, moved in to release the hostage and prepared injections of B-12, glucose, and adrenalin, to give the hostage energy for the trip to the evac. zone.

In the light from the quarter moon, four of my men moved into the hostage hut, as the rest of our team created a diamond formation surrounding them.

Then for no reason I ever understood, one of Morales' men fired an anti-tank missile at the jeep carrying the M60, but missed. It whizzed past the two guerillas at the jeep and slammed into a tree before they could react, but the explosion ignited them into action, along with the rest of the FARC. The M60 immediately started pumping tracer rounds into the area of the goat shed containing the hostage, which was surrounded by my men.

What had been a precision operation, degenerated in a matter of seconds to the insanity that is a firefight fuelled by panic. Seven of my twelve men were mowed down in the first bullet spray from the M60. The FARC fired at anything that moved. Morales' men emerged from cover firing their Israeli made Gali assault rifles from their hips like they were in some Rambo movie. The members of my team who weren't shot returned fire in three shot bursts while moving to find any piece of solid cover from which to continue the counter-attack.

For reasons only God knows I wasn't hit, and once the rain of death passed me by I focused the sights of my MP5 on the M60's muzzle flash and emptied my clip in bursts fore and aft of the flare. Then I unclipped a frag-grenade and heaved it towards the jeep before running to the hostage area, ejecting the spent magazine, and seating another.

Miraculously the hostage had also avoided being shot, perhaps because my two teammates, Crowley and Regan, the medical sergeants who were attempting to inject him with vitamins and adrenaline, had stopped several rounds each and fell gasping and gurgling on top of him. The Bull had arrived a moment before me, and pulled the engineer from under the two mortally wounded men like a rag-doll, and forced him into my arms. "I got these two," he said, ripping pressure bandages from his rucksack. "Get him out of here."

I jerked the hostage in the direction of the trail leading to the extraction point. A few hundred yards into the jungle I looked back at the camp, to see it lit up like a fireworks display gone awry.

We thrashed through the jungle in the dark, using my compass and a flashlight to search for the luminescent tape we'd used to mark the way to the extraction zone. It was slow going with the barefoot hostage, who I practically had to carry. It seemed like an interminable time before I could feel the rotor wash of our air support, and a retrieval basket was dropped on a line into the specified clearing, which was really just a shallow swamp. I strapped the engineer into the basket, but ordered the helo to stay in the area. While working my way back to the firefight, I confirmed more medical birds were on their way. I could hear the weapons fire less frequently, and I prayed that it was because our side was winning.

Fury pushed me back along that trail as fast as anyone could move in the mountainous jungle. This wasn't the first time that political maneuvering, and Washington's hunger for anything they could use to fuel the War On Drugs, had made our lives in the field more dangerous; it wasn't the first time that a mission had gone to hell because the Colombians were playing both sides of the fence, but it was the deadliest betrayal, and my men were paying the unnecessary price.

The Bull, T-bone, Sparky, and Kelly, had created a defensive position behind two dead cows felled by the M60, where they triaged our dead and wounded.

"They went fucking cannibal," was all The Bull said, nodding into the camp, meaning that Morale's men were shooting anything that moved, even if it was one of us. I looked at the nearby dead, and saw that Colombian soldiers lay amid the FARC who had tried to overrun the team.

I don't have a clear memory of what happened next. Shrinks have told me that my mind suppressed the memory to keep me from going crazy permanently, because I temporarily lost my sanity. The recollection I have is from what my men told me, and what was disseminated to me by the disciplinary investigators. It's like a scrapbook of collected images that I can see myself in, but can't connect with any feeling of being there.

The fighting was over. Morales' men were corralling the FARC who'd surrendered in front of the main house, stripping them of their clothes and equipment. Several of the GAULA soldiers were sifting through the bodies strewn around the compound and shooting the wounded.

A few of the prettier women had been dragged out of their hiding places and the men were taking turns raping them. The rest of the women and children were herded into the group of naked, surrendered men. Morales stood next to two of the FARC leaders and said, "A little something to take back to your friends," before ordering his men to pour kerosene on the group of captives.

It's what I've been told. I don't remember killing Morales, or shooting his men with the kerosene and the matches, or any of the others who put up a fight; I don't remember trying to smother the flames of the burning children with my body, but I have the burn scars, and I remember the smell...

What I'd done was an offense worthy of a Court Marshal, but the Army wasn't willing to risk the blowback of putting the facts on the record. I had too good a record and too many friends to just bury me in a stockade. My greatest regret was that I had not violated my orders sooner, moved to rescue the hostage, or fight Morales, when it might have saved the lives that were squandered. I could no longer be a good soldier, and the Army didn't want me to try…

Preferring physical pain to mental anguish, I sat up in the Mustang, to look at my face in the mirror on the back of the sun visor, probing my nose with my fingers, prodding where the cartilage and bone had been separated. I grabbed the end of my nose with my right hand, and pulled down with everything I had, while striking the area that was protruding with the edge of my left fist.

A feral shout escaped my mouth. I groped for the bag of iced peas and shoved it onto my face, rocking from side to side in the reclined driver's seat for a while, feeling nothing but the waves of pain and nausea course through my body, until slowly they subsided and I could take another shot of Tequila.

The burning liquid moved down my throat and then reversed. I opened the door and vomited onto the asphalt. The bottle of liquor rolled off my lap and clattered onto the pavement, spilling its contents.

Eventually, I gripped the steering wheel with both hands, and regarded my face once again. The nose seemed to be re-aligned somewhat. I felt as though the physical pain had reached its peak, and was now slipping away from me.

I felt empty, separated from my emotions, able to look at my life like I was watching a movie...

I'd cast about, laying drunk on different beaches, and in different women's beds after my resignation from the military was negotiated, taking my first protection job in LA just to have something constructive to do. Then once again, I found something I could do better than others, something that gave me purpose and direction. Instead of a uniform and a country, I had notoriety mixed with the intoxication of celebrity. My mission became success.

Yet with every accomplishment, and as I began to enjoy my life again, there were always the ghosts that would invade my dreams, waking me in the middle of the night, reminding me that their lives, the security of their families, had been taken from them, because I hadn't followed my instinct to do what was right.

The truth was, that I didn't want to have children because I was afraid to. I was afraid that if I loved something as much as you need to love a child, life would rip it from me in retribution...

I staggered out of the car, avoiding the mess I'd created, and walked up to the end of the block.

A marine layer had blown in off the water, and the bright lights of the stores around the UCLA campus were tinged with a halo of dewy mist. The cool air felt refreshing. I bent over at the waist, took several deep breaths, and then headed back to the liquor store. I purchased a package of paper towels and two bottles of water. Once again, the store clerk showed no reaction to my condition.

Outside the store, I downed one of the bottles of water without pausing to breathe. I used the other to dump over my head, and I cleaned away the dried blood with the paper towels.

I reached into the Mustang, picking my phone off of the passenger seat. I dialed Marianna's office number.

When she answered, I said, "What have you got for me?"

Chapter 17

Marianna wanted me to come back to the office, so I could see some of the research she'd uncovered while I was getting my ass kicked.

Bull was in the conference room with a big pile of trash dumped out on the long table, surrounded by four college kids Marianna hired. He was explaining how to sort through all the shredded documents from the Broken Dreams Productions dumpster, and then piece them back together.

Marianna came into my office and regarded my face. "I thought the Rocky Balboa look alike contest was next week," she said.

I shook my head, "What I want to know, is what the hell a pro with night vision was doing there? If it were the Feds, they'd have a warrant and would have arrested me. What the hell is going on?"

"Maybe you just surprised a high end cat burglar? Anybody can buy night vision online these days."

"You think a burglar could do this to me?"

"I don't know boss, you are getting older..."

"You are so fired when this is over," I nodded my throbbing head towards the folders she had in her hands. "What have you got there?"

"If you sit down like a good boy, I'll show you."

We moved to the leather couch and chair set that I used for clients that looked out over the city. The tall buildings of downtown were shining like the Emerald City in the distance. She dropped the files on the alabaster coffee table, sat next to me, and opened the folder from the top of the pile.

"This is Pemberton's file," she said. "The Joe that Kathy Sullivan told you about is probably Joe Banning."

She pulled out a downloaded image. It was the cover of a *Full Contact Karate* magazine from the '90's. Banning was big and muscular with longish dark hair, dressed in a black satin Karate Gi. The picture was taken when his foot was at the pinnacle of a roundhouse kick above his head.

"Could he have been the one that gave you that shiner?" she said.

I shrugged. "It was so dark. The size seems right."

"Banning was a drill instructor in the Marines. When Pemberton came to town with the movies he hired Joe as his right hand man."

"But why would he be sneaking around Cece Harris's house if they're working with her? Have you got a locate on him?"

"No. After Pemberton got sent up, Banning continued running the Dojo they set up together in Beverly Hills. His rent there, and the mortgage on his condo, is paid through the end of the month.

An instructor at the Dojo saw him last Saturday, he told me Banning was going out of town this week, but didn't know where."

"Did you look into what he owes on the condo?" I said.

Marianna leafed through the folder to a Real Property report that showed he'd just re-financed.

"Possibly pulling capital out to finance this job?" I said.

"That occurred to me too." She got a smug look on her face. "I called one of his ex-wives, who got all gossipy with me, and said that he has a taste for sex tourism. She said he was probably banging a room full of Asian girls…" Marianna pulled another piece of paper out of the sleeve that she was obviously proud of.

"This you would have to pay big money for boss, but for me it's free," she said, showing me a print out of his Dept. of Immigration stats, showing that he'd regularly traveled to Southeast Asia twice a year.

"And this helps me how?"

"There's no current activity, which means he's still in the States, unless he jumped the fence in Canada, or Tijuana."

"Or, he used an alternative ID…"

I leafed through the rest of the information she'd filled the file with. He'd been arrested on two assault charges, but not convicted, one against a woman. No other criminal activity. His service record was good. He'd gotten combat experience in Grenada, if you could call it that. He'd won a bunch of full contact Karate belts, was divorced twice.

"Hmm," was the most intelligent comment I could muster.

"These," she said, opening the next folder, "are all of the men Pemberton shared a cell with during his 'vacation'. Most of them are still inside or have been accounted for." She pointed to a dossier sitting on top of the thin stack. "This guy is interesting, since the kidnappers obviously have someone versed in cyber subterfuge assisting them."

The profile had a photo attached of a middle-aged man with dark hair and glasses. His name was listed as Paul Madison. There were also some wire-service printouts that Marianna had attached, chronicling his case. It took a few minutes for me to read through the pages of information. Marianna tried not to fidget too much. The case was quirky.

Madison had been arrested after an IRS audit seized his hard drive. He was a computer consultant, who was busted for setting up masking programs for child pornographers, and he never would've been caught, if he hadn't tried to hide his income from Uncle Sam. The only reason he was investigated, was because he'd put his cash in an offshore trust that was being managed by a guy the Feds were after. The Federal Prosecutor subpoenaed the records of all the trust's clients, and when Madison refused to cooperate, they got a court order to raid his house and office.

"He made okay money doing legitimate freelance programming and IT work, but his little kiddy-porn hobby turned a nice profit for him too," Marianna said. "I sent this info to Kaminoff and he knew who the guy was; went on about how this guy was really a genius, and described what exactly it was he'd done that was so unique, but it was all Greek to me."

I checked Madison's prison release date; it was several months prior to Pemberton's.

"He'd been staying with his brother since leaving prison," Marianna said, "but apparently moved out three weeks ago. The brother wouldn't give up any information, and there's nothing on the databases."

"Great," I said.

"But it gives us someone to be looking for, and Kaminoff said that knowing that it might be Madison, he can try some reverse worm options or something like that he hadn't thought of before."

She placed her hand on the final file. "For this last one, I'd like to bring in Jack Gillis."

"Sure, since you asked."

Marianna ignored my sarcasm and jumped up to use the intercom. Jack was the retired Sheriff's detective. He walked into the office wearing Hager slacks, a golden tweed sport jacket bulging under the left arm, with a green shirt open at the collar. With his close-cropped hair and mustache, he might as well have had a sign tattooed on his forehead that said, "Cop." We said our pleasantries, and he got down to business.

"Gave me a good one here," he said. "That phone number you got from Lauren's lover for her one night stand was for a throw away phone, and the name," he flipped open a little leather notebook, "Damiana Ambergris? Didn't show up on any of the databases as a person living within Los Angeles County." He leaned forward on the couch. "But it bugged something in the back of my head, and sure enough, Damiana and Ambergris are plants known as aphrodisiacs, so okay I think, good pseudonym for a hooker. Called some of my friends in Vice, did some research on the Escort Service websites and in the Hollywood Express, etc. Turns out there's several Damianas, so I scheduled appointments with each of them."

"What a guy has to do in the line of duty…"

"I have had worse assignments," he said.

"What'd you find?"

He checked his notes again. "Donna Anderson, aka Damiana Ambergris, apartment not far from here on Alta Loma. I didn't exactly identify myself as a police officer, but I didn't tell her I wasn't on the job either."

"Okay," I said. A PI could lose their license for impersonating a police officer.

"Anyway, I made it clear that if she didn't cooperate, she was going to have some serious problems with the Vice squad, which ended with her telling me that she'd been paid a retainer to seduce your subject."

"Lauren's lover Mika," Marianna said.

"She said the deal was she was given a thousand dollars, with the understanding that if she was called, she would drop everything, and do what she was told at $400 per hour until the job was finished."

"What was the job?" I asked.

"Get your subject to take her home, slip her a roofie, and then stick a flash drive in the security system."

"And she did," Marianna said.

"She said that when they called her and Mika was out cruising the bars, there were a couple of other working girls she recognized who were putting the moves on Mika too, but that your girl liked what our Damiana was offering that night."

Marianna's assistant crept in the door and gave her the signal that she had something important to interrupt with. Marianna excused herself and stepped out into the hall.

"Who hired her?"

"She wasn't giving that up. She said she didn't know who he was, but that she'd rather risk the Vice boys. She said he was nice to her, but seemed like someone you didn't want to piss off."

"Good work Jack," I said. "If we get you some pictures, can you go back and run them by her?"

"I'll try, but I doubt she's going to finger anybody."

"I'm relying upon your years of experience observing the finest of society, to tell me which ones she seems like she's lying about."

"That I can do."

I impressed upon him the need to keep all this confidential and told him that Marianna would get him a package. She came back in as he was going out.

"It's T-bone," she said. "They followed Cece Harris and her date to an estate in Mandeville Canyon. He needs instructions."

I got on the phone at my desk. While T-bone was briefing me on the surveillance that led him to the estate, I clicked on my computer to scan the email inbox. Marianna was on the extension taking notes regarding the address, and other particulars of the peculiar location the couple had retreated to.

An email entitled "Hey Asshole, Listen Up!" caught my attention. I'd passed it over on my IPhone, because I thought it was junk that crept by my filter, or some joke from a friend, but now I saw a return address on the big screen I hadn't looked at on the handheld. When it opened, I cursed.

From: <86521@brkndrms.com.
To: Richard Braddock <JB@StarShield.com.>

Sent: Tuesday, January 15, 2002 8:27 PM
Subject: Hey Asshole Listen Up!

Mr. Braddock,

I had hoped this would not have become necessary, but you have left me no choice. Please let me conclude my business and don't force me to do something else I will regret.

A photograph of my wife, bound and gagged was attached. There was no copy of the current day's newspaper as there had been with Lauren, but the clothes Victoria was wearing when she ran out of our house, and the look of fear mixed with outrage in her eyes, left me no doubt the image was authentic.

Chapter 18

Looking at the sickening picture of Victoria, a strange thing happened to me, it was like my emotions were shut off with a switch. I felt anything that was of other importance drop away from me like ice shattering off of a piece of steel in winter. The words, *So this is it*, were all that entered my mind. I saw clearly in a flash that the ghosts from my past weren't trying to warn me about some Karmic debt, they were the price I had to pay for that mistake. Now I'd made more mistakes, and how I dealt with them would determine the amount of regret I would have to live and die with.

The Bull and Marianna were saying things to me that I didn't hear. They both moved towards me, and I could hear my own voice like it was someone else's.

"The game just changed," I said. I felt as if I were outside my body, watching myself standing in the office, while time stopped for a moment.

I moved away from the desk so that The Bull and Marianna could see what I was looking at on the computer.

"Who are these guys?" The Bull said.

"Someone who did their homework," Marianna said.

"And found where we were vulnerable," I said.

"Hey man," The Bull said. "You know it's easy to ambush someone who doesn't think they're in enemy territory."

I didn't answer him, because I kept asking myself why I didn't start acting like I was in Indian country the minute I learned Lauren was taken. Why didn't I protect one of the few things that could be used against me? I looked out the window at the dark city, while my reflection mocked me in the glass.

"How do you want to play this boss?" The Bull said. "You thinking it's time to call the Feds?"

"Lauren is the high value target," Marianna said. "The probability of her being killed was always a variable, depending on the psychological stability of the captors and their level of threat tolerance. Now that Victoria has been added to the equation, they can afford to expend her for leverage and still remain relatively safe as long as the high value target is maintained."

"Don't sugar coat it Marianna." I turned from the window.

"What person," she said, "let alone an FBI agent, is going to want to be known as the person who got Lauren Hunter killed because they were trying to save your wife, except us?"

The Bull walked over and put his meaty paws on my shoulders. "Whatever you decide, we're with you."

I smacked him on the side of his ribcage in appreciation, and then moved over to the files of Kyle Pemberton and his associates. "You think this is the guy?"

"I feel it," Marianna said. "There's no one else with the motivation or the ability."

"Then let's find the son-of-a-bitch," I said.

"What about Cece Harris?"

"Of course, but she's a can of worms…"

"Let me see what I can pull up on her boyfriend," Marianna moved to my computer.

"Wait," I said. "Since they breached the security system at Lauren's house, and it's linked to our computer system, we have to assume they've hacked in and they're reading all our emails and who knows what else."

I pulled my laptop out of my briefcase, and plugged in the wireless card that worked separate from the Star Shield network. "Use this," I told her, "We have to keep moving forward, but I want it to look like we're backing off."

"If they've hacked our computers, they could also have gotten access to all our company mobile phones too," The Bull said.

"Marianna, we had the hardlines and the offices swept today right?"

She gave me a withering look while she typed the information she'd gotten from T-bone into my computer. "Unless they're using something new that our equipment can't pick up, the phones and the office are clean."

"Bull, break out the satellite phones for us," I said. "What do we have, four? We can get some throwaway phones from 7-11 for everyone else. We'll send out a cease and desist email and a text to everyone in the field, except for the guys keeping surveillance on Cece Harris, and I forget, is it Kelly who's tailing Bob Nilgore?"

Marianna nodded.

"Tell everyone but the two of them to stand down and report back here, so it looks like we're backing off. Get them hooked up with the new phones and brief them on the Victoria situation. Stop any work you're doing on this case using our PC's. Use laptops but only with independent wireless cards, not the wifi from our network."

The Bull went to get the phones. I had my own satellite phone, and used it to call Kaminoff. I wanted to see if there was any way he could reverse the hack that had been done on our system, and find out where our enemies were located. He agreed to come to the office and work on it. When I got off the phone, Marianna had a number of windows open on my laptop, with information on Daryl Pullman, the guy Cece Harris went home with.

The satellite photo from Google-maps depicted a sprawling estate nestled in a glen off Mandeville Canyon. The canyon is a long cul-de-sac of multi-million dollar homes, which branches off of Sunset Boulevard, a mile or two in from where it intersects Pacific Coast Highway at the ocean - about fifteen minutes drive from Lauren Hunter's house. It looked like there was a large house, a barn, and several other outbuildings nestled amid some pine trees, a few hundred yards from the canyon road. At maximum magnification, it looked to be laid out like a Kentucky horse farm.

"No neighbors within ear or eyeshot, plenty of room to hide utility trucks, close to the ambush zone, this would make a good base of operations," Marianna said.

"I'm still having a hard time understanding why these people would get involved with something like this?"

"Cece's boyfriend, Pullman, is a guy who could use ten million dollars," She clicked on other browser windows, from different databases, displaying Darryl Pullman's information. "He's a business manager. He used to work for some of our clients. He's the one who told everybody to invest in Lehman Bros. products right until the end. I haven't had time to run a full financial on him, but I can tell you that huge estate T-bone tracked them to is in foreclosure. He owes money all over town, and filed for bankruptcy last month."

"We've got several sets of problems," I said. "This could be the place where they're holding Victoria and Lauren. They might have Lauren here, and be keeping Victoria somewhere else. Or, neither of the hostages is here, and either these Hollywood big shots don't have anything to do with this, or they're keeping themselves an arms length away. That place could be set up with video, infrared, it's not some warehouse in the valley, guarded by a few reprobates."

"Why don't you talk to her second in command?" Marianna suggested.

"Nilgore?"

"Goody told you he had access to Cece's email account. Maybe he's got some information on her we could use... before you go storming the castle?"

"What's to keep him from squealing like a pig?"

"A day or two of his silence will be a lot easier to buy from him than Cece Harris or Darryl frigging Pullman, if we're as wrong about them as we were about David Holt in Van Nuys..."

It's hard to argue with a woman, especially when she's right.

"Besides," she said, "He might be a lot more willing to talk to me than you at midnight."

Chapter 19

Bob Nilgore owned a condo in a West Hollywood Gothic Revival building, complete with turrets, stained glass, and ironwork that made the place look like a castle with manicured lawns and bougainvillea. There's never any street parking in that neighborhood, so I parked the Mustang in a red zone across the street. Kelly walked over from where he'd been sitting on his motorcycle as Marianna and I exited my car.

"Far as I can tell he's in for the night," Kelly said. He was wiry, like a matador, with an aristocratic Castilian face, but he had the hair of an African from a Moorish ancestor, which made him look a bit like Jim Kelly in Enter The Dragon, and hence Marcello Diego ended up with the nickname Kelly. "He came straight here from the gym, his lights are out, and his car is still in the underground parking, but it's a security building, so I couldn't keep an eye on his front door without one of the neighbors dropping a dime. There're exits to the alley out back. Since it's just me, I can't say for sure he didn't skip on foot that way, but he didn't come out the front."

"Did you get inside the building?" I said.

"There's been a lot of traffic coming in, so it's not too hard to slip into the garage. His unit's in the back, but he had his curtains drawn. He almost made me when he came out to walk his dog, so I've played it kind of loose after that."

Marianna was buttoning her light leather trench coat against the chill. "What kind of dog?" she asked.

"Some kind of scruffy looking thing, medium size, I don't know my dog breeds too well."

"Did he seem nervous?" I said.

"No, just the opposite, he was whistling."

Marianna and I shared a hopeful glance. We got the placement and description of Nilgore's BMW Z4 convertible in the parking lot, gave Kelly one of the throwaway phones we'd picked up on the way over, briefed him about the security breech, and told him that my wife was now being held also. A repeated, "Holy shit," was the gist of his reaction before he told me not to worry, along with some graphic descriptions in Spanish of what he wanted to do to the kidnappers once we found them.

Marianna and I left him shaking his head and cursing. Soon, a two-seater Mercedes activated the gate to the building's parking garage. We slipped in while the sports car was parking.

"How do you want to play this? Quarreling couple or drunken lovers?" Marianna asked.

"I don't think I'm up for an argument with you right now," I said, and we wrapped our arms around each other like an amorous couple just back from the bar. She felt warm and soft, smelled spicy and clean, and I immediately felt guilty for noticing. Our acting wasn't necessary though, because the two men from the car were doing a better job playing the same role, barely paying attention to us when we shadowed them into the building.

Stairs led up to a well-manicured courtyard, filled with white rose bushes and agapanthus, growing amid flagstone footpaths, leading to each apartment. The faux medieval architectural style carried through to the interior, where the windows were fashioned in diamond patterned leaded glass, the doors, set in gothic arches, held large hammered steel hardware with strap hinges. The men from the garage stumbled into one of the doors, obliviously undressing each other, and several moments later thumping techno music rumbled out of their condo. The light of a TV flickered in another resident's window illuminating high-beamed ceilings. Since it was a two-story building with entries only on the first floor, I assumed that the units each had an interior staircase that led to upstairs bedrooms.

Marianna held onto me, until we got to Nilgore's apartment, and I let her. It was the only comforting thing that had happened all day. Then she untangled herself to ring his doorbell. The dog started barking from within, and a couple of other dogs from different apartments joined in. Shortly, we heard the clump-clump of someone coming down stairs. The dog barked half-heartedly a few more times from the second floor, before giving up.

Nilgore slid open a peephole that was cut into the door at eye level, the opening was cris-crossed with decorative hammered iron bars.

Marianna identified herself. "We've discovered some irregularities coming out of your office, that we feel could be dangerous to the production and we want to ask you some questions about them."

"Can't it wait until tomorrow?"

"I'm afraid it's seriously urgent," she said, "and we felt you might be more comfortable talking with us privately."

His eyes rolled over to me and widened slightly. "Can I put some clothes on?"

She told him that would be fine, and we waited while he clumped up the stairs again. I'd seen Nilgore just about every day when Lauren was in Mexico, but had very few conversations with him. Everyone on the Production referred to him as Cece's slave behind his back. He was one of those guys who pumped up his body at the gym like a balloon, thinking that muscles signified strength. The few times I'd dealt with him, he'd been peevish and bitchy, referring to me as Lauren's boy when he thought I was out of earshot.

Marianna was just about to ring the doorbell again, when we heard him descending the stairs, this time accompanied by the jingle of the dog's tags. The deadbolt clacked open and Nilgore said, "Come in," as he pulled the door open with a broad smile. His other hand held the collar of a good-sized Airedale terrier. Just as my mind was registering the straps of a backpack on top of the gray sweatshirt he wore, and I realized there was something wrong, he shrieked, "Brutus, help me."

The animal who'd been standing alert but calm at his master's side as the door opened, exploded with the sound of claws scratching against the hardwood floor, into a flying mass of growling teeth and fur across the several feet between us.

The flashing jaws clamped around Marianna's arm that she raised to protect her neck as I moved too late to intercept the beast. She let out an involuntary cry of pain, beating at the dog's head with her free hand. I was completely focused on trying to grasp the dog's ears, gouge its eyes, do something that would get him to release Marianna, when Nilgore barreled by me like a blitzing linebacker, smashing me off balance, so that Marianna, the snarling dog and I, tumbled off the landing, down the couple of stairs, into a frenzied heap on the flagstone.

Marianna's screaming stopped when the dog and I landed on top of her, but the animal kept tearing at her arm, while his paws kicked and scratched at us, trying to find a footing. After a long few moments of righting my own equilibrium and using the dog for leverage, I was able to raise my arm and bring it down with a hammer fist, directly onto the terrier's large black nose.

The animal yelped, and I tried to hit it again, but it let go of Marianna's arm to direct its gnashing teeth at my face. The first snap missed, and I was able to get hold of an ear, and yank, but it only directed the biting towards my left arm, where I felt sudden searing pain. For what seemed like hours, I tried to keep him from getting a better purchase in my flesh by using my upper position, getting hold of his other ear, and yanking on it repeatedly, tearing the skin at its base.

His claws gouged at my chest, arms, legs, and stomach, while I battled for control of his head, until he yelped again and convulsed violently. I looked up, following the wires from Taser darts sticking in the dog, which were attached to the weapon in Marianna's shaking hand.

"Are you alright?" I said.

"No I'm not alright, my arm was just chewed off," she said, her finger poised on the trigger, ready to give the dog another jolt of electricity if he acted aggressively. "Go get Nilgore, so I can use this on his balls."

I ran through the courtyard, to the front of the building. All the dogs on the premises were yammering, the techno was thumping from the gay guys' apartment, but I could still hear the squeal of tires on concrete, below in the garage. I ran through an expansive foyer that held mailboxes, a bulletin board, and a counter, which harkened back to when residence hotels had clerks in their lobbies. By the time I burst through the large wood and ironwork entry door, Nilgore's BMW Z4 was nosing out of the garage gate.

"He's running. He's running," I shouted to Kelly, who was jamming his helmet onto his head and firing up his bike, as Nilgore smoked the tires out of the driveway, racing up the street, headed north.

I leapt down the stairs leading from the entry and sprinted to the Mustang. When I tried to turn the wheel with my left hand, after I'd jammed the gearshift into reverse, I realized how much damage the dog had done to my left arm by the pain that struck me like a pickaxe. I used my right hand to spin the wheel, and screeched the tires, shifting through the gears up the street.

My last sight of Kelly's bike was of it turning left on Fountain Avenue, where I slowed down just enough to gauge the cross traffic, down shifted into second, and skidded across the lanes, causing the oncoming cars in both directions to lock up their brakes noisily, swerve, and no doubt call me everything but the Son of God.

I was cursing too while I accelerated westbound on Fountain, because of the arm that felt like it had nails driven through it, and the fact that I had no way to contact Kelly without using our compromised communication system. The guys all had their phones connected to Bluetooth headsets in their motorcycle helmets, so that normally I could have speed-dialed Kelly, even driving eighty miles per hour while avoiding traffic going half that, but I only had a paper list of the new phone numbers stuffed between the seats, and even if I were to call Kelly, if he stopped to answer, Nilgore would get away.

A red light and cross traffic forced Nilgore to stop at the tee intersection where Fountain hits La Cienega, and as I closed rapidly, I watched Kelly skid to a stop beside the BMW's passenger side door, and begin to draw his sidearm.

Seeing this, Nilgore launched his vehicle into the northbound cars on La Cienega, who had the green light, clipping the tail end of a Toyota, before he slid into the southbound stream of cars. I could see Kelly aiming and considering a shot, but there were too many civilians who could be hit by a miss or a ricochet, so he didn't pull the trigger.

Cursing again, I accelerated into the oncoming lane, around the car in front of me, and then I cut a left, into the last side street before the intersection, which parallels La Cienega between Fountain and Santa Monica. We had to coral Nilgore quickly, before one of the citizens - who was no-doubt dialing 911 that moment - brought the LAPD swooping in on us. I prayed that the roar of the Mustang's bored out exhaust would keep any innocent pedestrians from stepping out from between the parked cars, as I redlined the tachometer down the normally quiet street of apartment buildings.

I had to squeal to a stop for cars on Santa Monica before jumping out to the right, and squirreling my way into the left hand turn pocket for La Cienega. The traffic light showed a red arrow, but there was enough space before the next oncoming car for me to hammer the gas pedal, pop the clutch, screech and slide across the intersection to the southbound lanes of La Cienega.

I spotted Nilgore's taillights a few cars ahead zigzagging erratically, trying to move forward through the two lanes of cars. The center median clogged with vehicles turning left or right, headed to or leaving from, the restaurants and clubs located on either side of the wide boulevard. Checking my mirror I could see Kelly trying to cross La Cienega against the light.

When I looked forward again, the center median had opened up, and Nilgore was angling the little sports car to take advantage of the open space, where he would be able to gain a considerable lead. A car still faced me, between us in the median, trying to turn left, but no cars approached in the nearest oncoming traffic lane, so I punched the Mustang to the left, power-shifting into second gear, then flashed my brights at the oncoming traffic. Nilgore's little BMW two-seater might give the Mustang trouble if we got into some serious curves, but on the flat it was no match and shortly I was nosing up on his rear fender.

The only problem was that there was a car dead ahead of me in my lane, who either didn't see me hurtling towards it, or couldn't get out of the way. I eased off the gas and was about to tuck in behind the BMW, when the car ahead swerved out of my way to its right.

I gunned the Mustang and pulled abreast of Nilgore, who had to brake for the cars waiting in the left turn lane at Beverly. He ducked back into the number one southbound lane. The light ahead turned green, and I blew by the vehicles in the left turn pocket to my right, down shifted when I hit the crosswalk stripes, and swung the car right, through the two directions of left turning cars edging their way into the intersection, and slipped the Mustang into Nilgore's lane, in front of the car ahead of him.

I braked down, slowing the lane, so that the BMW was boxed in by the traffic in the right hand lane, which was going faster. When Nilgore tried to jump out into the median, I moved to block him. The car between us was blaring its horn, and angry arms were gesturing from the windows on either side, but behind them, I could see the single light of Kelly's motorcycle pulling into the blind spot on Nilgore's passenger side.

There was half a car length of space in the lane to my right, so I nudged the nose of the Mustang into it, causing the upcoming car to jam on its brakes and lock up both lanes of traffic, preventing Nilgore's car from moving in any direction. Everyone was honking and screaming at me now, as Kelly came skidding to a stop between the lanes, threw the kickstand down, hopped off his bike, and reached Nilgore just as he was scrambling out of the vehicle. Kelly launched himself into the air with a diving elbow that hit the side of Nilgore's head with all of Kelly's weight behind it, crumpling the bodybuilder against the open driver's side door.

I lurched the Mustang forward, freeing up the traffic jamb, and parked it in the median. When I got out of the Mustang, the angry young driver of the closest car I'd cut off was out of his vehicle and coming toward me, but something about my demeanor caused him to change his mind and move out of my way. Perhaps it was the blood dripping from the dog-bites, or the expression on my beat up face? My appearance also caused several of the women in the vehicles, gawking from the opposing lanes, to emit frightened exclamations.

Unconscious, Nilgore was one heavy piece of meat. Kelly and I grunted as we dragged him to my car and stuffed him into the back seat, amid calls of, "Hey," "What are you doing," and other assorted heckling from passersby.

I could hear the wail of sirens sounding closer than I wanted them to be.

"What about his car?" Kelly said.

"It'll give the cops something to deal with when they get here besides looking for us. Go help Marianna."

As I got back behind the wheel of the Mustang, and Kelly sprinted to his bike, I pulled my gun out and placed it between my legs in case my passenger woke up feeling frisky.

Kelly worked his bike into the traffic headed back the way we'd come on La Cienega. I eased the Mustang into the flow of traffic southbound, before turning right into the residential streets of Beverly Hills as soon as I could. I made a number of consecutive right turns, to make sure I wasn't being followed, before finding a parking space where I could stop and pop the trunk. I pulled out some plastic zip-tie cuffs, a roll of tape, and a Leatherman tool from my tactical bag. Nilgore came to while I was binding his wrists, so I chopped him on the temple with the edge of my hand, shutting off his brain switch for a little longer. Once I had his ankles and hands bound together so that he couldn't kick out my windows or the back of my head if he regained consciousness again, I covered his mouth and eyes with tape.

Then I called The Bull to give him a sit-rep, before continuing to drive cautiously along backstreets towards the Star Shield office.

Chapter 20

Nilgore regained consciousness during the drive to Star Shield, causing me to crank the Mustang's sound system. Lupe Fiasco's song *Words I Never Said*, drowned out his muffled expressions of displeasure, protest, and query. The subterranean garage at the Star Shield building was mostly empty at that hour of the morning. The base reverb echoed off the concrete as I wound down the three levels to where the Star Shield parking spaces were located, near the ready-room used by our operatives commonly known as the Pit.

The Bull was waiting for me when I pulled up. "I told dispatch to tell any of our people who were coming in or going out to a regular assignment that the Pit was off limits until further notice," he said.

We dragged the bodybuilder out of the car, and carried him into the Pit, where we dumped him on the floor.

I turned on the lights, illuminating the two walls of lockers, the mismatched couches, chairs, coffee and card tables covered with magazines, dominos, and chess sets. Nilgore wriggled on the floor making muffled sounds of complaint. I motioned for The Bull to follow me outside.

"How's Marianna?" I said.

"I sent Willie to pick her up. She's on the way to the doctor." He looked at my arm and said, "You should probably do the same."

"There'll be time for that. Right now I want to ask Mr. Nilgore a few questions."

"And if he's not answering?" The Bull looked me in the eyes.

"Let's hope he's smart. If not, you can go upstairs, I'll take the responsibility."

"Not a problem for me boss," my friend said. "I'm not planning on leaving any marks."

Anything I said would have cheapened his willingness to go to the mat for me, so we both just stood there for a moment, sharing the knowledge that we would do whatever needed to be done, together.

Back in the Pit, I went to the battered refrigerator for a Diet Coke, and guzzled it. The Bull cut the plastic-cuffs from around Nilgore's ankles, and then grabbed his ear, pulling him over to one of the card tables, where he shoved Nilgore into one of the folding metal chairs.

I flipped open my Spyderco knife and cut the straps off Nilgore's backpack, then put on a pair of latex gloves before emptying out the contents of the pack onto the top of the table.

Nilgore's eyes darted from The Bull to me, as I laid out the contents of the rucksack: a laptop, a change of clothes, toilet kit, chargers, other sundries one might bring on a short trip, as well as a nylon envelope containing five thousand US dollars and roughly forty-five-hundred dollars in Mexican Pesos. The envelope also held an American Express card, and Argentinean passport with Nilgore's picture, but both were in the name of Robert Nestore. Also a First Class plane ticket to Acapulco on Aeromexico, scheduled for the following day at six o'clock p.m. I opened the laptop, but it was password protected. I handed the laptop to The Bull. "Kaminoff's here right? Let's see if he can crack the password."

The Bull called upstairs on the hard line for someone to come down and get the computer to Kaminoff.

I returned to the table and regarded my bound prisoner. "Okay, Mr. Nilgore... or Nestore as the case may be, since you set your dog on my partner and I when we tried to interview you the polite way, what I'm really tempted to do right now is get down with some old-school, clip a car battery to your nuts type of questioning."

He couldn't meet my eyes.

"The only reason I don't have my friend here whacking you on the side of the head right now with a phone book, is that I can't figure out why a guy like yourself would be in the business of kidnapping movie stars, unless you were somehow a victim too."

Sweat was soaking Nilgore's forehead and dripping through his eyebrows, causing him to blink rapidly. Or he was crying.

Knocking sounded on the door. The Bull handed the computer to one of our staff and returned. I placed the non-incriminating items back into the rucksack, arranged the money, the passport, the plane ticket, neatly on the table in front of Nilgore.

"Now I'm going to take that tape from your mouth, and I'm going to give you a chance to help us. If you don't work with me, we'll let your friends think that you did when we catch them, and then you'll be in County Jail all by your lily-white self. I doubt you'll ever get to cost the taxpayers the expense of a preliminary hearing."

Quickly, I swiped the tape free of Nilgore's mouth. His eyes watered, as little spots of blood dimpled around his lips where the tape yanked out whiskers or stripped off skin. His chin quivered and dimpled, but he didn't cry or scream.

"So Bob," I said, "what do you have to say for yourself?"

"I'm not saying anything without a lawyer," he said.

That made The Bull and I laugh without humor.

Then The Bull yanked Nilgore upright and punched him in the stomach with one swift motion. "Do I look like someone who gives a shit about your Miranda rights?" He waved his meaty hand over the items we just pulled out of Nilgore's backpack. "Boy, you're sitting here with all this shit on the table, and having just sicced a dog on my friends… Unless you start telling us pretty quick how you're mixed up in this shit, you're going to need a doctor more than you're going to need a lawyer."

When Nilgore could finally breath, and stopped gulping in air, we hauled him off the floor onto the chair again. No color remained in his face, and he seemed like he was trying not to cry.

"You scared Bob?" I said. "You should be. You're in way over your head, and the only way your going to see the shallow end of the pool is if we help you."

I let him think about it for a moment. He continued breathing heavily. Rivulets of sweat were streaming from his temples.

"Of course if you do cooperate, maybe nobody has to know? You're a little fish Bob. Help us out, and we can keep you from being snagged in the net that's going to catch the sharks."

He just stared straight ahead, without responding.

"Is this all just a misunderstanding? Maybe you didn't realize what was really going to happen? Maybe you're what they call an unwilling accomplice? Maybe you were coerced into something that then you couldn't get out of? Did they threaten a family member, someone you care about?"

Nilgore looked at me distrustfully.

"The good news about us not being the police is that we don't have to worry about booking slips and detention paperwork. We only care about one thing, getting our client back, not enforcing the law. It might even be in our interests to have you back at work in the morning like nothing happened... You've heard of double agents, haven't you Bob?"

I felt like I'd struck a nerve, because I could see him thinking.

"The bad news is, that we could dump your body in the ocean if we had to get too rough with you," The Bull said laying his big hand on Nilgore's shoulder. "See, whatever someone else has over you, you're here now..." His hand then dug into the Brachial plexus, located in the hole between Nilgore's neck and his collarbone, causing Nilgore to call out in pain, and say, "Okay...okay...Okay stop. Please!" until Bull let go.

"It's up to you Bob..." I said, pouring out some bottled water into a Dixie cup and putting it to his lips.

Because he was hyperventilating, he inhaled some of the liquid, which caused him to cough violently for a little while, leaving him spent and bent over.

When he sat up, I said, "You okay?"

"No," he said, sardonically.

The Bull and I coaxed and prodded him for a while longer, building Nilgore's belief that I thought he was just a good guy who had made a mistake, while also explaining that with the evidence we had laid out on the table, he was going to need someone like us on his side. We worked him like a big trout on a fly line. Until I said, "Listen, we already know about the emails. We just need you to fill in some details…"

"How did you know it was me?" he said. "I always used her computer."

The Bull and I exchanged a look like that was the dumbest question he could have thought up, "It's what we do," The Bull said. "Someone wants a movie made, they call you. Someone wants to know who's misbehaving, they call us."

"What I'm curious about is why Bob?" I said. "You don't seem like the kind of guy who needs to get involved in something like this?"

Though outwardly it appeared as though I had all the time in the world for him to fill in the small parts of the puzzle I hadn't figured out yet, I felt more anxious at that moment than I had all night. The truth was that I was struggling like mad to figure out how he fit in, without revealing how much we didn't know.

"It was supposed to go so easy," he said speaking towards the ground, "A win/win for everybody."

I pulled up a chair, and sat on it backwards, facing Nilgore at his level. "See, I suspected that you just got roped into this somehow, and that's what we wanted to talk to you about earlier." I kept my mangled arm hidden by the back of the chair. "Now I'm willing to start from square one, to see if we can work something out, but you're going to have to be straight with us, and no bullshit. Do you think we might be able to work together?"

Nilgore hung his head. "I can't believe this is happening…" He was barely audible.

"How was it presented to you as a win/win?" I said.

He looked up at me imploringly. "They're taking really good care of her, as soon as they get the money she'll be able to complete filming and everyone will be covered by the insurance claim."

"Do you know where Lauren is being held?"

Nilgore smirked. "He'd never tell me something like that."

"Pemberton?" I gambled.

Nilgore barely nodded. His expression was the greater confirmation.

I glanced at The Bull, and though neither of us showed any emotion, I knew he was probably feeling the same excitement that I was.

"You just provided the information?" I said.

"That's all I did, I swear."

"I know, I know. But maybe you overheard something? Saw something you weren't supposed to?"

He shook his head.

"Who else is involved? Maybe you know one of the people we haven't turned up yet?"

"Kyle was the only person I ever met with. All we talked about was the type of information he wanted on Lauren and Tom, how to get it to him, and how I'd be taken care of."

Again I caught The Bull's eye for a brief moment. This was the first time that Tom Grayson, Lauren's co-star had been mentioned.

"How were you supposed to be taken care of Bob? You make a good living; I still don't understand why you would risk so much? Was Pemberton threatening you in some way?"

Nilgore looked disgusted and just shook his head. "I can't believe this is happening," he said again.

I held back from prodding him.

"A million dollars," he said almost silently. "I was supposed to get a million dollars for sending a few emails." Then he became more animated. "And he said that if anything went wrong that they'd go after that bitch first, and if anyone suspected me, it would take so long that I'd have plenty of time to get away first. That's what I don't understand, why don't you have her down here instead of me?"

"Cece?" I said.

Again, almost to himself he said, "I wouldn't even be in this mess if it weren't for that cunt."

"How's that?"

"It's because of her that I'm broke." He said. "I invested all of my savings with her stupid boyfriend, and he put it all in Lehman Brothers. With that and the condo I'm upside down in, I make less now than I did when I was a PA."

I glanced over at the Pesos and the ticket to Acapulco. "And a million dollars would get you a fresh start in Mexico?"

He laughed sadly, shaking his head. "Argentina. I was going to open a gym down there… Today, when I actually thought it was going to happen, is the first time I've been happy in years."

"Why don't you cut those cuffs off him Bull?" I said.

We got Nilgore something to drink and settled him in a more comfortable chair. For the next hour we cajoled his story out of him.

Bob Nilgore had worked for Cece Harris for years. He was her Production Secretary when she was a Production Coordinator, and stayed with her as she rose to Unit Production Manager, becoming her Production Supervisor. "So, basically I did all the shit work, and she got all the glory," he said.

Nilgore got to know Kyle Pemberton when Pemberton was hired as a Military Advisor. Pemberton eventually dated Cece for a while on a movie preceding the one Pemberton got in trouble on. When I asked him if he knew what the real story was behind Pemberton getting arrested, Nilgore said, "Denise Morton threw him under the bus, and Barry could have pulled him out from under that bus, but didn't."

"Why do you say that?"

"I was in a meeting with Barry and Cece where they were talking about Kyle getting in bed with Denise Morton, and how that was going to be a pain in their asses, because Kyle could just run up his budget as long as he had Denise to protect him."

"What budget?"

"Explosions, extras," he made air quotes, "safety - which means hiring your stunt friends. There were a lot of battle and action scenes that everyone was looking to Pemberton to make real," again he made air quotes. "If he's banging the star, who's going to tell him he can't have six more explosions, or a few more tanks? It becomes what she wants, and nobody tells those people no once shooting starts…"

"So you don't think that Pemberton sexually assaulted Denise Morton?" I asked Nilgore.

Nilgore shrugged, "What's sexual assault? Did she maybe say no that night? I wasn't there, but if he did force himself on her, it was only because she'd given him the green light - until that night when her husband showed up."

"I still don't understand how Barry Sheldon is at fault here?"

Nilgore shrugged, "Pemberton's whole defense was that he had been having consensual sex with Morton for a couple of weeks, but all of the housekeepers from the camp," air quotes again, "went back to Mexico, before the trial... None of the actors were going to risk their relationship with Morton or Paragon, so they saw, heard, and spoke no evil, which left Barry as the only person with actual knowledge of the existing relationship, and he told the court that he didn't know shit about it."

"If he'd never seen them sleeping together, he'd be telling the truth?"

"That's what I was getting to before you started asking me about Kyle's budget. The reason Barry called that meeting, was because he'd walked into, what was supposed to be a private, hand-to-hand combat training session between Kyle and Denise..." Nilgore laughed sardonically, "Barry said, Kyle must have been teaching her how to get someone's mouth off her pussy..."

The Bull and I exchanged glances, and Nilgore shook his head.

"Kyle just got his dick caught in the Hollywood machine. I felt sorry for him. That's why I started hanging out with him when he started working out at my gym."

Nilgore explained that he'd first run into Pemberton during one of his regular workouts, shortly after Pemberton was released from jail. Looking back on it, Nilgore felt that the meeting hadn't been as accidental as he'd first assumed, but he said he felt sorry for the guy.

The two men developed a friendship, that again Nilgore had to admit, was mostly initiated by Pemberton. They each had common gripes against Harris, Sheldon, Paragon, and life. "I mean," Nilgore said, "Do you have any idea what it's like to work all your life thinking you've made it, then to be forty years old and living paycheck to paycheck?"

I commiserated, and Nilgore went on to rail against Cece Harris, and how she'd abused him over the years.

"Is that why you decided to contact Pemberton using her email account?" I said.

"No," Nilgore shook his head again with the shame of being duped, "It was his idea. He had six years in prison with nothing to do but plan this."

He explained how Pemberton patiently encouraged him to participate and constantly downplayed the risk, in the end making Nilgore believe that it was just a matter of sending a few emails. However, once Nilgore accepted the getaway money, passport and plane ticket that Pemberton provided, and Nilgore started divulging any information he could get about the film's two stars, Pemberton made it very clear that if Nilgore got cold feet there would be dire consequences.

He confirmed that Pemberton used the Broken Dreams production company as a front to set up the operation, and that Pemberton had shown equal interest in the travel and security information Nilgore was providing on both Lauren and Tom Grayson, Lauren's co-star. Since Tom was one of the hottest male stars in

Hollywood, he also made twice as much as Lauren, and his deal provided for a four-man security detail at all times from my biggest competitor, Blackthorn Security. Coupled with the fact that Tom lived at his mansion in the thick of Beverly Hills most of the time, it seemed that we were selected as the more vulnerable target. Which was a relief in one sense, because it meant that it was unlikely that someone from within Star Shield betrayed us.

We spent time going over the details of how Nilgore was supposed to receive his payment. An account had been set up for him at a bank in Hong Kong. He could use the American Express card he was carrying, in the name of Robert Nestore, and the balance would be paid automatically from the Hong Kong account. Pemberton told him that Paragon was supposed to wire-transfer the ransom payment to an account in the Caymen Islands, which had been instructed to make a blind disbursement of any deposit it received, by percentages, to the accounts around the world, set up for the people working with Pemberton. Whatever the amount of the ransom, Nilgore's Hong Kong account was supposed to receive ten percent of it.

When we felt that we had milked all of the usable information out of Nilgore, The Bull called upstairs and got someone to bring our captive something to eat and stand guard over him.

Chapter 21

In the office kitchen, the black sludge that I dredged from the bottom of the coffee pot tasted more like chemical waste than refreshment, but with the clock moving towards two a.m. I hoped the nasty flavor meant the liquid's stimulant qualities would be enhanced.

Marianna was back from the doctor with her bandaged arm in a sling, and when we finally emerged from interrogating Nilgore she had some nasty words for us because we wouldn't let her have a go at him herself.

Our people had come in from the field to get their new phones, but because The Bull had left explicit instructions that we were not to be disturbed, they looked to Marianna for guidance, and not being able to give them clear direction made her even crankier than her injury. She was eager for the information we'd gained, and I suggested that we gather in the conference room. "Perfect," she said, "I put everyone to work there piecing the trash together while you were having your ménage a trios. Do you want Kaminoff to be part of this meeting also?"

I'd sought the coffee while she was rounding up Kaminoff.

When I walked into our state-of-the-art conference room, it looked like the location of a strange puzzle competition. At one end of the table, piles of shredded paper The Bull brought in from the dumpster of the Broken Dreams Productions office were heaped in mounds. On every other flat surface in the room, the members of the team were huddled around taped together shreds of pages at the beginning of re-assembly. The college kids we'd hired as temps were shuttling little strips of paper between the big piles and each of the documents under reconstruction, trying to find pieces that matched. The Bull was watching it all with a bemused grin.

I called a halt to the activity, gave the college kids the list containing the new phone numbers, instructed them to collect each operative's new phone and program the speed dial numbers, so that we could quickly contact each other. I also suggested they make themselves, and everyone, some fresh coffee.

Marianna prodded Kaminoff into the room and they opened their laptops on the conference table. The rest of the team made efforts to protect the small pieces of reconstructed documents they'd been working, on before making themselves comfortable for the briefing.

When everyone was settled, I brought the group up to speed regarding the events leading to Nilgore's attempted escape and subsequent questioning. I outlined what we knew about Pemberton's background and motives, then Marianna flashed photos of Pemberton on the video screen, as well as his suspected accomplices Joe Banning and Paul Madison, while she spoke to what we knew about each of them.

"Nilgore was attempting to get to the airport when he fled," The Bull said. "He was carrying a phony passport, ten thousand dollars in cash, and a ticket to Mexico scheduled to leave…" The Bull checked his watch. "In fifteen and a half hours. Pemberton told Nilgore that the money would be in his account by noon, so we feel strongly that they are going to attempt a hostage exchange this morning. It's also what they stated in their ransom note."

I directed my attention to Kaminoff. "Did you get into Nilgore's laptop?"

"Yes I did," the hacker said. "The person who set up the Hong Kong account for Nilgore was very careless in hiding her tracks."

"Her?"

"I emailed Marianna with the woman's details so she can run a locate. Her name is Marnice Belstein, someone who's worked as a free-lance accountant for the studios."

"Nice going," I said.

"It's the first bit of IT work on this job that's been sloppy. It looks like maybe Nilgore, and this woman Belstein, were set up to take the fall if anyone came looking for the money."

"Interesting," I said. "If Nilgore used his laptop at work, and had access to the Paragon network, could you use it to mask your access to the system, so that you could override their security?"

"Theoretically."

"Good, I'm going to need you for some field work." I addressed the rest of the room. "We may not be able to find Pemberton before the exchange, but I want to be in the best position we can to monitor the hand off. We need to get whatever surveillance technology we can into the offices of Barry Sheldon, Cece Harris, and Rikki

Wymen at Paragon. The Bull, Kaminoff, T-Bone, Sparky, Kelly, and I, are going to set that up."

"We also know from Nilgore's confession that Pemberton was definitely using the Broken Dreams Production office as a front for his operation, so Willie and Pernell, let's get those temps back in here and finish work on the shredded documents, focusing on anything that might refer to another location they could be using as a headquarters where they are keeping Lauren, Dale and Victoria, or a location to make the hostage exchange."

"I was working on something that looks like a lease agreement," Willie cranked her head to look at the patched together paper around her.

"That's the kind of thing we want," I nodded to Willie, "Get 'er done."

"All over it."

"I want everyone else scrambling to get any thread of intel on our suspects that might give us an edge."

The Bull clapped his hands. "Let's get on it people."

We received a tired, "Hoo-yah," from the group.

After the meeting I went to my office, so that I could change out of my tactical gear into a spare set of jeans, shoes, oxford shirt, and black blazer that I kept in my closet; I was clipping my holster onto my belt when Marianna walked in.

She stood fully in the doorway, and it was the first time I'd really looked at her since I left Nilgore's apartment. I hadn't yet registered how bloody and torn her expensive silk dress was, or, that for the first time since we'd known each other, her hair wasn't perfect. "Do you really need to go to Paragon?" she said.

"I was planning on it."

"They're going to bug some offices in a movie studio, not break into Fort Knox. You need to go to the doctor."

"Bullshit, I didn't get bitten nearly as badly as you did."

"But you did get bitten, and Dr. Saperstein said she wanted to see you also, because puncture wounds are the most likely to get infected if not cleaned out properly."

I flexed the hand Nilgore's dog used as a chew-toy. It was stiffening up and shot a burst of pain up my arm that made it hard for me to breathe. "I'll throw some Hydrogen Peroxide on it, and it'll be fine."

"You don't have a choice in this matter," she said. "I've just talked to The Bull and the other boys, they all agree with me. It's not just your arm, it's everything, and the doctor has some good stuff, believe me." She waived the arm wrapped in gauze and belayed by the sling, "I couldn't stop crying it hurt so bad. Now it's bearable and I don't feel woozy; she fixed me a nice upper cocktail, with a to-go package to keep me sharp. The crew can keep things moving forward for an hour while you get taken care of."

My initial feeling was to argue, but I could hear the wisdom in what she was saying.

"He's not giving you any trouble is he?" The Bull moved into the doorway behind Marianna and spoke to me. "You don't want to start snapping like a twig when it's nut check time tomorrow. Let the Doc give you a flashlight to help get through Ghost Town with."

I nodded, making a half-hearted effort to grin. Ghost Town was how we referred to the time when you're sleep-deprived, stressed, and there's no end to the mission in sight. We'd experienced it together many times, the achy, itchy pain of sleeplessness, where motor response time slowed perceptibly, and all experience is muted by a gauze of mental and physical fatigue; but like anything, if you train for it, the human body can adapt, function, and often surprise you with the resilience it can afford. Naming the feeling brought a strange sense of comfort, enabling me to realize that on top of that condition, I'd suffered some physical and psychological abuse that could use a little patching up too.

"You guys are ganging up on me aren't you?"

"And we'll call back up if we need it," The Bull said.

They wouldn't even let me drive my own car. One of our guards, Tony Evans, who'd just come off a shift shadowing a TV star on a date, was assigned by Marianna to put me in an Escalade and not take any shit from the boss. Tony was a professional, he didn't say a word, just raised his eyebrows at me to see if I was going to give him any trouble before he escorted me downstairs and packed me in the back seat of the vehicle.

Riding as a passenger through the blinking neon and flashing digital billboards illuminating the streets of Hollywood, where the traffic consisted mostly of driver's spilling out of the bars and clubs, cruising with the stilted care of those trying to avoid a DUI, or the erratic slinking of Johns and junkies looking for a fix, I couldn't evade the feelings of foreboding. Though I was doing my best to maintain a positive mindset and exude confidence in our plan, my experience wouldn't let me lie to myself. Whatever scenario I extrapolated from the facts, resulted only in questions regarding the extent and scope of casualty and damage.

Tony turned the Escalade up into the maze of winding streets in the hills above Sunset Plaza, looping higher and higher, until he finally parked in front of a large Craftsman style house nestled behind a hedge of Fichus trees. He jumped to get the door for me as if I were a client. I told him to relax, but he wouldn't even let me punch the key code that opened the gate to the guesthouse of Myra Saperstein, a doctor who was willing to make house calls or discreetly receive VIP patients in the middle of the night. We'd brought more than our share of clientele to her door at all hours, suffering from overdoses, pregnancies, hypochondria, misplaced foreign objects, psychotic episodes, headaches and heartbreaks. She was also who I used personally when Victoria or I had need of a physician. Saperstein's ministrations carried not only a highly educated knowledge of medicine, but also a bedside manner that never felt judgmental or clinical, she had one of those uncanny abilities to make anyone feel comfortable, and acquitted of whatever they were feeling guilty about in their moment of weakness or shame.

Saperstein opened the door to the building that she used as her "office," wearing fuzzy suede slippers, gray flannel pajama pants, a black t-shirt with the Coca-Cola logo written in Thai, a white lab coat, and a stingy brimmed fedora with a snakeskin pattern. She gave me a brief, but strong hug hello, and ushered me into a room that was furnished as a plush den, which incidentally used the occasional piece of medical equipment for avant-garde decoration.

She led me to a large, comfortable chair, upholstered in soft leather, where she turned my face left and right, examining it in the light, then inspected my hand and arm. "You're going to have to take off your shirt so I can clean out those puncture wounds. Marianna told me about the dog, who did the job on your face?"

"When I find out, I'll send him to you."

She helped me out of my shirt and jacket, handing me a dark blue 'scrub' shirt to put on. "I don't want you to get cold."

She went to one of her handcrafted chest of drawers, selecting some items, placing them in a wicker tray, and setting the tray on a low table next to my chair where it was out of sight. "I know you could tough it out," she said, "but I'm going to give you a local anesthetic before I clean out those bites," and with the fluid motion of an artist, she had the needle in my arm so smoothly, that I didn't see it, and barely felt it.

"Nicely played doc."

"They don't call me Myra Saperstein for nothing," she said, "We need to give that a little time to do its magic, lay your head back and I'm going to put some ice on your face. Marianna told me you've got a big day tomorrow, and we can't have your face looking like a kielbasa. Once the ice has numbed you, I'm going to shoot you with some anti-inflammatory in the bad spots, that sound okay?"

"Sure." I rested my head back, and then she applied an ice pack to my face that looked like an old goalie's mask made of soft cotton, I'd seen actresses use them to tighten their skin. After a few moments I got the feeling that she'd shot more than a local painkiller into my arm.

"I'm going to go and get some more things," her voice sounded close to my ear. "Just rest for a few moments and I'll be right back."

A Miles Davis tune was playing in the background, and while I rode on the clear melodies of his trumpet, the day's events slipped from my mind... until the doctor's voice broke the trance.

"Richard?"

The question caused me to spasm involuntarily like when you wake from a dream where you're falling.

"Whoa hoss," she said, touching my shoulders with warm hands. When I settled she said, "This is going to sting a little," and started digging in the puncture wounds in my arm with her swabs and instruments. It definitely hurt, but whatever she'd injected me with kept me from caring.

"I need to ask you a question," she said. "As doctors, we're not supposed to operate on loved ones. Is it wise for you to be trying to rescue your wife?"

"So Marianna told what's going on?"

She shrugged and returned her attention to my arm. "Doctor / patient privilege."

A team of specialists paid for by the Joffrey had tended Victoria's injury, but Saperstein was whom Victoria went to for pap smears, and other routine doctor stuff, since we'd been together. The two women had become friendly, and several times we'd had dinner socially with Saperstein, and her partner Paris. On other occasions when I was out of town, Victoria had spent time with the women shopping, going to museums and other fun things.

I didn't say anything while she disinfected and bandaged my arm, wondering what concerns about our marriage Victoria had shared with Dr. Saperstein.

She removed the ice-mask from my face. "This is going to hurt quite a bit, would you like something to bite on?"

"I'm good," I said.

The doctor wasn't kidding. Whatever she injected into my face burned and throbbed almost as badly as the blows that had caused the injury.

When she was finished, she said, "You didn't answer my question."

"Doc," I said, "If someone you loved was injured, and there wasn't another doctor available that you trusted, would you go ahead and operate, or let just anyone else do it because you weren't supposed to?"

She looked in my eyes for a moment gravely, and then smiled. "Okay," she said, producing a little plastic container with several compartments containing different pills. "I've put together a little care package to keep you sharp. I need to go over it with you."

Chapter 22

When I returned to the office, there was a quietness in the building that felt heavy with expectancy and promise, the way things can seem at five-thirty in the morning, when the demons of the night before are expending their last gasps and the new day has yet to undress itself.

I found Marianna in her office, surrounded by stacks of file folders, staring intently at her computer screen, talking into her new safe-phone. "I've got no shared addresses, if his name is on the box, I don't know what to tell you. He may have a new girlfriend and is staying at her house, he may be out of town; the databases are only good for so much. Wake up the neighbors and call me back."

I knocked softly on her door.

Marianna shifted her eyes away from the screen, rubbing the bridge of her nose. "The doc fix you up?"

"You could say that."

"I feel like I've had eight hours sleep."

"Me too, on Mars."

"Yeah, there is a weird feeling to it, but I'm definitely happier than I was a few hours ago."

"Where is everybody?"

"Powell and Willie finished piecing that lease agreement together from The Bull's trash haul. It was for a commercial building, except the shredder destroyed any legible address information. However, we were able to decipher the name of the real estate broker. His phone is just going to voicemail, so they went to roust him at his house."

"I take it that was them on the phone?"

She nodded, running the fingers of both hands back through her dark hair. "He's not home or not answering the door, or dead, or doing something else that is not helping us."

"What's the status at Paragon?"

"Barry Sheldon and Cece Harris's offices are bugged, Kaminoff is tied into all of the *Forced Conclusions* production office phones and email, but he's having a tough time getting around the security set-up for Rikki Wymen's office."

I checked my watch. The studios always had at least a few people working twenty-four hours a day, but the lot started to get busy around six a.m. when the first of the shooting crew workers arrived. The Bull's time was running out, pretty soon assistants would start arriving to make the morning coffee, cull through email, and would start calling security about strange men in the Executive Building.

"They're going to call me when there's an answer." Marianna sat back in her chair with her arms folded.

"Did you check the realtor's website archives? See which commercial properties have dropped off his list?"

"He's leased thirty properties in the last six months. Do you want me to find someone to do thirty door knocks?"

I didn't have a day for an investigator to go from door to door, trying to locate a building that Pemberton might be hiding my wife in. "Where's the realtor's office? The file will be there."

"Downtown, but we don't have anyone to send right now, and it's in a security building."

"What's the address? I'm just going to make everyone miserable if I don't have something to do."

Marianna remained stationary for a moment before she rocked forward in her chair, shuffled some papers, selected one, wrote the address on a post-it that she affixed to the page, and then held the page out to me. "This is a copy of what we pieced together from the first page of the lease agreement. I'll call you if anything breaks."

I transferred my tactical gear from the Mustang to an Audi S4 I kept in the office parking lot, for those times when I wanted to drive something less conspicuous. It's a rather innocuous looking four-door sedan that comes stock with a supercharged V6 and a racing suspension. I exited the parking structure onto a sleepy Sunset Boulevard, and pointed the Audi downtown towards the CB Commercial Real Estate office.

I took Santa Monica to the Hollywood Freeway South, and spent a couple of minutes weaving through the pre-dawn traffic before downshifting onto the Temple Street off-ramp. I cruised by the marble and glass edifices of the Mark Taper Forum and the Dorothy Chandler Pavilion, then swung a left on First Street. The Disney concert hall, Frank Geary's homage to stainless steel, was refracting the first rays of the new sun as I made a hard right onto

Grand Avenue, into the canyons created by LA's few monolithic skyscrapers each bearing the name of a different financial institution, huddled together like a group of boys measuring their penises.

Approaching the corner of 3rd and Grand, I slowed to a normal speed, so that I could examine the structure that held the realty office I was searching for. The building itself was a trapezoidal pillar, striped with alternating bands of russet colored granite and dark tinted glass windows. The space surrounding the ground floor was nicely landscaped, with neatly trimmed hedges and trees as well as a few abstract metal sculptures, which softened the otherwise severe architecture. I noticed a security camera housing mounted under a sign reading, *Milton International*, spelled out above the fifteen-foot-tall glass of the bank's first floor façade. At the end of the block I noted an entry to an underground parking garage, but a gate made of steel grating blocked access to anyone without a key-card. The next cross street was Hope Way, which ramped up on the south side of the building. I turned right onto it, noting that along its length, the building only offered a granite wall next to the sidewalk, with an occasional vent painted black, and no workable point of entry. However, turning right again, the façade that faced Hope Street proper to the north exhibited a large sloping glass lobby, used for gaining entrance to the building's upper floors, and it reflected the four mirrored cylinders of the Bonaventure hotel, two blocks away. On the brick patio, between the stairs leading up from the sidewalk and the entry doors to the building there stood a large, white, abstract steel sculpture. Café tables surrounded the art piece, also some planters, filled with assorted colorful flowers and nicely pruned trees. At each end of the lobby a security camera bubble stuck out, mounted on a steel rod, so that their lenses could cover the entire glass enclosure and its surroundings.

Because there'd been no call from Marianna, I knew the real estate agent hadn't been located, so I looked at the printout Marianna sent with me and noticed that the suite number of the realty office was 2700, which either meant the second or twenty-seventh floor. In either case, I was going to have to access the inside of that building.

I drove up and down the surrounding streets, familiarizing myself with their layout and my avenues of escape, since most streets downtown only allowed traffic in one direction. Then I parked and thought about my options. I wondered if Pemberton had even anticipated this move, making the deal for his hideout with a realty company that housed its offices inside a building, which also maintained security for a bank? If he had, then all he'd done was make me angrier, which made me care less about the consequences of the plan that was forming in my mind. I got out of the car, popped the trunk, pulled the things I thought I could use out of my tactical bag and the spare tire compartment, debated for a moment about whether I was being too stupid, then got back behind the wheel and guided the Audi away from the curb.

I un-holstered my gun, pressed the 'down' button for all the windows in the car, opened the sun roof, then as I rolled by the target building I fired three shots into the tops of the fifteen foot tall windows of the bank's lobby, saying a silent prayer that a ricochet wouldn't accidentally find its way into the flesh of an innocent watchman or cleaning person. Even with the car windows open, my ears were tingling with that strange whining noise and semi-deafness that comes from discharging a firearm in a closed space without ear-protection, but I could still hear well enough to register the building's alarm screaming loudly into the dawn.

Casually rolling up the windows, while guiding the car another block down Grand Avenue, I turned right onto 5th Street, where I parked in the loading zone in front of a Coffee Bean and Tea Leaf. I turned the car's blinkers on before locking it with the engine running, and taking off on foot.

In the middle of the block, across from the Los Angeles Public Library, a wide pedestrian stairway climbs past a few shops and café's, connecting 5th Street with Hope Street. I took two steps at a time, getting my heart rate up when I reached the top, where I looked over at the part of my target building sporting the angular lobby. The alarm siren was still wailing. Elsewhere in the city I could hear the whine of patrol cars, by now alerted and on their way.

I paused for a moment to put on latex gloves, then I crossed the street, keeping my face away from the video camera, and walked up to a part of the glass next to the building that was obscured from the street and the camera by trees and shrubs in the landscaping. Peering inside, I didn't see anyone in the lobby, so I removed a lug-wrench that I'd kept hidden under my blazer, and swung it at the glass.

The police sirens were getting closer, and so it didn't make me happy when the lug-wrench bounced off the large pane of glass without doing any damage. I cursed, remembering something I'd heard once about the strength of tempered glass. I didn't want to use my gun. I was calculating that the building's internal security personnel were on the bank side of the building, investigating the window that I'd already shot out, and I didn't want another gunshot to bring them my way. I hit the glass several more times, but it just shuddered with resilience, and then I remembered that tempered glass was more vulnerable to small sharp impacts. I yanked my gun out again, but this time held the point of the forward sight against the glass, striking the barrel of the pistol with the lug wrench. The first strike created a small spider web of cracks in the glass, which a second blow magnified across the entire pane, turning it into a million small crystals. The cracked pane easily gave way to prodding from the tire iron, until there was a hole in the glass large enough for me to enter the building through.

The lobby presented a large expanse of marble floor that I crossed quickly, keeping my gun out of sight under my jacket, but ready in case I encountered anyone. If security were still watching the video monitors, I was going to have company soon, but I gambled that the building used one of the many uniformed security services who only paid minimum wage, which would mean at that moment there were only two old men, or a couple of immigrants who could barely speak English hiding until the police arrived. There was a large, black desk, centered between two sections of elevator banks, designed for a receptionist, which was currently vacant. I could hear the police cruisers pulling up to the Grand Avenue side of the building, but the area was obscured by a partition that contained graphic advertisements, depicting the different services Martin Bank offered its investors.

I located the building directory, and was grateful to see that the CB Commercial Real Estate offices were on the second floor, rather than the twenty-seventh. I sprinted to the row of elevators that served floors one-to-fifteen.

Exiting the elevator, I encountered two sets of double doors, bordering either end of the elevator lobby. One set were adorned with two large brass embossments of the letters "C" and "B", each to a separate door. The braying of the alarm still resonated, but not as loudly as it had been outside or in the lobby.

I jammed the flat end of the lug wrench into the area between the two door handles, and heaved against it. The latch gave way, only creating a small crack in the door's face. I thought, *Thank god for small favors* as I entered the realty office, closing the doors behind me.

A reception area led to another set of doors, which opened onto a vast maze of cubicles. I checked the document Marianna sent with me to find the agent's name. During the several minutes it took to locate Drew Lepinski's desk, the clanging of the building's alarm silenced, which told me that the police had entered the building. The realtor's file cabinet was locked. The drawers gave way to the tire iron but were left mangled badly. It took me almost as long to locate the file as it had taken to get into the building. The realtor organized his files alphabetically, by the name of the listing client, and the Wilburton Holding Company owned the property, leased to Pemberton's shell company, Broken Dreams Productions. I yanked the entire file out of the drawer and helped myself to some full sized color brochures for CB Commercial that were in one of the realtor's other drawers. I also took a few of his business cards, shoving them into the breast pocket of my shirt. Then I neatened up his workstation as much as I could, walked back to the broken entry door, and listened.

All I could hear was the whirring of air blowing through a ceiling duct, so I opened the door, stepped out into the hall, closed the door behind me, and then removed my rubber gloves, shoving them into the pocket of my blazer.

Either the cops hadn't started their sweep of the building, or they hadn't paid enough attention to notice the destruction I'd caused to CB's door and had moved to an upper floor.

I debated taking the elevator down to the garage, but since I hadn't noticed an exit, other than the one that would require the weight or mass of a car to activate it, I chose to risk the lobby again. When the doors opened, I looked out to the same empty area that I'd entered through. I moved towards the exit doors with the file cradled in my hand. The only sound I heard was the click-clack of my shoes on the marble, until I was three quarters of the way across the expanse, when a loud voice said, "Hey you, stop right where you are."

Chapter 23

The glass exit doors of the Milton Bank building were about twenty feet in front of me. I knew why the police officer was telling me to stop, but I slowed my steps and looked behind me with an impatient and quizzical look on my face. One uniformed officer of LA's Finest trained his weapon on me, and I could hear the clank and rattle of an equipment belt, as his partner ran towards us, to provide back-up from the far side of the lobby.

"Who me?" I said, stopping and turning towards the officer. He was thirty feet away and closing, a young Mexican looking guy, in good shape, with enough years as a patrolman so that he wasn't visibly nervous.

"Yes, you sir, don't move. Hands out to your sides."

I walked towards him irritated, "You've got to be kidding me. What's going on here?"

I could see him assessing me, debating his options, now not as secure as he was a moment ago.

"I've got your six Javier." The partner said, taking cover behind the reception desk, training his weapon on me.

"Sir, just stand still please," the first officer said, advancing.

"Is this about the alarm? You think I would break into my own office?" Using the same tone in my voice I used when training a new recruit, authoritative derision, challenging their decisions. He was now ten feet away.

"Sir, please just stand still and raise your arms away from your body."

I stopped and raised my arms to the side dramatically, opening the blazer enough so that he could see I wasn't packing a piece in either a shoulder holster or the front waistband of my pants. I held the folder I'd taken so that it would be plainly visible to each officer, as well as my other empty hand, while making a face indicating that I thought this was the most ridiculous thing in the world.

The young officer approached closely enough for me to identify his pistol as a Browning 9mm. When he came within striking distance, he retracted the weapon from the two handed shooting position he'd maintained while closing, and brought his gun hand down next to his waist, where it would be hard for me to reach before he could pull the trigger. He'd been trained well.

With his left hand he reached out to pat me down. I sighed, hoping that I was conveying a put-upon attitude, that said, "Go ahead, do what you have to do kid," belying the effects of the adrenaline rushing into my arteries. I had my Kar .40 shoved into its holster in the small of my back; if his hand moved into that area, I was going to have to disarm this young, strong, well-trained policeman, while maneuvering him so he presented enough of a human shield to his partner. Otherwise, I was going to end up in cuffs, on my way to Parker Center, where it could take all day or longer, before I made bail.

"Can you at least tell me what this is all about?"

He patted under my arms, checked the breast pockets of my jacket, the waistband and pockets of my pants. "Someone shot out three of the windows in the bank, we just need to check out anything suspicious." He didn't reach around to my back, go near my crotch, or ask me to turn around. My outraged citizen act seeming to have sold him, though he still had his gun trained on me.

"What are you doing in the building so early?" he said.

"I have to show a property at eight o'clock. I was just running down to the Coffee Bean, to review the file before my meeting. Here's my card," I reached slowly into my breast pocket with my left hand, so neither of the men would confuse it for an aggressive gesture. While I was handing the officer the realtor's business card, I looked past his shoulder to see that his partner had relaxed, which made me nervous, because if the partner looked to his left, he'd notice the window I'd broken out to get in.

"What happened to your face?" the officer moved a little closer, squinting slightly as he studied the still visible effects of the punishment I'd taken, despite Saperstein's anti-inflammatory shots.

"Alumni rugby match last weekend, where I forgot how old I am," I tried to look embarrassed.

The Latino officer nodded slightly, looked down, and squinted at my card, "Alright Mr., ah – Lipinski, a detective may be in contact with you later," he said, pocketing the business card.

"The cell number's the best way to reach me." I offered him the cheerfulness of a professional salesman, smiled, shrugged, and turned towards the exit.

I didn't hear the officer move away. I knew he would be wrestling with the instincts that were telling him something was not right about me, while his reason would be considering the trouble harassing an innocent citizen might create. I didn't fit the profile of someone who would just randomly shoot at a building, nor did I particularly seem like a bank robber, so I made it out the door without further restriction, but as I headed down the steps, outside the building, I glanced back. Young officer Javier was still standing where I'd left him, fighting with the sixth sense a good law enforcement officer has that tingles when something isn't quite as kosher as it seems.

Descending the stairs leading down to 5th Street, I anticipated the possibility that police cruisers might converge on me at any moment, if officer Javier's gut overrode his desire to avoid conflict, but I made it back to the Audi and pulled away from the curb without further incident. I drove straight ahead on 5th Street, entering the onramp for the Harbor Freeway North, wanting to quickly gain as much distance as possible from the building I'd just burgled.

When I determined there was no one following me, I took the Hill street exit, which loops back around and dumps out into the east end of Chinatown. I found the first open parking space, which was across from a building that looked as though an architect tried to cover the exterior with a sample from every different type of Asian ornamentation. The rising sun slashed strange shadows across its front and glinted off the green enameled tiles of its roof.

I dug into the real estate file, finding the address I was looking for, 387 Mission Road, along with pictures of a white, one story, concrete block building with no windows. The words Kramer Electric Cable Company were painted on the front of it, in faded, peeling, blue letters. I plugged the address into the Audi's navigation system, and the little checkered flag popped up on the map indicating the destination, just south of the 101 Freeway overpass, in Boyle Heights, where Mission ran parallel to the LA River, only a couple of miles away.

I called Marianna while I sped past the seafood restaurants, trinket shops, fish and food markets lining Hill Street. I instructed her to send Pernell and Willie to meet me at the Mission address. I implored her to indicate they should travel as fast as they could. She told me that Kaminoff had been successful in breaching the security to Rikki Wymen's office, the listening devices were placed, and The Bull's team was set up with a listening post at Paragon.

As the sun probed the shadows of the city tentatively, I left the colorful griminess of Chinatown, via Vignes Street, then turned to enter Caesar E. Chavez Avenue, which traveled by Union Station and the MTA building, before fancy architecture gave way to the junk yards, tire dealers, and Spanish billboards that lined each side of the street leading to Mission Road. There I turned south under the freeway, spilling into a neighborhood containing a strange mix of dirty, run-down clapboard bungalows, interspersed with utilitarian commercial buildings, some bustling with rattling forklifts, loading palettes of wholesale foodstuffs onto trucks of all sizes, and others, including the building pictured in the real estate folder, seeming as if they were quietly waiting to be opened by occupants yet to arrive.

Older cars and pickup trucks were parked on the street, as well as a few tractors for big-rigs, but there were no vehicles in the small parking lot of the building I was interested in.

Rolling down the street, I felt an embarrassing wave of disappointment wash through me, making me realize that I'd been secretly hoping to find several utility trucks parked outside, or perhaps a neon sign flashing 'Kidnapper's Hideout.'

I mentally chided myself while I scanned the rest of the street, before turning right at the next intersection. The block-long street ended at the service road, running in tandem with the railroad tracks, which also ran parallel to the wide concrete storm-drain, laughingly called the Los Angeles River. A lone locomotive sat idle on the railway, steam billowing out of its rusting body, with a beautiful panorama of downtown's tall buildings spread out behind it, glinting in the amber glow of first light. To my left, the road snaked along the trickle of water that is the river towards the First Street Bridge. I turned the car to the right, where the road looked as if it went for a quarter mile before ending at another bridge that carried the 101 freeway over the river. It wasn't really a street, as much as a wide gravel drive where even more trucks of all sizes waited, were being loaded or moved around the chain link bordered yards and loading docks. A scarred and broken concrete loading dock, that looked like too many trucks had backed into it too hard, ran along the back of the Kramer Cable building. A tin awning covered the dock, but no vehicles were parked in front of it. The only details breaking up the gray concrete block wall of my target building were a metal roll-up door painted yellow, one window covered with expanded metal security screen also painted yellow, and a black steel door with the words "Receiving" hand painted on a piece of wood above it. From the amount of plastic bags and other garbage that had collected by the building and the surrounding area, I received the impression the loading dock hadn't been used in a while.

I was debating where to park, so I could query people at some of the neighboring businesses, when I saw something that caused a tingle of excitement to rush down my arms. A hundred yards in front of me, the bridge carrying the 101 freeway across the river descended to this side of the bank in a series of broad, colonnaded, Art Deco arches, built during an era when an effort was still made to instill some line of beauty even in utilitarian public structures. This support system created caverns under the bridge, which were closed off by individual chain-link fences; only the fences were cut through long ago, in many places. The caverns were being used as an ad-hoc storage area by the local businesses in some instances, and as a shelter for the homeless elsewhere. Backed into the arched opening between the concrete pillars of the freeway bridge closest to the river, sat the boxy shape of a panel truck covered in the ochre yellow paint used on Department of Water & Power vehicles.

Weeds, some large enough to be called shrubs, grew up through cracks in the pavement all along and away from the bridge, several clumps in front of the truck obscured the license plate, but they also showed signs of having been driven over recently.

Instead of stopping, I rolled up to the bridge, and then turned right into the alley that led back to Mission Road, where I found a parking space a block away. Opening the trunk of the car I quickly exchanged my blazer for a dark blue windbreaker and a clipboard, then returned on foot towards the river. Every Star Shield vehicle has a clipboard, hard-hat, and a tape measure, in its trunk. Displaying any or all of those items, accompanied with an air of intent, will make most civilians dismiss you without much notice, and I was hoping that anyone looking at me would assume I was just another salesman or trucking company supervisor, making my rounds.

I didn't head directly to the utility truck, but rather walked towards the grouping of vehicles waiting their turn to load at the dock of the nearest warehouse, which had a sign reading "Ichikawa," surrounded by pictures of different vegetables. Using the trucks as a blind, I walked down towards my target building to get a closer look for any type of video or other security measures, but none were visible. However, that didn't mean there weren't any, or that there wasn't someone behind the darkened window keeping an eye out, so I didn't venture too close an inspection.

I had to fight the insistent urge to know if Victoria was in that building *right now*. That impulse was telling me to throw rocks at the door until they opened up, and then shoot anyone who came out, or got in the way of finding my wife.

Instead, I examined possible assault points and fields of fire, making notations on my clipboard. I made my way down closer to the bridge. As I got closer I tried to see into the tunnel where the utility truck was parked, but it was just a black abyss. Even at its zenith the sun probably wouldn't provide enough horizontal light to see much beyond the entrance. I was able to read the plate number though and see the DWP insignia applied to the driver's door. No one appeared to be inside the truck, but I couldn't see much past the two front seats, and I didn't want to risk getting made.

Walking back out towards Mission Road, I counted seven bodies huddled under cardboard, ratty blankets, and other make-shift shelters nestled in the other places where the chain link had been breached and the local businesses hadn't stacked used crates, barrels, or other junk. I needed to set up my surveillance team and start bribing these homeless for what they knew about the comings and goings of that truck, and anything else they'd seen.

When I was far enough down the alley I phoned Marianna and gave her the license number to run. "I don't care what comes back though, as long as it isn't DWP. If I were running this operation, I would have replaced the original with a stolen plate," I said. "This place is hot, I can feel it. If they're not here, they were not long ago, and I want heavy surveillance here as soon as possible."

"Pernell and Willie are on their way, but they're not outfitted with a surveillance vehicle, or anything special," Marianna advised me.

"Get anyone down here in a surveillance van, two if possible. The building has multiple exits, and there are a number of escape routes."

"They're going to have a tough time getting downtown quickly, rush hour's starting."

"I know, I know, just do the best you can," I said, and hung up. I crossed Mission Road and then walked down the sidewalk on the opposite side of the street from the Kramer Cable building. With all the cars parked on the street, it was going to be tough to set up surveillance in the front of the building. We were going to have to wait until one of the resident vehicles moved and then take their space.

I lounged against the bed of a pickup truck surveying the Kramer building, which was built in the shape of a horseshoe around a parking lot. A steel gate, topped with rolls of concertina razor wire, closed off the parking lot from the street between the two portions of the building that formed the legs of the horseshoe on either side of it. Each leg of the horseshoe contained a rollup door, as well as a regular door covered with a security screen. Dried out weeds grew up through cracks in the asphalt of the parking area, indicating an absence of recent heavy vehicle traffic. The address was written in small block letters on the wall facing the street, to the left side of the parking lot. That wall also contained an entry door I hadn't noticed the first time by because it was hidden in a little alcove, between the sidewalk and where the gate was attached. Everything had a coat of dusty white paint on it, so the alcove blended in, hiding its door, which was also painted white.

Litter and sandy dirt had accumulated in the door alcove, but as well as I could see from across the street, it looked like the swing of the door had scraped away the trash in front of it in the shape of a quarter circle. Evidence that, even though the place looked abandoned, that door was used recently.

I thought about trying to gain access to the roof from one of the surrounding businesses, to see if there was a hatch or some other way into the building. While I was slowly searching the area for any good point of access or entry, mulling over the options, my phone rang.

It was Marianna. "They've made contact," she said.

Chapter 24

My mind was so tied up with concocting ways that I might gain access to the building where I suspected Pemberton was holding my wife, it took me a moment to comprehend that Marianna was telling me the kidnappers had sent another email message.

I looked at my watch; it was twenty minutes after six. "Damn it. They're early."

"Well," Marianna said, using a tone usually reserved for petulant children, "I'll bring that up at the next kidnapper time-management seminar."

"What's it say?"

"It instructs Barry Sheldon to go to the Hollywood Post office, and pick up a package that's waiting there for him. It tells him to come alone, be sure to have everything necessary to transfer the money, and it threatens that the deal's off - that Lauren's safe return can't be guaranteed - if Sheldon involves law enforcement or isn't there by 8:45 a.m. There's no mention of your wife. It's very brief."

"Who's read it?"

"Only our people. Kaminoff has everything going in and out of the mailboxes he hacked stopping at his computer first, right now he's holding the message before sending it to Sheldon's inbox."

"Do we have eyes on Sheldon yet? Has he arrived at the studio?"

"That was a negative when I talked to The Bull just a few moments before calling you."

"What's the call time for the shooting crew?"

I heard Marianna's fingers clicking on her keyboard, checking the call sheet, before she said, "Seven A.M."

"Tell Kaminoff to hold that email until we know where Sheldon is, he's pretty good about being on time."

"What if he's late?"

"We have his cell number, get someone to ping it for us, see where he is."

"That's not always reliable."

"Since we've got a little time, let's roll the dice. It would take too long to get someone to his house or try to intercept him on the way to work. We can't have him getting that message on his phone and then charging off from someplace we can't track him."

"There's a time stamp on the email, what if someone notices the delay?"

"Doesn't matter. It'll give them something else to wonder about. I want to push this so that they're forced to deal with it where we have microphones. My guess is Rikki Wymen's office will be where they'll decide on their response."

"One other thing," Marianna said, "That license plate you gave me is attached to a Ford Econoline van, registered to a Mario Soto of Van Nuys. I made a pretext call and confirmed that his license plates were stolen last week."

"Bingo," I said. "I could feel it. What's happening with the additional surveillance?"

"I've called everyone who isn't booked for this morning and they're on their way in. I have one van rolling to you with two of our people who were out all night on assignment, and two more are turning around from their drive home and will pick up a van here shortly."

"Let's push the next pair who are ready to the Hollywood Post Office, and get everyone else headed towards Hollywood, so we can deploy them when we see what's developing. Call the helicopter and get in it. With traffic the way it is, we're going to need eyes in the air and you can quarterback from up there. But make sure you've also got a shooter with you."

After we finished our call, I kept watch on Kramer Cable, not wanting to leave the building I'd just found until at least one of the team showed up, yet I had no patience for surveillance. The only thing that kept me sane was trying to figure out how a package at the Hollywood Post office reconciled with this real estate Pemberton's crew rented downtown. My guess was that the package contained a cell phone that the kidnappers could use to give further instructions and track Sheldon with. Perhaps make some sort of rolling switch, and use this location as their fallback position.

I also couldn't figure out why they'd left that utility truck out in the open. With the number of roll up doors in the building, they could have driven a small fleet of vehicles inside, out of sight. I started to feel that the utility truck might be bait for a trap of some sort.

The probability was, that they were going to exchange Lauren, while keeping Victoria for insurance, and that they were holding Victoria on the other side of the concrete block building that I was burning with my eyeballs. Adding to my impatience was the frustration of only being able to watch one side of the building at a time. I chose to stay in the front, since there were more ways to gain access, and I could also keep an eye on the two alleys that fed to Mission Road from the rear, but if someone did leave or arrive in the back, and drove or walked along the river from farther down, I was going to miss them.

After what seemed like a hundred years my phone rang again, this time it was Pernell, letting me know he was approaching the Mission Road off-ramp, and wanting to know what I wanted him to do.

Willie was in a second car behind him. I instructed them to find a parking space for one of the vehicles as soon as they got off the freeway, and then come together in the other car, which they would use to pick me up from where I was stationed down and across the street from our target.

When we were gathered together in Pernell's black Chevy Tahoe, I directed him around the area, showing them the parked utility truck, the homeless that I wanted interrogated, and the building. We discussed where to place the other operatives that were on their way and how to best cover all avenues of escape for a rolling surveillance if there was traffic out of the building or the truck moved.

"If it looks like they're moving with Lauren, or both women, hold back because they may be on their way to a negotiated exchange. However; if they make a move with only my wife, or even if you think it's her, stay on them like glue, call the cops, swarm the vehicle and wait, but make sure that someone is watching the other side, in case they pull some sort of decoy maneuver," I told them.

Willie patted my shoulder from the back seat, "We won't let them get away. Once the rest of the team gets here, I'll dirty myself up and hustle the homeless."

"Do you have cash?" I asked her.

"A couple of hundred. That ought to buy what they know and some made up stories too."

We all laughed at that. The problem with incentivizing witnesses was that they often told you just what you wanted to know, whether it was true or not.

Pernell and Willie were professionals with years of experience. When I got back into my car I was feeling for the first time in twenty-four hours that we were gaining high ground on our quarry.

I guided the Audi to the northbound onramp for the 101 freeway and gunned it towards Hollywood. The southbound side was already clogged to a standstill, with a glut of commuters making their way into downtown, but happily the northbound section I was traveling was still able to handle a fifty mile-per-hour pace. Passing the rise north of Alvarado Street, where Hollywood spread out in front of my windshield and the strengthening sun glinted golden off of the windows of homes dotting the hills, my phone buzzed again.

"Sheldon just pulled into his parking space," The Bull told me.

"Get a GPS transceiver on that car, and his body if you can."

"T-bone's going to hit the car, and Sparky is going to follow him and place it with a pickpocket bump when he can get away with it."

"Good. Good," I said. "Am I being too much of a mother hen?"

"A little, but it's okay I'm used to you being a nagging bitch."

The man could always make me smile.

"Kaminoff releasing the email?"

"Just did, soon as we ID'd Sheldon. Matter of fact I'm looking at him get it right now on his phone."

"What's he doing?"

"Standing there like a baby who just crapped his diapers, trying to figure out what the smell is."

I listened to dead air for a moment, noting that I was passing the Silverlake exit. "I'll be there in a few minutes."

"Now he's heading in towards his office," The Bull said. "For a moment there I thought he was going to bolt on us, or drive straight to the Post office."

"What are your positions?"

"I'm with Kaminoff in an Escalade, parked in the visitors parking lot adjacent to the spots reserved for VIPs. The rest of the boys have a motorcycle parked at each exit."

"How did you get the vehicle on the lot? I thought our passes were revoked."

"Kaminoff used Nilgore's laptop to email in a drive-on pass for himself, and we just hid in the back."

"That's using your head for something other than a hat rack," I said. "Give me a heads-up if Sheldon rolls before I get there?"

"Will do," he said.

The next few minutes I spent navigating off the freeway onto Melrose Avenue, where the traffic was bumper-to-bumper crawling into Hollywood.

When I was two blocks from the studio, I checked in with The Bull again and he said, "We've got a problem boss."

"Lay it on me."

"Sparky was tailing Sheldon, who started making calls on his cell phone immediately after receiving the kidnapper's instructions. He was walking to his office, when all of a sudden he does an about-face and goes to the executive dining room. This is good for us in one way, because Sparky gets the opportunity to plant the GPS on him, but it's not so good for us, because Sheldon meets Rikki Wymen at the executive dining room where she's having breakfast. Though Sparky can see that they're arguing, and each talking on their cell phones, the two hours we just spent risking our asses getting mikes into their offices isn't doing shit, because they decided to have their pow-wow off the reservation."

I asked if they were still in the dinning room.

"Fighting with each other like a couple of cats," Bull confirmed.

It was frustrating that we couldn't get a fly on the wall for that conversation, but you have to roll with the punches. "Okay, we've got new assets coming in from Marianna," I said. "We know Sheldon or someone has to go to the post office, so I'm going to scout it out for good surveillance positions, and set up the new people when they get there."

We then discussed the logistics of following Sheldon once he left Paragon. As long as we were getting a good signal from the GPS transponders, it would be prudent to hang back, in case the opposition was tailing him also for their own security.

"Pemberton has thrown us a curve ball at every turn so far," I said. "This whole post office thing could be a ruse to get us looking in one direction while they move in another. They could snatch him from his vehicle at a traffic stop, call his cell phone with alternative directions once they know he's moving, or make some other play we haven't thought of, because we haven't been planning this for six years like he has…"

"I hear you," The Bull said, "I'll stay a block back in the Escalade, with Kaminoff reading the GPS, while Kelly, T-bone, and Sparky will do their best to box him in on flanking streets with their motorcycles."

"Marianna will be overhead soon with the helicopter too."

"I don't know what other angles we could cover boss," The Bull said.

I double parked on Windsor Boulevard, the street opposite the Paragon gate, and fished out my radio, clipped in the earpiece, and tested it, to make sure that I was reading on the same frequency as the Paragon team.

I received a variety of affirmative responses from each member, before pointing the car towards the Hollywood post office. The radios worked on a repeater system that could keep us connected anywhere in the city, but the transmissions were easily intercepted by anyone with a scanner, so our communications would remain as few, and as cryptic, as possible.

By the time I'd traveled to Vine Street and Santa Monica Boulevard, about half the way to the post office, I heard Sparky's voice over the radio say, "Both items are moving." It meant Barry Sheldon and Rikki Wymen were leaving the Paragon executive dining room.

"Dietrich building," was Sparky's next transmission, identifying a landmark the subjects were passing. All the structures on the lot were named after an old star or a famous filmmaker.

"I have the items also, and will take the big one," T-bone's voice soon added. He was joining the tail in case the subjects separated, and would pick up Sheldon, since Sparky had already made close contact.

I was turning west on Selma Avenue when I heard Sparky say, "Damn it, items now in Demille, unable to continue," indicating that Barry Sheldon and Rikki Wymen had entered a building where they couldn't be followed without it being noticed, because there was a receptionist or a different obstacle. A few more short transmissions transpired between Sparky, T-bone, and The Bull, requesting that Kelly join them, because the building had three exits that needed to be covered. The frequency was quiet while I drove by the post office, through the intersection of Selma and Wilcox, and found a parking space around the corner.

The Hollywood post office, with its brass light fixtures, fluted marble pilasters, and vermillion art-deco frieze, stands in stately grace despite its surroundings of flophouse hotels and liquor stores with their faded and pealing neon signs, catering to Tinsel-Town's transient population, either newly arrived on dreams with meager budgets, or who have been broken by one of the many disappointments the city offers. I put on a baseball cap and walked the streets surreptitiously, looking for someone who might already be placed to pick up Sheldon for the kidnappers, but none of the vehicles in the area contained anyone loitering inside, nor did any of the street people seem interested in much other than their own private hells.

I was calling Marianna to get an update on who was headed my way, and what their ETA was, when I heard Kelly's slow, deep voice, say, "I've got the larger item," over the radio. Thirty seconds later he said, "I think it's time to mount up."

Chapter 25

I ran back to my car, following the chatter on the radio as the team monitored Barry Sheldon leaving the Demille building, then walking to his Black Mercedes SL550 and driving it off the lot.

I got Marianna on the phone. Reinforcements were stuck in traffic and wouldn't be getting to my position for another twenty or thirty minutes. She would be airborne soon, but couldn't give me an exact time. I told her to tune into the radio frequency we were using to follow Sheldon, so that she could keep track on what was developing and steer help our way.

I maneuvered the Audi around to Wilcox Avenue, parking in front of one of the flophouses at their loading zone, where I could see both entrances to the post office. The radio was chirping with Kaminoff's nasal voice, as he called out street names, and the direction Sheldon was traveling whenever he altered his position. It wasn't long before Sheldon's shiny German car slid around the corner at Selma and turned north on Wilcox, then crept to the parking lot opposite the post office, hesitated, and then turned in to park.

The time was 08:25, and a few people had moved in to congregate around the main entrance to the building, which was scheduled to open at 08:30. Sheldon got out of his car, looked around as if he were trying to find someone, checked a piece of paper in his hand, and scowled at his watch.

I was impressed. He didn't look flustered, just annoyed. You didn't get to be a high-powered producer in Hollywood by being a pushover. You needed *chutzpah*, a Yiddish word that translated as audacity, but in practice meant having such a belief that one could bend a situation to their will that it kept someone forging ahead, despite all indicators of failure. I could almost hear Barry Sheldon saying something like, "What? It's just another negotiation. So these guys have guns, how much worse could a gun be than Harvey Weinstein's breath?"

Slowly Sheldon crossed the street and mounted the broad steps of the postal center, to take a place with the other customers waiting for the doors to open.

I clicked my mike on and notified the others over the radio that I had the item. None of my guys were visible from where I sat, but they'd all called in their positions on the surrounding streets.

The minutes it took for the doors to finally open seemed to elongate maddeningly. I searched for anyone who looked like a bogey, but if the kidnappers had a tail on Sheldon they were blending well into the banality of regular folks dealing with something to send or receive through the mail. Eventually the brass doors swung inwards, sucking the patrons into the building.

I was nervous losing sight of our subject. "Do we still have GPS tracking on the item?" I asked the radio.

"Affirmative," The Bull said.

He would have to exit through the area restricted for postal workers if they weren't going to use the two exits we had covered, so I resisted the urge to get out of the car or send one of the boys inside. Several minutes elapsed before Sheldon stumbled out of the building again. He carried a small manila envelope tucked under one arm, and was looking at something I couldn't decipher in his hands. After descending a few of the exterior stairs, Sheldon glanced about, as if he needed to be reminded of where he was, then strode purposefully to his Mercedes.

Sheldon's black sports car nosed out of the parking lot and turned north towards Hollywood Blvd., where the light was red. Sheldon clicked on his left-hand turn signal as he slowed towards the intersection.

When the light turned green, I heard the throaty sound of a motorcycle engine firing up behind me. Moments later a rice-rocket, like the ones we used, shot past me towards Sheldon, who was waiting for opposing traffic before turning. The bike slowed as it neared the intersection, letting Sheldon's car make the turn, and then creeping forward to turn, several beats later.

"Did anyone leave their position?" I queried the radio.

I was met with silence.

"We may have company," I said. "Bogey number one is on a Jap bike, black leather jacket, reddish helmet, westbound on Hollywood behind the item."

"Confirming," T-bone acknowledged. "Visual on both item and bogey-one." He was one block west of me on Cherokee, and Sheldon must have just passed his viewpoint.

"Stay with them Bone," I said, "but don't get burned." I pulled my car away from the curb and turned left on Selma, which ran parallel to Hollywood Blvd. I screamed up through the gears, ignoring stop signs and the speed limit, until I reached Highland Avenue, the next major cross street, and turned right. A number of cars idled ahead of me waiting for the light to turn green at Hollywood Boulevard, but craning my head I could see up to the intersection, where Sheldon appeared, and made his turn, just before I heard Kaminoff's voice say, "Northbound, on Highland."

A quarter mile north was an entrance to the 101 freeway where he could head out to the valley, or possibly towards downtown and the building we already had under surveillance.

But then Kaminoff's voice said, "He's making a left turn, but there's no street indicated on the map."

I couldn't see far enough ahead to catch the action, but T-bone's voice crackled on the radio, "It's the Renaissance hotel, the item is in valet parking, the bike with bogey-one turned into the gas station just north and is stopping to observe."

The light in front of me turned green and traffic surged forward. Electronic Billboards flashed on the Northwest corner of Hollywood and Highland mounted on the giant shopping and entertainment center attached to the Grauman's Chinese and the Kodak Theater, where the Oscars were held. In the middle of the block, on the west side of the street, a driveway led to the underground parking for the complex, and just past that was the main entrance of the chic, high-rise, Renaissance hotel. The hotel's small parking area was sprinkled with a number of palms in five-foot tall black lacquered pots and featured an onyx obelisk fountain. A louvered glass awning sheltering the arriving and departing guests dominated the area, and at that moment Barry Sheldon was moving under it towards the hotel's entry.

"Item is entering the hotel," I said. "Bull get here quick. Meet me in the strip mall across the street."

T-bone was straddling his motorcycle between two cars, parked on the opposite side of Highland from the hotel. I passed him and turned into the parking lot of the two-story shopping center containing the Highland Hookah Parlor, a Philly Cheese Steak joint, Paradise Beauty supply, as well as the Hollywood Academy of Dramatic Arts. While backing the Audi into a parking space facing the hotel so that I could just drive straight out if I had to leave quickly, I briefly wondered if anyone had made it to stardom studying acting in that mini-mall.

"The guy from the motorcycle, bogey-one, is now on foot going after the item," T-bone said. "He's got blonde hair, jeans, he's still wearing the leather jacket with some sort of blue shirt underneath."

"I'm going to need someone inside that hotel," I said. I didn't want to go myself because I was certain that our enemies knew what I looked like.

"Be there in seconds," Kelly's voice announced. The Bull's Escalade slid quietly into the parking lot from Yucca and he parked as I had done. I stepped over to the passenger side where Kaminoff was rolling down his window, and said, "I need another locater."

Kaminoff dug in his bag of goodies, from which he handed me a small plastic rectangle. Kelly parked his bike on Yucca, and jogged up next to us. I handed him the GPS tracking device. "Take this and get over there," I said, "We need a vertical match-up."

Once a subject with a tracking device went into a multi-story building, it was hard to determine what floor they were going to. The GPS gave an altitude reading above sea level, but unless you knew the exact floor heights of the structure, it became guesswork.

"There's a side entrance," I radioed Kelly, as he waited to jay-walk across the six-lanes of traffic on Highland Avenue, "It's off the entrance to the parking garage." A number of our clients would stay at this hotel on Oscar night so that they didn't have to deal with the horrendous limo-jams in and out of the event. They could get right to the drinking and other distractions that made celebrating or mourning their losses more enjoyable. Most of our operatives had worked inside the Renaissance at least once and were familiar with the layout. His dismissive wave told me that he had already planned on avoiding the main lobby entrance.

I clambered into the back seat of the Escalade, where I could look over Kaminoff's shoulder to the screen of his laptop, which displayed a map, magnified to contain only the surrounding blocks. Three different colored icons, each representing one of the tracking devices we deployed, were blinking inside a big area of gray that outlined the structure of the hotel.

"Which is which?" I asked.

"Green is Sheldon, red is for his car, and blue is the one we just issued," the computer man replied.

Each cursor displayed a dot, with a directional arrow and an altitude reading. While I was trying to register the details of the information, the red icon moved south. I looked across the street, through the windshield of the Escalade, where I saw a man in the white shirt of the hotel's parking attendants driving Sheldon's

Mercedes into the entrance for the underground parking garage, which serviced the hotel as well as the entertainment center next door.

"Why would he park his car?" I said.

We stared at the screen, watching the red dot twisting into the depths of the garage, until suddenly it disappeared.

"That's not good," I said.

"Under a certain amount of concrete, you're not going to get a signal." Kaminoff's words were garbled, because he was chewing on a mangled, plastic toothpick.

I keyed my radio mike. "Sparky, please verify how many exits there are to the Hollywood/Highland parking."

"On it," Sparky said. His motorcycle engine roaring to life was the last sound of his transmission.

"Bogey-one is loitering in the lobby, talking on a cell phone," Kelly reported.

Kaminoff followed on the radio with, "The item's leveled at 546 feet and moving northwest." He'd taken the toothpick out of his mouth.

"Going up. Where should I start?" Kelly said.

"We're about four hundred above sea level on the street here, try twelve."

When the elevator arrived at the twelfth floor, Kelly got his altitude from Kaminoff, showing below Sheldon's reading by twelve feet. When Kelly hit the fourteenth floor, he matched the altitude reading on Sheldon's tracker. Kelly walked down the hallways until the blip of his cursor lined up with Sheldon's.

"There," Kamioff radioed. "On your left."

It took a few moments before Kelly transmitted back. "The reading is between two doorways, but it's either 1438 or 1440."

"Is there anywhere you can observe?" I asked.

"Negative. Fire stair has an alarm, and no cover elsewhere."

"Goddamn it," I said. "Okay, just keep walking up and down the hallway. If anyone comes, jamb a credit card in a door lock and act like your key-card isn't working, or head to the elevator, whichever seems less risky."

"You got it boss," Kelly said.

"Where the hell are those new people Marianna was sending us?" I asked The Bull, making sure my mike wasn't keyed.

He just shrugged his big shoulders, and said, "Traffic's a bitch this time of day."

I looked at my watch and fidgeted, I wanted to get out of the vehicle and move around. I felt like we were on the verge of a critical moment, but were undermanned. "Kaminoff," I nodded at his laptop. "That thing doesn't need you to run it, does it?"

He took the toothpick out of his mouth again and said, "No, but…"

"Go across the street and see if you can book any rooms adjacent to where Sheldon is, I need a listening post."

"I'm not a field operative," he said.

"I'm just asking you to book a friggin' hotel room not assault a beach, if either of us could do it," I nodded at The Bull, "we would."

"Just go ask if you could take room 1440," The Bull said, using his soothing baritone. "If they don't have it available, tell them that it's the anniversary of a wild night you spent with your girlfriend in that room and you wanted to surprise her tonight, so do they have anything available near it?"

Kaminoff looked even more uncomfortable. A situation where he had to interact with new, unknown human beings, was as daunting to him as reading a programming code would be to me. He started to shift like he was going to do what we asked though, either because of The Bull's encouraging expression or my murderous one, when Kelly's voice crackled in our earpieces.

"The item is moving towards the elevator," Kelly whispered, "He's wearing different clothes."

The three of us in the Escalade looked at Kamioff's computer screen, where the icon representing Sheldon, was in the same place it had been for the preceding minutes.

"Son of a bitch he's ditched the GPS," I said. "Kelly you have to get on the elevator with him, because if he gets off anywhere but the lobby we're fucked. T-bone, get your ass across the street, and Sparky, where are you?"

T-bone didn't acknowledge verbally, but I could see him starting his bike and getting ready to navigate across Highland to the hotel.

Sparky's voice came over the radio saying, "I'm on Orange Avenue with eyes on the second exit to the parking garage. Where do you want me?"

I hesitated, because I wasn't sure of the answer to that question. If Sheldon went underground to pick up his car, without any GPS, he could leave through the alternate exit before we picked up the monitor in his car, and he would get a huge jump on us. Conversely, if the kidnappers were smart enough to have him change his clothes to get rid of any electronic surveillance measures, perhaps they'd rented him a clean car too? "Stay where you are, and make sure none of the vehicles that leave there are containing our item."

"Roger," Sparky said.

T-bone was out in the rush hour traffic on Highland, zigzagging his way through the slowly moving cars, like a trout wriggling against the current in a shallow stream.

"This is Marianna," came over the radio. "We just got airborne and will be over Hollywood in a couple of minutes."

"Thank you baby Jesus," I said off-line, making The Bull smile, "Roger that, Marianna," I said, giving her our location and telling her to hold at an upper altitude for further instructions once the helicopter was overhead.

"Kelly do you still have the item?" I asked.

After what seemed like too long, the only response was the click-click of a mike being keyed twice with no verbal transmission, which we all hoped was Kelly's way of replying in the affirmative, because he was too close to Sheldon or someone else to talk.

Of course it could also mean that he had been ambushed, and the mike was keyed inadvertently while he fought.

Chapter 26

"Kelly," I spoke evenly into the radio mike, "Give us another signal if you're okay?"

Many long seconds passed with no contact before we heard, "Sorry, I was in the elevator with the item. We got off on the Mezzanine level. Item is traveling towards the conference area. I'll maintain visual as long as I can, but I have to hang way back, there's no one else up here so he'll see me if he turns around."

"Without the GPS we're not doing any good here," I said to The Bull. As we jumped out of the Escalade, I shouted to Kaminoff, "Get in the driver's seat, keep it running, and stay on the radio."

I could see T-bone was already across the street, off his bike, and moving towards the side entrance of the hotel.

Stepping in front of the first cars that offered even a small break in the traffic, The Bull and I trusted the car's squealing brakes to protect us. At the median we had to pause again because no driver southbound would even make eye contact since they had a green light ahead. The Bull and I made a quick scan of all the rooftops and everyone we could see on the street, to see if there was a pair of eyes that were overly interested in what we were doing, but we didn't see anyone who looked like they'd been caught monitoring us.

"Hey," T-bone whispered harshly over the radio, "That guy that followed Sheldon into the hotel - bogey-one - just sprinted up the stairs to the mezzanine, while staring at an iPad."

I had to hold my hand up to my ear, to hear what he was saying over the street noise.

"Shit I'm glad you said something," Kelly came on, "I would have run right into him at the top of the stairs. He's definitely tracking the item too. I'm dropping behind bogey-one, so that if anyone gets burned it's not me."

"I'll be there to spell you in a moment," T-bone said. His breath heavy on the microphone, so that I imagined him mounting the broad curved stairway that led from the lobby of the Renaissance up to its mezzanine level, where the ballrooms, restaurants, and conference facilities were located.

The southbound cars on Highland Avenue started to slow for the light that had turned red at Hollywood Boulevard, so The Bull and I once again jumped out into the first gap, drawing more blowing horns and skidding tires. We were scrambling like a bunch of unprepared amateurs, but we had to play the hand we were dealt.

A three story arched entryway welcomes visitors into the Hollywood Highland arcade next to the hotel. The Bull and I loped up the deep steps leading through the huge edifice into the main shopping plaza. I remembered that there was an entrance into the hotel's mezzanine from a bridge on the second floor of the entertainment complex, and that seemed like the best place for us to join the chase.

The courtyard of the mall was built in homage to the Babylon scene from D.W. Griffith's film, Intolerance. Huge sculptures of elephants and mythical creatures, decorated like ancient deities, loomed everywhere over the tourist shops. If an archeologist were to find ruins of this Mecca buried in the future, they might think that our civilization worshipped animal gods, offering sunglasses, ice cream, and t-shirts that read, "You've just jumped the shark," as homage. However, the absurdity of the architecture wasn't on my mind when we ran through the circular courtyard towards a bank of escalators located in the breezeway to the Kodak Theater on the opposite side of the plaza.

"The item is heading out onto the concourse," T-bone said.

The Bull and I looked up to where an overpass connected the shopping center with the hotel. I could see Sheldon's upper body as he walked along the bridge. I could also see the unidentified blonde male we'd tagged as bogey-one following Sheldon, peaking out from behind a column inside the mezzanine of the hotel. I snagged The Bull's shoulder and we took cover behind a cell phone kiosk in the middle of the plaza, which hadn't opened for business yet.

I broadcast that we had the item in sight also, while we watched Sheldon stride purposefully towards the bank of escalators Bull and I had been headed to. He had on a dark blue hooded sweatshirt with no logo or other apparent marking, and kaki pants. When Sheldon arrived at the hotel, he wore jeans and a polo shirt, with a black jacket bearing the name of a movie he'd produced.

When Sheldon chose the moving stairs going down, bogey-one walked out onto the bridge and watched Sheldon for a moment before referring back to his iPad.

"If I were to bet," The Bull said, "that guy looks like he's using that iPad for GPS tracking."

"He doesn't match any of the photos that we pulled as possible accomplices," I said. "So who the hell is he?"

Sheldon got off the escalator at our level. He skirted the courtyard, moving in the direction of Hollywood Boulevard, where the exit was framed by another huge, decorative archway.

The Bull and I did our best to act like a couple of tourists window-shopping for cell phones as Sheldon's unknown tail went to the escalator. T-bone moved out onto the bridge, and Kelly remained back inside the hotel.

"Kelly," I said into the tiny microphone in my hand, "You've already been seen. Get back to your bike, it looks like the item's headed to Hollywood Boulevard, see if you can gain a position there."

"I could make it there in seconds," Sparky's voice chimed in.

"No, stay put. I want you and Kaminoff to be ready on our flanks."

Again I checked everywhere to see if our little game was being observed by anyone else, but other than a Mexican looking guy in a maintenance uniform, who was pushing a big plastic cart from one trash can to another, and four Japanese people gawking at the giant elephants seventy feet in the air, we were the only people visible on the concourse.

"Don't forget I'm up here too," Marianna's voice announced, backed by the engine noise of the helicopter.

Her transmission caused me to look up; where high above us I could see the helicopter circling. I felt like we were back to gaining the advantage of a well deployed hunting team.

As Sheldon moved past the clothing stores and novelty shops that wouldn't open for another hour, bogey-one stayed about forty feet behind. The Bull and I separated, he taking the western side of the shopping center and I the east. We pretended to window shop, as we each eased our way along behind our prey, preparing for him to go either way once he hit the walk of fame.

Another wide cascade of steps lead down from the main plaza to the street, and as Sheldon headed down them he began moving to his left, diagonally across the stairs, towards my side of the area. He turned around once, as if he were checking to see if he were being followed, but his blonde headed tail hadn't ventured onto the stairway yet, bogey-one was nestled under the awning of a storefront, consulting his iPad, and I too was still at the edge of the plaza watching Sheldon in the reflection from the plate glass of The Gap storefront, which bordered the descending concourse.

With little hesitation, Sheldon turned left towards the east as soon as his feet hit the black terrazzo squares on the walk of fame.

"I'm going to grab my bike and get onto Highland," T-bone panted as he sprinted away from us.

I couldn't figure out where Sheldon might be headed. I thought that a vehicle might be picking him up on the boulevard, or that perhaps he would go west, where there were a number of offices and parking lots. The Bull and I hung back, as bogey-one consulted his iPad and moved down the stairs after Sheldon. By his actions, I was sure he was using the computer to monitor a tracking device on our target. Which made it a high probability that he was the enemy.

The blonde man stopped, looked up, looked back at his iPad, then up again with a worried expression, and ran down the stairs. The Bull and I exchanged a glance across the plaza, and then cautiously started pursuing him down either side of the forty-foot wide esplanade steps.

I reached the sidewalk first, and tried to see in the direction Sheldon had gone by using the reflection off the building signage, but it did me no good, so I poked my head around the corner, facing down into my cupped hands as though I were trying to light a cigarette while looking up.

The blonde man was fifty yards away from me, searching around everywhere, the way one does when someone they were following has just shaken the tail. He had a cell phone to his ear and kept staring back at his iPad, as if hoping it would revive itself as his oracle.

Then he looked up to the top of a pillar that he was standing in front of. I followed his gaze to a large sign for the Metro.

"Son of a bitch," I said and keyed my mike, "I think Sheldon has just ducked into the subway station."

As the words left my mouth the blonde guy made the same connection, and leapt towards the stairs leading down into the subway.

I gave Bull the *Let's go* signal before stepping onto the sidewalk, attempting to look like just another commuter a little late for his train stop. The entrance to the Metro is a simple opening set between two storefronts, with a swooping, stainless steel awning. I looked down the first set of stairs and escalators, but there was no sign of Sheldon or the man who had been following him. I hit the stairs two at a time, wending my way past the men and women trudging up and down with rush-hour grimaces on their faces.

At the bottom of the stairs the landing turned to the right, heading off to the series of tunnels and stairs that led down to the trains. I hunted through the sea of bobbing heads. I thought I could pick out bogey-one's golden hair, pushing its way through the crowd towards the end of the ovoid, green-tiled tunnel, where people were bunched up at the next set of escalators and stairs going down. I started thrusting my way forward also, taking a quick glance back, to see The Bull starting down the stairs from the street.

Kelly's voice sounded in my earpiece. "I just pulled my bike onto Hollywood Boulevard and there's something going down here."

"What does that mean?" I responded, annoyed by his vague description.

"I... shit, trying to park my bike," he started, then went silent for a moment, "Okay, two black SUV's roared up to the curb and four guys jumped out, then ran past me towards the subway. I recognize two of them from Blackthorn."

"Are you sure?" I asked. Blackthorn Security was one of our two most serious business competitors.

"As sure as I can be, seeing them for ..." the transmission stopped.

I was about three quarters of the way through the tunnel, and I cursed as I realized that the mass of concrete above me was probably cutting off any signal from the repeater towers that transmitted our radio signals.

I looked back and saw the four Blackthorn ops coming down the stairs, closing on The Bull and me. I pushed forward even harder and more rudely, no longer worried about decorum, because I had a feeling any semblance of cover was about to get blown if I didn't hustle.

Bogey-one had chosen the stairs instead of the escalator, where there was enough room to gain some ground without knocking people down, and I followed suit. The next tunnel curved to the left, making it difficult to see ahead, but the traffic shuffling out of the station thinned as the last of the passengers from the train that recently off-loaded straggled their way up to the street. I used the opening to sprint to the end of the tunnel, where a vestibule containing the ticket machines was located. The opposite side of the expanse contained a bank of turnstiles, separating the ticket hall from the final bank of stairs and escalators descending to the train platform. Most of the people were going straight to the turnstiles and using their monthly passes.

I could see Sheldon at one of the turnstiles trying to pull something out of an envelope, and to my right, Sheldon's tail was in front of a ticket kiosk, pulling his billfold out of his pocket.

Behind me, The Bull turned, and using the crowd to his advantage blocked the men coming after us. "Can I help you gentlemen?" he said.

I heard, "Stand down McCoy, this is our operation," as I continued to push forward.

"We're doing this together, or you're not going anywhere," The Bull said, followed by the sounds of struggle. I turned to see The Bull grappling with one of the Blackthorn agents, while another tried to get his arm around my partner's neck. I stood frozen for a moment, torn between running to my friend's aid and continuing after Sheldon. The Bull got hold of his frontal assailant's hair, and slammed the man's head against the tile wall of the tunnel, dropping the Blackthorn op to one knee. The Bull was a formidable force, but despite what kung-fu movies would have you believe, the odds against one man beating four other trained fighters in close quarters were impossibly high.

I checked on Sheldon, who was now through the turnstile, and in line to descend the escalator to the train platform. If I was going to have any chance of affecting the outcome of my wife's or Lauren's capture, I couldn't afford to let Sheldon get away. I didn't know if Blackthorn had been hired by Paragon to protect Sheldon, or to make sure I didn't interfere, or if they had some other stake. Whatever the case, they had a reputation for being heavy handed, and I knew their priorities would not be the same as mine. I couldn't let them stop me now.

Looking back one last time at The Bull, I saw the black steel of a telescoping baton flash into the air and come back down again, followed by a bellow of pain and anger from my friend.

I pushed over to a ticket machine, listening for the sound of a train entering the station; if one did come, I'd take my chances and vault the turnstiles, but for now I wasn't willing to risk attracting the attention of the transit police for something as stupid as an unpaid fare.

Because the public transportation system in Los Angeles was destroyed by the automobile, oil, and rubber companies in the forties, and the recent attempts to reinstate it were more a joke than a practical way to do business in this city, I'd taken the Metro perhaps once or twice before as a novelty. I had to spend several moments reading and understanding the instructions on the ticket kiosk, but thankfully The Bull was able to occupy the Blackthorn men long enough for me to figure out how to buy a one day pass, which I snatched out of the machine before hustling for the nearest turnstile.

Once again I chose the stairs down to the platform for their expediency. On a small landing, half of the way down to the platform, I stopped and tried to seem as casual as possible while still searching for either Sheldon or his tail, and to see who was coming behind me. I spotted Sheldon down towards the end of the platform on the side headed downtown. He was looking up the tracks for a train, and then he checked his watch and muttered to himself before taking another look. I didn't see his tail, but I assumed Blondie was hidden in the crowd somewhere. I was more concerned with Blondie's friends, who hadn't reached the stairs yet.

Passengers riding the escalator down beside me were excitedly talking about the fight in the hall, wondering what it was all about, but nothing they were saying gave me any useful information. So I jogged down the remaining stairs, then moved to the nearest of the tile columns that were spaced regularly in the center of the platform, sequestering myself so I could keep an eye on Sheldon and also stay hidden while watching the people making their way down to the trains.

Before long, two of the large men who I'd seen back in the tunnels, appeared at the top of the stairs, scanning the crowd below them. The stairwell was approximately eight feet across, and each man took a side, stepping down slowly, looking from person to person. I concealed myself behind the pillar, and checked that Sheldon was in the same place I'd last seen him, considering my options.

My Kar .40 was the only weapon I was carrying, and drawing it with so many civilians around would cause a panic, not to mention the fact that it was useless unless I didn't care about innocent people being killed by stray bullets. Even if I shot accurately, at this close a range the bullets would exit my targets and careen around the station, likely stopping in bystanders.

The Blackthorn men were both dressed in our industry standard, dark blazers over sport shirts, and dark slacks. The one on the right seemed closer to my age, possibly Slavic, bulky, with a dark mustache and shaved head, he might have been limping, and seemed to be carrying something in his right hand, which could be the collapsible steel baton like the one I'd already seen them use on Bull. The one on the right was younger and leaner; he had the longish hair that guys usually went for right after leaving the service and probably still had foreign soil under his fingernails. In a few moments they were going to be on top of me.

CHAPTER 27

The two Blackthorn men stopped on the same stair landing I used and similarly scanned the platform. I needed to get them away from Sheldon, and wherever Blondie was lurking nearby. So I stepped out from behind my hiding place on the side of the platform where people were waiting for the train bound for the San Fernando Valley, acting as if I were unaware of the Blackthorn men coming down the stairs, and as though I was still searching for Sheldon. With my peripheral vision I could discern my assailants on the landing of the stairs and register their excitement when they spotted me.

With inspired vigor I threaded my way down the length of the platform, so I could get as much distance from Sheldon as possible before they caught up with me. The distant rumble of an approaching train infected the station, along with the rising odor of ozone and flint, but I was too preoccupied with searching for some sort of advantage to discern which direction it was coming from.

I traveled from the center of the waiting area, to where the fewest passengers stood waiting, providing less cover but more room to maneuver. In the far quarter of the station, an elevator shaft dominated a large portion of the platform, reserved for the handicapped and others not wanting to ride the escalator. I took a quick glance behind me, seeing both Blackthorn men following me to the northbound side of the tracks, with the younger man slightly in the lead fifteen yards away.

As I ducked around the far corner of the elevator shaft the air being pushed through the tunnel by the approaching train blew gum wrappers and other paper trash skittering across the floor of the platform. I really wished I'd brought a Taser or some other nonlethal weapon, but the only thing available to me was a nearby trashcan. It was a concrete job, too big to wield, but it had a steel top with a hole in the middle. I ran to it and started wrestling the top off.

It was harder to remove than I'd expected. The panic I felt at the prospect of my assailants reaching me while still hunched over the waste bin supplied frantic strength, which I used to heave the top up and off, feeling a searing pain in my fingers from a few of my fingernails splintering as they scraped over the can's concrete when the top gave way.

The blur of subway cars rushing into the station appeared on the downtown side to my left. I spun rapidly to my right and hurled the steel lid like a Frisbee at the younger Blackthorn operator who was now five feet from making contact with me.

He was quick, and protected himself as well as he could before the steel disc slammed into him, but it threw him off balance enough for his shoes to lose their grip on the smooth platform floor, spilling him to the ground. The kid rolled away from me as soon as he'd hit the deck, and would have been up and on the attack if it weren't for his bad luck colliding with the back of a middle-aged woman who was waiting for the train, now coming to a stop on the downtown tracks.

His Slavic looking partner already had his baton telescoped out to its three-foot length and was moving in to strike downwards at my head. I continued to spin three hundred and sixty degrees before uncoiling my right heel into his exposed ribs with the full momentum of a spinning back-kick. Feeling the sweet disintegration of bone and tissue as I followed through with all of my weight. The Slav flew backwards into the wall of the elevator shaft, his face registering surprise and agony. He crumpled to the ground, gasping for the air that had just been smashed out of his lungs.

The kid had knocked the back of the woman's legs out from under her, landing her right on top of him. He was just pushing her off and starting to rise when I picked up the trash can lid, bringing its edge down into the fragile area of his collarbone, and then I raised it again, dropping it flat against the top of his head for good measure.

The doors of the last car on the downtown train were open directly in front of me, and the commuters getting off were standing with their mouths open and eyes wide, staring at me like the rabid man I was. The boarding passengers were either too intent on entering the train before the doors closed to have been bothered by the fight, or, were also frozen in expressions of shock and fear.

I bolted onto the train, which was packed with commuters, filling all the seats and most of the standing space. I muscled though the salesmen, working mothers, city employees, and school children towards the front of the car - a few of the passengers saying,

"Whoa," and things like, "Hey watch it asshole," but not daring to interfere.

As I reached the passageway to the next car, the doors to the station closed with a whoosh, and the train eased into motion. In the short time it took to reach the next stop at Hollywood and Vine, I was only able to push my way through two more cars of packed humanity smelling of cheap perfume, nicotine, and coffee breath.

When the doors to the next station opened, I battled ahead a car and a half on the platform, all the while desperately searching the people exiting the train ahead of me for Sheldon's graying hair and Sephardic nose. When the electronic ding from the station's speakers announced departure, I jumped back on the train, hoping that I hadn't made the wrong decision, though I didn't see Sheldon in the crowd on the platform before we slipped into the darkness of the tunnel.

By the next stop, at Western and Hollywood, I was able to finally relax when I was able to bully my way forward enough so that I could see Blondie wedged into the rear of the lead subway car. Sheldon was standing miserably amid the masses, hanging to an overhead strap in the front third of the same car.

I jumped into the car directly behind my quarry, and as politely as possible, edged my way next to the glass in the doors at the passageway between the trains, where I could see through to a piece of the black leather jacket Blondie was wearing in the lead car.

I pulled the radio earpiece out of my ear, and hid it inside my collar, since it wasn't doing any good. I also checked my cell phone for a signal, but it showed zero bars. I could only imagine what was happening on the surface between my men and Blackthorn. I was hoping that someone was attempting to follow the subway, though at this hour traffic would be prohibitive, even on motorcycle.

The train slid along through its route south, under Vermont Avenue, before weaving through the Wilshire corridor into the business district downtown. At each station I readied to elbow my way out through the crowd, but in the jostle of passengers disgorging and entering the train, Blondie stayed in place, and I could catch a glimpse of Sheldon morosely enduring the shuffling crowd.

The majority of the train's occupants got off at the Pershing Square and Civic Center stops, leaving only a dozen or so passengers in Sheldon's car, making their way to the terminus of the Red Line, at Union Station.

Barry Sheldon took a seat, and Blondie stared at an ad on the wall of the train, keeping his back to the producer, but in less than a minute the train's brakes squealed their protest as the platform of the final Metro-stop came into view outside the windows. Sheldon rose from his seat, and I lingered behind the passengers in my car who were eager to get off.

Out on the platform Sheldon moved uncertainly towards the nearest escalator, Blondie falling in twenty feet behind him. I pretended to be confused about which way to exit, so that I could look for anyone else who might be honing in on any of us.

Nobody caught my eye, so I followed the back of Sheldon's and Blondie's heads up the escalator into a long hall like the ones we'd entered through. I was the last of the exiting passengers, and I kept checking behind me, but didn't notice anyone else dropping into the chase. If there was a second tail they were very good. Blondie hadn't turned around again so I closed the gap a little, hopping on the escalator several steps behind him. As we rode up, I re-assessed the Blackthorn operative one more time. He didn't seem like a fighter, he was fit and tall, but didn't carry himself with the presence of someone who was used to being physically imposing, but that also could be part of his game. Several of the most deadly men I knew looked more like accountants than assassins, and they used that to their advantage, but my instincts were telling me to make a move on this man, and either co-opt or eliminate him.

Blondie pulled out his cell phone, checked the screen, and then started to text. I checked mine, but didn't have a signal yet. As the escalator spit us into the short hallway leading to the train station, I moved ahead quickly behind Blondie, then pretended to stumble, and snatched the cell phone out of his hand.

Blondie took a furtive look at Sheldon passing through the doorway into Union Station, and then said under his breath, "Give me that."

"Come and get it." I said.

He hesitated, so I went after Sheldon. A few commuters looked our way, while Blondie followed within striking distance, but didn't attack.

I read, "@ union " on the text screen of his phone. When the service bars came back I punched the menu button that chose to dial the telephone number, instead of send a text message.

After one ring, I recognized the Israeli accented voice of Blackthorn's Los Angeles Chief Operations Officer, Yuri Herzog, who said, "We just picked him up on the GPS."

"Yuri, this is Richard Braddock. You better tell your man to start working with me, or you and I are going to hold hands going down the toilet together."

"I don't think you're in a position to be giving orders, my friend," Yuri said.

"Don't fuck with me Yuri, I'm the one with nothing left to lose," I tossed the phone back to the Blackthorn agent, and turned towards the doors Sheldon walked through moments before.

Sheldon was standing about twenty paces inside the 30's era train station gazing around, lost and annoyed for a moment, before he dug into the manila envelope he was carrying. He pulled out a cell phone that looked very much like a throwaway model. I assumed the kidnappers had provided it in the package from the Post Office and were using it to transmit instructions. The flow of commuters were spilling around Sheldon like water passing a rock in a stream, splitting into those who were headed towards the broad concourse leading to the embarkation platforms, and those who were headed towards the Alameda Street exit on the other side of the old Mission Style building's grand hall.

I made my way to a large leader board that posted the status of the various arrivals and departures in red electronic letters, where I pretended to scrutinize the information while keeping an eye on Sheldon. He was walking into the main station area haltingly, fumbling with the phone and a piece of paper that may have held his instructions.

The blonde Blackthorn op ambled up sheepishly, and said, "So what's the play?"

"What's your name?" I said.

"Mike."

"Well Mike, as far as I know," I nodded towards Sheldon, "he's going to tell us what the play's going to be." Sheldon was holding the phone to his ear. I nodded at Mike's iPad, "How'd you get him on GPS?"

Mike seemed to have forgotten about the GPS in the recent commotion, and looked sheepish. "We gave him a suppository."

That explained how they'd been able to track him after the clothing change, and I wanted to hear more about how Barry Sheldon got a transmitter shoved up his ass, but he appeared to be receiving instructions on the phone and turned slowly around until he was facing the concourse.

Union Station is a beautifully cavernous building, sheltered by a richly stained coffered ceiling containing colorful hand-painted illustrations in each of its panels. Chandeliers, crafted like enormous bronze and glass flowers, provide a dappled, sepia lighting, which plays handsomely with the earthen tones of the sage plastered walls, thickly varnished woodwork, and the mosaics of Spanish tiles covering the floors and many of the walls.

I scanned its expanse for someone else that might be watching Sheldon, possibly talking on a phone, but there were just too many people. Twenty or thirty men and women sprawled in the large leather benches around the waiting area, many of them on the phone or reading. Any one of those people could have been monitoring Sheldon, or me and my new friend.

Sheldon started to move down the concourse. It was about forty feet wide, with a low stucco ceiling. The floor was a blood red concrete. Richly colored Spanish tile-work ran halfway up the sides of each wall as a wainscoting. The concourse was divided into fifteen arched openings, spaced symmetrically on either side, which allowed entry to the train tracks via ramps and stairs.

I pumped Mike's hand like I was damn glad to have run into my old friend, and said, "I'm going to shadow Sheldon. Stay here and see if anyone picks us up. What's your number?"

He looked unhappy, but we exchanged phone numbers. "How long until Yuri gets backup here?" I said.

"He said ten to fifteen minutes. They're having trouble with traffic."

As I moved away, Mike added, "You'll let me know what's going on too, right?"

"Of course, besides you've got that thing," I said, glancing at his iPad.

Tracking the back of Sheldon's head as it moved down the concourse, I worked the radio ear piece back into my ear and keyed the mike, "This is number one, I have the item at Union Station. I don't know if it's getting on a train or headed to the parking lot for more hide and go seek. I've made contact with Blackthorn, and have one of their ops working with me here."

Marianna said, "We've been flying over the train route, so if they go back on the street, we'll be able to track them from the air."

"What's the situation with The Bull?" I asked.

"Blackthorn have The Bull and Kelly in custody. They are stating that they've been hired to protect Paragon Studio's property, and that we are placing that property at risk."

Sheldon stopped in front of the entrance to track number twelve, and then looked into the archway to his right. Sheldon nodded his head slightly, put the phone in his pocket, and turned into the entrance to the tracks.

"Yuri's a dead man," I said, picking up my pace, to close the gap with Sheldon.

Marianna continued to tell me that T-bone, Sparky, and the agents who were too late getting to Hollywood were following the train route on surface streets, but still weeding their way through downtown.

When I got to the entry area for track twelve, and looked the way Sheldon had gone, he was nowhere in sight. I said, "Stand by," into the radio.

A broad stairway was set back a few feet from the concourse. Peering up the stairs I could see the canopy of the train platform at it's top. On either side of the stairs the floor rose at a slight incline and then converged behind the stairwell into a long ramp that also led up to the trains. A little way along the right hand ramp there was a door that looked like it might lead to a janitor's closet or some other utility area. I didn't see Sheldon anywhere.

I took the stairs two at a time while dialing Mike's number. At the top of the stairs, I looked each way on the train platform. No sign of Sheldon. The gleaming silver body of an Amtrak train stood huffing, with its doors open, accepting passengers.

When Mike answered, I said, "Get down to track twelve, I've lost him."

"I'm halfway there," the Blackthorn operative said. "His signal disappeared."

Chapter 28

"Alright Barry, where are you?" I said to myself. I looked back down the stairs where some college kids and an elderly couple were making their way up to the train. Past them I saw Mike turn in from the concourse. I went down to meet him halfway up the stairwell.

"He's got to be on the train," I said. "I need you to get on it and see if you can spot Sheldon."

"How did you lose him?" Mike said.

"Get on that God damned train."

He glowered at me resentfully for a moment before heading up the stairs.

Mike was reaching the platform when the door that I thought was a janitor's closet swung open with a bang and Sheldon stepped out frantically trying to get his bearings.

He looked up through the railing, and seeing me, gave a start of recognition before scrambling towards the concourse.

I leapt down half the stairs and then vaulted over the handrail, intercepting Sheldon and slamming him against the wall.

"Barry, what's going on?" I said.

"I'm not doing it. Fuck this. Let me go," Sheldon said, squirming in my grasp, "Where's the guy that's supposed to have my back?"

"You're not doing what?" I asked, ignoring his question.

"I'm not going down there, fuck that," he said.

Some of the commuters were staring, but kept moving.

"Calm down Barry. What were your instructions?"

"Braddock," Mike called from the stairs, "I think we've been made." He was pointing into the concourse, where a woman in a tan coat, jeans, white tennis shoes and curly red hair was talking into a phone and looking our way.

She averted her gaze when we saw her. I shouted, "Go get her."

I started pushing Sheldon towards the door he'd come from, and said, "What were you supposed to do in there?"

"No, no goddamn it," Sheldon said. He wriggled and punched at me ineffectively, trying to resist being maneuvered through the door. We stood on a small landing at the top of a very long, narrow, metal stairwell. The stairs were lit with a single light bulb, mounted halfway down the ceiling, and the steps ended at the head of what looked to be a thin, dusty corridor filled with pipes and conduit running along each wall.

"What is supposed to happen down there?" I said, pushing him to the edge of the steps.

"They just said to walk down the corridor and not to stop until someone met me."

I wanted to wait for backup, but if that woman had been working for the kidnappers, they might already be retreating.

"How far did you get?"

"Not far, I felt like I was going to shit my pants."

"Well you may have to Barry, we're not taking any bathroom breaks now." I un-holstered my gun and pushed Sheldon ahead of me down the stairs.

As we negotiated the steep steps, I clicked on the radio and notified everyone listening that I was going underground and might be off-grid once more.

"I'll give you the codes, you can do it yourself, you don't need me. I'll just get in the way, this isn't what I do…" Sheldon said.

"It is now Barry," I said, and hustled him down the stairs a little faster. "There's a reason they wanted you. You've lost your free choice privileges. From here on out, just shut up and do what I tell you so you don't get us all killed. Am I clear?"

Barry didn't say anything and I didn't care, none of us would be here if he hadn't testified against Pemberton. If Pemberton wanted to make a business deal, I didn't care about Paragon's ten million, my reputation, or any of that bullshit if I could get the women back alive. If Pemberton wanted blood more than the money he had a better hand than I did, but it was too late to fold.

The bottom of the stairs revealed a tunnel barely six feet across, and maybe nine feet tall at the apex of the arched ceiling. Dust was caked on the ridges of board-formed concrete. Cobwebs laced themselves between the various pipes and conduit attached to the walls and the ceiling. The corridor made a slight curve to the left, obscuring its end because of the turn. Caged incandescent bulbs, spaced about 30 feet apart on the right wall, illuminated the passageway poorly. The odor was more a taste of mildew than a smell.

Then my body tingled in warning from what I saw mounted on the ceiling at the end of two brand new strands of electrical cable. A Claymore Directional Anti-Personnel mine hung facing in our direction. I knew it contained thousands of ball bearings and an explosive C-4 charge that would shoot the bearings through the small space at a high velocity. A mini video camera was taped to the mine with its lens pointed at the area where we stood.

"I don't know if you can hear me," I said directly to the camera. "But I'm just here to see if everyone can leave happy today." I flashed the peace sign with my left hand, feeling confident that the gun in my right was concealed from the camera behind Sheldon's back.

"I hear you fine?" Sheldon said, trying to turn around, "What's your problem?" I pushed him forward into the passageway.

"They've got us on video Barry." I didn't want to spook him any more than he already was, so I said, "That's a good thing. It means we won't surprise them and get shot by accident." I nudged him ahead of me. "You're doing well, I'll have you out of here in no time," I lied, and then tried to change the subject. "I heard there were tunnels like this under all of downtown Los Angeles, but I thought it was just an urban legend."

Sheldon said, "What are you the Disney Channel? Who gives a shit?"

After approximately one hundred yards, we arrived at a Y shaped intersection, where Claymore mines and video cameras were clamped to the ceiling pipes pointed in each direction. A few paces further into the left-hand corridor I could also see a doorway set in the wall.

Pemberton's traps were set to defend against attack or escape in all directions.

A voice beckoned with resonance from inside the doorway, "Come in Mr. Braddock, I think you've got a good understanding of my handy-work."

Barry Sheldon stiffened with recognition, and frantically whispered, "I know that voice."

I pushed him towards the door.

"No! No! No! Let me out." Sheldon clawed to get through me. "He wants to kill me."

"He might have reason to," I said shoving my gun under his chin. "But here's the deal Barry, if you don't get in there and take care of business I'll kill you myself."

I may not have been bluffing, and pushed Sheldon ahead of me into a large storage room. Packed shelves, spools of cable, and carts laden with tools or supplies filled most of the space; everything was covered with grime and dust. To the right Lauren sat gagged in an alcove, her hands cuffed in front of her. Our eyes met and she lurched to stand up, but couldn't, because the man with a mustache and sandy hair clipped in a neat crew cut, who I recognized to be Kyle Pemberton, held her in place, using her as cover. And he was pointing a large caliber automatic pistol at me.

"Easy now," I said, using Sheldon as my own cover, with my weapon aimed at Pemberton's head. I knew the only reason Pemberton didn't shoot me, was the same reason I didn't squeeze the trigger on him – we couldn't be sure that the other's dying act wouldn't be a shot in return.

"It's going to be very easy," Pemberton said. "Barry's just going to call in the codes, make the wire transfer, and you can take Miss Hunter back to finish the movie. When I'm safely away, I'll release your wife."

"What about Dale?"

"Your employee created an obstacle for us that had to be eliminated. I'm sorry."

He sounded almost sincere. It made me wonder if Victoria's status would change to obstacle once he had his money.

"Lauren, how're you doing?" I said.

She nodded her head vigorously and met my gaze. Even with the unwashed hair, the streaks of mascara striping her cheeks, the tracksuit she'd been captured in grimy with dirt from the tunnel, she still looked more beautiful than most women ever will.

"She's a feisty one," Pemberton said. "This has been a little like the ransom of Red Chief."

"Forgive me if I don't feel to sorry for you," I said, edging into the room, Sheldon between us. I tried maneuvering for a position with a clear shot.

"Braddock, there's another one of my little toys behind you. If you did get me with a headshot, my partner will detonate it, and the three of you will die with me. You don't strike me as someone who's that impractical."

I checked my flank and saw that he wasn't bluffing. A Claymore rested at chest height on a broad plank shelf, next to a video camera. At this range, the blast of ball bearings would shear our upper bodies off at the waist.

"You're very thorough," I said, feeling sweat trickling down my neck and hoping I sounded more confident than I felt.

"I would've liked to have a big enough team to weed you out, but this was the best I could do under the circumstances."

"Can we just get this over with," Sheldon said.

Pemberton beckoned to the phone on the table, "I'm not the one that's holding things up Barry."

"I get Lauren first," I said.

"We trade," Pemberton countered.

"Fuck you," Sheldon said to me.

"Calm down Barry, it's a show of good faith," I said. "If you're waiting for the Blackthorn cavalry to come, they might make Mr. Pemberton more nervous."

Pemberton studied me looking for a tell that I was lying.

"You're not scared of me are you Barry?" Pemberton said. "We used to be buddies."

"I warned you not to play with fire," Sheldon murmured.

"There's a difference between playing with fire and getting stabbed in the back Sheldon. You took six years of my life." I could see sweat beading on Pemberton's forehead, and I knew it wasn't from the temperature.

I said, "Can Lauren walk Kyle?"

"Yes Richard," Pemberton said, "We've tried to take good care of her."

"Lauren," I said, stepping away from Sheldon but keeping my gun pointed at Pemberton, "Why don't you walk over to me, and Barry how about you go help Mr. Pemberton collect his money?"

Lauren sprang out of her seat and rushed to my side.

Barry Sheldon stood immobile, looking furtively over his shoulder at the exit.

"You can still talk on the phone if you're shot in the ass Barry," Pemberton said, "Come over here like a good boy."

"Fuck you both," Sheldon said, looking at me, suddenly calm and sounding like he was negotiating a deal, "What's to keep him from killing me once I release the money?"

Pemberton lowered his gun, then the sound of it firing was deafening in the confined space. I grabbed Lauren and held her tight to me.

The shot was aimed into the outer muscle mass of Sheldon's right thigh, and sliced nicely through and through, clear of the femur and its major arteries that lined the inside of the bone. I admired the shooting. Sheldon just looked puzzled for the seconds before Pemberton got to him, and started dragging him towards the phone, shouting, "I'm done fucking around with you Barry, now call the Goddamned bank."

Sheldon started to howl like an animal. "You shot me? You fucking shot me?"

My ears were ringing, adding an odd reverberation. I yanked the gag out of Lauren's mouth saying, "Are you okay? Can you run if you have to?"

"Yes, yes," she gasped.

Pemberton was yelling, "Shut up," to Sheldon. "If you want to live, you'll make that fucking call." Yet he still had his gun pointed in our direction.

Sheldon cursed even louder, as the pain in his leg started to register.

"Kyle!" I shouted. Pemberton glanced my way. "How do you know that your partner won't cut you out of the deal by blowing us all up once the funds are transferred?"

"We all take our different chances," Pemberton said. Then he hauled Sheldon up by his collar with one hand, and pitched his upper body onto the table.

I was impressed with the man's strength.

Sheldon stopped howling for a moment when he hit the table, and we heard a voice coming from the speakerphone shouting, "Boss, boss, they're coming in. They're coming down the stairs."

Pemberton looked at the computer monitor. From where I moved to intercept Lauren, I could see that the monitor was broken into multiple squares, each showing the feed from a different camera.

Pemberton looked at me, and said, "Are you an idiot?"

In one of the little screens I could see men in black battle gear descending the stairs from the train station.

"Hit them now!" Pemberton shouted at the phone.

We heard a muffled blast, the little square on the monitor went black, and then silence followed for a moment, before cries of those who were not yet dead seeped down the long hallway.

"Those aren't my people," I said.

"But they followed you here," Pemberton said, the veins pulsing like worms on the side of his neck and his gun barrel eight feet in front of my face.

"Are we going to do this? Or are we going to die?" I said, my own weapon pointed right back between Pemberton's eyes.

The room stank from cordite, fear and sweat.

"Where's the number?" Pemberton shook Sheldon.

"It's in my pocket," Sheldon said, the color gone out of his face.

Pemberton dug in the pocket of Sheldon's sweatshirt and pulled out a folded piece of paper. He punched the second line on the telephone that emitted a dial tone over the speaker before he pounded in the telephone number. Pemberton held the barrel of his gun to Sheldon's head saying, "Your only chance to live is not screwing this up."

"Deucha Bank California," a male voice said eerily from the telephone speaker.

Pemberton prodded Sheldon. "This is Barry Sheldon, I need to make a wire transfer," the producer panted.

"I'm ready sir," the banker said.

Pemberton gave the banker the account number. We could hear keys being tapped through the speaker.

The banker said, "We are ready sir, we just need to confirm the amount and the password."

Barry Sheldon looked at me pleadingly. I nodded my head in encouragement. "Ten million. Schnauzer 6314," Sheldon said.

"Could you spell that please sir?" the banker asked pleasantly.

"Oh for God's sake, just send the fucking money," Sheldon said hoarsely.

"I'm sorry sir, I need the correct spelling of the password."

Barry spelled "Schnauzer," starting to laugh halfway through.

Lauren gripped me tighter. I whispered, "He's in shock."

"Thank you sir, we're processing your transaction," the voice on the phone said.

"Do you need anything else from us?" Pemberton asked.

"No, sir. Is there anything else I can do for you?" the banker said.

"We'll call you if there's a problem on our end," Pemberton said, and pressed his finger on the button that switched lines on the phone. "Joe, it's happening," he said. "Let me know when you have confirmation."

"You got it boss," the husky voice said from the speaker.

The room was quiet except for Sheldon's labored breathing. No more cries could be heard from down the hall.

"I don't see any more incoming," Pemberton said after scanning the monitor.

"So what now?" I asked.

Pemberton looked up as if he'd forgotten that we were there. "I'd be lying if I didn't tell you that I'm a little pissed that you've interfered with my plans Braddock."

"You've got your money," I said, keeping my gun trained on Pemberton's head and my body in front of Lauren's.

"But what about six years of my life Barry?" Pemberton leaned in close to the producer's face. "What about the rest of my life?"

Sheldon just closed his eyes and whimpered, "I'm sorry. Please … please…"

"It's in the account," Joe's voice from the speakerphone said.

Pemberton smiled. "Joe, you know what to do," he said to the phone. Then edging towards the door, hesitating for a moment at the entry, still pointing the gun at us he said, "I'm sorry," and backed out of the room.

I immediately turned, wrapping my arms around Lauren, driving her off her feet with every ounce of strength in my legs towards the wall, below the shelf where the Claymore was mounted.

As I felt Lauren's body collide with something hard and crumple under my weight, every other sensation was obliterated by the blast, but not before I could think, *Oh no Vic I wasn't fast enough…*

CHAPTER 29

The pain from ball bearings ricocheting into my back, and especially into the back of my legs, burned like red hot nails driven into my flesh, but the feeling turned me almost giddy with the realization that I was alive. I couldn't hear or see anything, because the mine exploded inches from my ears as I'd driven us just under the blast pattern, and the room was a whirling storm of dust and smoke. I felt movement underneath me, which meant that Lauren was alive.

I asked her if she was hurt anywhere, but I couldn't even hear my own voice, let alone Lauren's. I remembered that I still had the earpiece from the radio stuck in my right ear, and when removed, it became obvious that the piece had supplied some protection from the noise of the explosion, because I could faintly hear Lauren screaming, "Get off of me. Get off of me, I can't breathe," as if she were somewhere far away instead of squirming right underneath me.

I pushed myself off her and the effort brought more complaints from the areas where my skin was bruised, punctured and torn from the shrapnel of the Claymore. Not so much pain or damage though that my limbs refused to move, and again another wave of silly joy swept over me, with the realization that I had been able to tackle Lauren so that we fell under the funnel shaped body of the mine before it was detonated, escaping the direct impact of the projectiles.

I'd held onto my weapon. I shoved it into its holster, coughing and gasping with Lauren as we tried to suck in whatever oxygen hadn't been displaced by the dust and the concussion of the explosion. In the dim light that spilled into the room from the doorway, I could see the shredded remainder of Barry Sheldon's body, shredded from the full impact of the blast, and I was grateful for the lack of visible detail.

"Are you alright?" I asked Lauren.

I couldn't really hear Lauren's answer, but I could make out her face, and after knowing her for so long I understood that it was something to the effect of, "No I am not alright. What kind of a stupid question is that you asshole?"

Again I almost laughed out loud, because I was so deliriously happy that she wasn't injured so badly that I would have to choose between providing her first aid and going after Pemberton.

"Don't move," I said, "Stay here until I come get you." I knew that I only had moments before the dust cloud would begin to subside, and anyone monitoring the cameras in the hallway would be able to see me escape.

I ignored Lauren's protests as I crawled out into the hall on my belly, and scrabbled to the left along the grimy floor until I felt like I'd passed the fifty-yard effective range of the Claymore that was pointed my way. Then I got to my feet and started to run down the hallway. I had no idea which way Pemberton had gone when he left us, but since I had to make a blind choice, I chose the one that seemed the most likely and the least risky.

As soon as I felt completely out of range I slowed down and searched the walls, as well as the arched ceiling of the tunnel. Even this far from the blast it was difficult to see in the low light and the dust, requiring me to feel with my hands for the cables that carried signals to the cameras and anti-personnel mines. After thirty seconds I found the new cable trail nestled along the top of a two-inch piece of conduit, which was part of the many metal pipes and steel tubes lining the corridor.

I looked around for something that I could use as a cutting tool, but the only substance not fastened to the walls was dirt, so I followed the cable to where the next light bulb feebly illuminated the area around me. I tore the bundle of cables away from the wall until I had enough slack to get the cables down to where the light bulb was attached to the fixture. Then I broke the bulb, and used the jagged edges of what was left to cut through the insulation to the tightly wound copper strands in the five lengths of electrical and phone cable that provided command and control for the mines and cameras. If I had to double back, if Lauren or anyone else ventured out into the hallway, I didn't want them to fall victim to any more carnage.

Eliminating that threat took longer than I'd hoped, the fragile glass of the light bulb broke repeatedly from the pressure of the copper wires, but eventually all the strands were cut, and thankfully I hadn't heard any further detonations.

I drew the Kar .40 from its holster, finding that it was now slick with blood from the wounds to my back. I continued following the tunnel for what seemed like a long time, choosing to track the direction of the cable at the several intersections I encountered, groping my way along in the dark through the portions where the lighting was non-existent. A part of me was amazed by the extent of the tunnel network, and wondered where under the city I was traveling. At the same time, the pain from the flayed flesh on the back of my body lanced me with every move, concerning me about the loss of blood. Since there was nothing I could do about it, I just pushed forward until the band of cables wound up into a metal stairwell, much like the one I'd first come down with Sheldon, except that here the tunnel didn't dead-end, it continued on. I chose to follow the cables up. It was dark at the top of the stairs, and I knew that I'd be at a serious disadvantage if anyone was waiting for me up there, yet once I topped the steps I arrived in another storage room, with a doorway on the opposite side that was slightly ajar, letting in a small amount of daylight.

Until that point, I hadn't thought about trying my phone, and I hadn't replaced the earpiece for my radio, both of which I immediately attended to. I didn't have a signal on the phone yet, nor did I hear anything from the radio, so I continued to inch towards the rusted, metal fire door, finding it to have been battered in from the other side. Where a doorknob and deadbolt once rested, there were now just two holes with a chain hanging slack through them.

I listened for activity on the other side, but didn't trust my hearing, since it now sounded like I had the Pacific Ocean breaking on the beach inside my head and a throbbing headache had joined my list of physical complaints.

Carefully I nudged the door open, noticing a gravel floor on the other side of the threshold before scanning the open space diffused by the light coming from an opening to my right, which was blocked by something big and boxy that took up most of the area.

Again I paused before moving forward. When I didn't receive any warning signals I pushed the door completely open and followed my weapon into the void. My feet skittered on the gravel as I spun to the right and left searching for targets or threats, but the only thing that assaulted me was the powerful stench of urine and feces.

As my eyes adjusted to the new light I started to discern that the boxy structure was the rear of a truck. My right ear started to register sounds through the earpiece attached to my radio, but I couldn't make out what the voices were saying.

I edged my way towards the rear of the truck, turning at each step to swing the gun across my flanks, seeking movement.

The strange noises in my head and the physical pain were making me feel nauseous, but I kept moving until I was at the rear bumper of the truck. The cable that ran out of the tunnel snaked its way into an opening cut in the sheet metal of the vehicle's rear door.

I knew I wouldn't be able to discern sounds from inside, so I reached up to the handle, turned it, and swung the door open, immediately crouching back down to make the smallest possible target behind my pistol sweeping the cargo compartment.

Nothing met me but blackness, and I stood up slowly before hopping up on the bumper and stepping inside.

A makeshift monitor panel was set up on a tool bench that ran the length of the cargo compartment. The screens were black, and a crude multiple switchbox lay on the bench that no-doubt was the control for detonating the Claymores. I froze for a moment, with the thought that if I were going to abandon a command post like this, I would leave a surprise for anyone following me. I searched for trip wires or other devices, without finding anything, and was careful to retrace my steps exactly as I'd come in. Perhaps they were confident enough in their Claymore defense, or didn't have the time or the resources to booby-trap the truck.

I started to catch pieces of the radio transmissions being broadcast in my earpiece by the team, trying to make sense of what was going on at Union Station. I turned up the volume on the transceiver clipped to my belt, but I still seemed to be under too much concrete and steel to receive a clear signal.

Tossing some loose dirt from the ground into the air along the left side of the truck created a little cloud of dust that would reveal a trip-wire, but no threat appeared, so I stepped around that side of the vehicle. For the first time I could see what kind of garage or other enclosure I was standing in. The recognition of where I was hit me like a blow.

I stood beside the utility truck I'd witnessed earlier that morning, which was tucked into the alcove underneath the freeway overpass.

The tunnels I'd been following had brought me south, under the freeway and then east beyond the L.A. River. I recognized the DWP insignia on the driver's side door of the truck, beyond which I could see out into the parking area that ran along the river and the railroad tracks, abutting the building on Mission; the building that supposedly my people had under surveillance.

I fumbled to activate the switch on my radio mike, "This is Braddock. What channel are the people using, who are watching the Mission warehouse?"

Either my ears, or the radio, hadn't recovered sufficiently from having the clump of C-4 in the Claymore go off a few feet away from them, because I could hear sounds, but I couldn't understand the words, as if someone were shouting at me from a long way off. When the transmission stopped I gave my position, and explained that I was deaf because of an explosion. I also notified whomever was listening of Lauren's location, and told them I'd deactivated the Claymores.

I couldn't understand what the response was, but it was short enough that I felt comfortable believing I'd been understood.

I moved up to the mangled chain link gate that once closed off the area and peered around it, through the tall weeds growing on the other side to see if I could locate any of my people. I began doing a radio check, searching for my surveillance team through the nine radio channels on my transceiver, when I sensed motion in the weeds to my left. I rolled to my right, and came up with my weapon pointed at a homeless woman. She held up her hands and said, "Richard it's me, Willie. Hold your fire."

I wasn't sure if I really heard her, or if it was because I could see her lips move that it made the words easier to understand, but I recognized her as my employee, Natalie Williams, who had smeared dirt into her face, hands, hair and clothes as part of her cover.

"Willie," I said, "You scared the shit out of me."

I had to slow her down, and ask her to repeat several times, so that I could follow her lips, when she told me that a few minutes earlier, two men matching the description of Pemberton and Banning, exited from behind the truck and ran to the door of the Kramer Cable building.

"And?" I said.

"Nobody had intel on the hostages, or could figure out what happened to you, so we let them go. Then Marianna just radioed that you were here."

Then she held up a finger while she listened to her radio earpiece.

"Copy. Copy, I'm with Richard now," she said into her mike, then looked up at me and using exaggeratedly loud and articulate speech she said, "The loading doors of Kramer Pipe are opening on Mission."

Instinctively I grabbed Willie's arm and started to run, dragging her with me.

"Radio your team to get on channel one," I said. "Then Call 911," I shouted, "Tell them we've got a hostage situation with shots fired and one dead."

I looked over at her face and knew she wanted more details, but I let go of her arm and she stopped to key her mike, at the same time that she dug for her phone with the other hand.

As I sprinted across the dirt and gravel parking lot, I could see the roll-up door at the back of the Kramer Pipe building begin to open.

I switched my transceiver back to Marianna on channel one, and keying the radio mike, said, "Marianna, get the helo to my position. They're starting to rabbit."

I was closing on the back of a dirty white cube van, with Asian writing on it, halfway to the building. Garbled noise issued from my radio earpiece, as the roll up door on the back of the Kramer building reached its zenith. Gulping air into my burning lungs, I reached the van and peered around it to the open door, but all I could see was the trash on the empty loading dock, and one brick interior wall. Then a dark green older model Jeep Grand Cherokee burst out of the opening and launched off the four-foot drop of the loading dock. It landed hard, sparks spraying from the front bumper and undercarriage, but it continued to careen forward, the driver cranking the wheel hard right and slamming on the brakes to avoid colliding with a tractor-trailer that was driving parallel to the railroad tracks in the parking area.

The big-rig driver locked up his brakes just before the jeep skidded broadside into the trailer, creating a turbulent haze of gravel dust. The impact sounded strangely muffled to my damaged ears. Either the car stalled, or some entangled metal kept it from moving for several moments, and in that time I tried to cross the fifty yards separating me from the crash-site faster than I'd ever moved in my life. Through the windshield I could see Pemberton struggling to get the Cherokee rolling again, and next to him in the passenger seat, Victoria was trying to pull her hair away from her face, with hands clamped at the wrist in silver cuffs.

Chapter 30

Pemberton must have sensed me closing on him out of the corner of his eye, because he tore his attention away from the dashboard to stare straight at me as he worked the gearshift into reverse. Even my injured ears could hear the engine rev past its red line, followed by the shriek of scraping metal as the Cherokee lurched backwards, freeing itself from the trailer.

Pemberton slammed the shift lever down, and the Cherokee accelerated forward, turning straight for me, where I stopped, took aim, and squeezed off three shots into Pemberton's side of the windshield, which reflected the morning glare.

When the car's grille got within a few feet of me, I dove forward onto the hood, trying to turn as I leapt, so that my back was the first thing to catch the impact. I was tumbled up the windshield and onto the roof of the car, where I attempted to grab onto the bars of the luggage rack, but couldn't. I continued to roll, slipping off the back of the Jeep, landing hard on the gravel.

I was still conscious though, and looked up to see the car accelerating away from me towards the alley that exited to Mission Road.

Staggering to get my legs under me, I fumbled to activate the radio mike, "Pemberton has Victoria. Green Grand Cherokee, coming from back of building. Don't let it get away," I croaked.

Then the Cherokee started to swerve, first a little to the left, and then an over correction to the right. It turned left again in the right direction, but not quite on track, before it started to wobble, and then nosed into the side of the vegetable wholesaler's building, grinding to a stop.

I stumbled as quickly as I could towards the green Jeep, but before I could cover more than a few of the two hundred yards that separated me, Steve Kelvin's black Tahoe shot across the parking lot, skidding to a stop, so that its front bumper wedged the Cherokee against the building. Kelvin flew out of his door, crouched behind the hood of his own vehicle, and pointed his weapon at Pemberton's window.

I'm sure Kelvin was screaming orders to Pemberton, but I couldn't hear them. I was running to Victoria, certain that Pemberton was a dead man, after taking three of my hollow points in his upper body. Only I was feeling the effects of the punishment my body suffered in the past twenty-four hours, and it seemed like one of those dreams where you're exerting every bit of energy to move forward and yet it seems like you're traveling through molasses.

Then the jeep lurched forward, dragging the Tahoe with it, knocking Kelvin to the ground with the vehicles open door.

I wondered if I was hallucinating - until it struck me that of course Pemberton was wearing body armor. My weapon was loaded with hollow point rounds, which are designed to expand and shatter on impact, causing terrible damage to the unprotected target, but useless for anything other than causing a massive bruise to someone wearing a Kevlar vest.

Gravel, dust, and trash, flew into the air, as the four tires on the Jeep churned, tearing the vehicle free of the Tahoe. On the ground, Kelvin rolled into a prone firing position, and emptied the clip of his pistol into the rear tires of the Jeep.

My ears registered the sounds of the gunshots, and the tires rupturing, as I closed the last thirty yards to the Tahoe, leapt behind the wheel, threw the vehicle into gear, and tromped on the accelerator.

The four-wheel-drive Jeep's front tires were still intact, dragging the vehicle forward, while the rear wheels sprayed sparks and a plume of dirty smoke and burning rubber. The Grand Cherokee lurched around the corner, into the alley that ran between the bridge and the last of the warehouses bordering the river.

I followed the Jeep up the alley to Mission Road, where Pemberton turned right and pushed his injured vehicle as fast as it would go past the open gate of Kramer Pipe. "Pemberton has Victoria… Green Cherokee southbound on Mission… abort all other pursuit," I barked into the radio. My mouth was dry and brackish from dehydration, also from inhaling the smoke emitting out of Pemberton's melting rear tires.

The Jeep reached the next intersection, where he scraped a left and drove uphill on a street lined with low-income apartment buildings. From my earpiece, I thought I heard Marianna calling out coordinates for the other pursuit vehicles in our team, but couldn't be certain.

I gained ground on the Cherokee as we roared past the entrance to the Gabriel Garcia Elementary School, where the street started sweeping to the right following the hedges and fencing that bordered the campus.

The black plume of smoke the Jeep was creating obscured my view of Pemberton or Victoria, but as we rounded the broad corner, I could read the brake lights illuminating through the haze. The Jeep swerved left and I could see past it to the next intersection, where one of our surveillance vans was parked broadside, blocking the street. Then Pemberton swerved to the right, jumped the curb, and the Jeep crashed through the chain-link fence separating the school's playground from the sidewalk.

Gym teachers and young children no more than eight or nine, dressed in their Phys-Ed uniforms of dark blue shorts and white t-shirts, scattered or stood paralyzed as the Jeep careened into their midst.

I skidded the Tahoe to a halt on the sidewalk, but I couldn't pursue the Jeep, because frightened youngsters were running past the hole in the fence that Pemberton's Jeep had created.

I leapt out of the SUV and used the hood to steady my arm, aiming for a headshot, but Pemberton was moving too quickly and there were too many civilians crossing my line of fire in front and behind of my target.

Pemberton threw the car door open, looked up, and raced around to the rear of the vehicle where he opened the back hatch and pulled a long green tube out of the cargo area. He then disappeared from my view on the passenger side of the vehicle.

I ran around the hood of the Tahoe and pushed my way past the distraught children, who were trying to get out of the schoolyard through the fence. The children screamed and ran back towards the Jeep when they saw the gun in my hand.

Once I was through the fence I moved cautiously towards the vehicle, trying to understand what my adversary was doing. I could see my wife's hair in the front seat. It looked like she was bent over, but I couldn't tell if she was trying to protect herself somehow, or was in a bad way.

Leaves, aluminum cans and dust, began to swirl into the air all around the schoolyard, and I was trying to understand what was happening, when a flash erupted from behind the Cherokee and something streaked into the air, followed by an explosion so loud that my damaged ears had no trouble processing it.

I looked up, and saw a helicopter with its engine area aflame only several hundred feet above us. In what seemed like slow-motion, the aircraft wobbled in the air, then the body began to rotate as it dropped from the sky in a smoking heap, crashing into the roof of an apartment building adjacent to the far side of the schoolyard.

Even before the helicopter impacted the building my mind registered that Pemberton had just killed Marianna, the pilot, and whomever Marianna had chosen to be her shooter.

I found myself running at full speed towards the Jeep and when I was a few feet from the driver's side I launched myself into the air, diving over the roof of the SUV, because I saw Pemberton trying to pull Victoria out of the vehicle.

When I collided with him, I was trying to butt him in the face with the point of my hairline, but missed, and we sprawled onto the pavement of the schoolyard. My momentum crushed him into the pavement and then bounced me off, spewing me along the tarmac.

I was disoriented for a moment after hitting the ground, then scrambled to right myself. I must have lost my weapon when we impacted, because I realized I was barehanded.

Pemberton was attempting to get his feet under him, and it looked like he was digging for a weapon at the same time. As he stood and was twisting, drawing his weapon from a cross body holster in his tactical armored vest, I drove my right shoulder into his torso.

He grunted satisfactorily as my weight crushed him into the ground, and I felt sure that he was suffering from the beating his chest took from the three bullets that impacted his vest. I struggled to gain control of his gun hand, but the best I could do was keep his arm pinned to his body. I was spreading my legs to leverage an upper body control position when his weapon discharged, and my leg felt like a spike was driven through it.

Five more blasts erupted from his firearm, some hitting my legs, some not.

I felt the surge of panic, knowing that I would not be able to fight much longer, and put all my efforts into keeping him under me until help arrived.

Pemberton was also fighting with the crazed ferocity of someone knowing their life will be weighed by the outcome of their exertion.

My strength was ebbing perceptibly, I tried to neutralize his legs with hooking maneuvers, but I felt his lower body twisting away. Pemberton was gaining position, and despite what force I was able to apply, he was close to where he would have enough advantage to roll me off of him.

I sensed someone moving near us, and I heard the sounds of a woman's voice, but I couldn't understand what it was screaming.

Then a weapon fired four times near the back of my head, and Pemberton's face disintegrated from the impact of hollow-point shells.

I rolled over to see Victoria, holding my Kar .40 in her cuffed hands, with an expression of hatred, disgust, and disillusion on her face.

Epilogue

The Sunset Tower Hotel rises above the core of the Sunset Strip with the elegant beauty of a bygone era. Much like the stars who once adorned its penthouse such as Marilyn Monroe, Zsa Zsa Gábor, and Clark Gable, the building casts an image of sensuality, glamour, and pulchritude, which seem inimitable today. It was also notoriously rumored at one time for maintaining the best-kept call girls in Hollywood. The fact that Holiday Landau chose it as her personal residence suggested that the building's reputation wasn't as anachronistic as its allure.

I hobbled into the sun of the Terrace Bar, where a view of West Hollywood and the entire South Bay created a backdrop; leaning on the cane I'd acquired since abandoning the crutches I'd hopped around on for too long. Holiday was reclining on a chaise by the pool, in a pomegranate colored bikini and large, floppy hat.

She waved when she caught sight of me, scissored her long lean legs girlishly, and sprang to her feet. She wrapped a flamboyant Colin Heany silk sarong around her waist, slipped into a pair of high-heeled Manolo Blahnik sandals, before sashaying over to me. Watching her, it was hard to believe that there was anything masculine being veiled artfully. She kissed me Parisian style, smelling of coconut oil but mindful not to stain my clothes with it.

"How are you darling?" she said, stepping back and regarding my appearance with a critical eye. "The cane makes you look very old world chic – scrumptiously sexy as always."

She hooked my arm proprietarily, and we moved to a table that Holiday had reserved for our lunch.

Once the formalities of ordering and small talk were behind us, she said, "How is your heart, love?"

I shrugged and looked out at the panorama of Los Angeles falling away from us. "You know," I said, "when I was a little boy the fairytales all told me that all I had to do was rescue the fair princess and we would live happily ever after... but that's not really working out."

"Oh," she shook her head, took a sip of her Kir Royale, and said, "Those fairytales lied their ass off to me too honey – but then Cinderella didn't have to find a slipper that fit a men's nine and a half..." She laughed at her self-mockery. "Is Victoria being nasty?"

"No." I shook my head. "No, it's a very civilized divorce. We still care for each other, but as a friend of mine said, 'A fish and a bird may fall in love, but where shall they build a house?' It's like that."

"That sounds like the story of my life." She finished the remainder of her drink, and hailed the lean, tan, male server, for another. I nursed my Tom Collins.

"I thought about visiting you in the hospital, but I figured you had enough going on without having to explain why this old whore was bothering you."

"You're one of the most decent people I know, Holiday."

"Flattery will get you everywhere," she said, batting her long lashes. "Seriously though, I didn't want to bother you while you were mending, but now I want to know everything." She elongated and emphasized the last word theatrically.

"With all the lawsuits I'm involved in, I don't want you to be called as a witness."

"As if a jury would take anything I said seriously."

"You'd be surprised."

"Then why don't we play a little game?" She smiled at me devilishly.

"When I was asked that question as a little boy, it got me in a lot of trouble with Marcy Mednic."

"Well, wasn't she lucky. My game however, will keep your clothes on – for the moment."

"Okay, shoot," I said.

"I'm going to tell you what I've heard, and if it's true you don't have to say anything, then all I would have to testify to is where I heard it. If it's not true, then you have the opportunity to set me straight, so that whatever I say on the record is, La Vérité. Ne C'est Pa?"

"Okay." I smiled.

"Well," she said dramatically, "I heard that you had a meeting with Rikki Wymen, where you explained all of the embarrassing things about her behavior and goings on at Paragon under her watch, which would come out in discovery if they went after you?"

"Our insurance companies are battling it out behind closed doors," I said.

"I also found it interesting that Paragon's parent company made a large donation to the re-election PAC of our D.A., which coincided with a plea bargain for Robert Nilgore, and Marnice Bellstein the ex-studio accountant who'd set up the offshore ransom banking distribution network, in exchange for their portions of the ransom and their silence?"

"Amazing coincidence," I said.

The deaths of Barry Sheldon, the Blackthorn men in the service tunnel, and the lives lost from crashing helicopters, were an embarrassment for the LAPD and difficult for any government official to explain, so they stonewalled the press, saying that they couldn't comment about an ongoing investigation, until the twenty-four hour news cycle found more juicy subjects to prey on. Nobody wanted to advertise how easy it was to eliminate the low-flying aircraft, or that one could obtain with little difficulty the Russian SA-18 missile that Pemberton used. Joe Banning, Pemberton's accomplice also carried an SA-18 slung over his shoulder on the motorcycle he used for his escape, and unlike his unfortunate boss, Banning disappeared after downing the helicopter that was sending police cruisers after him. The LAPD didn't want criminals all over LA shooting down their eyes in the sky, which made escapes from pursuit so rare these days.

"Did you know that I use Leslie Kaminoff's company for my various websites?" she asked.

"They're a good outfit," I said.

"He just paid cash for a 1.2 million dollar house on Lani Kai, in Hawaii."

I sipped my drink.

"I also found out, that the house belonging to the widow of the guard who died trying to save Lauren's life, was also paid off in cash last month. What was his name? Dan Irvin."

"Dale," I said.

"A little birdie also informed me that even though you lost most of your client base, you only laid a few people off, and that Star Shield kept everyone on payroll, even if they didn't have assignments?"

Our lunch was served. I'd ordered Cioppino, which required a lot of physical attention, skewering tender morsels out of the mussel shells, dealing with the tails on the shrimp, sopping up the rich broth with crusty pieces of fresh baked bread. All of which I paid great attention to, saying nothing, while Holiday picked out only the candied pecans from her roasted beet arugula salad with gorgonzola, and continued to horrifyingly impress me with the information she'd obtained from her network.

To perpetuate the Studio's ruse that the ending of the movie was being re-written to make Lauren's character stronger, Rikki hired writers who actually accomplished that task. Lauren was a trouper, and five days after paramedics evacuated her anonymously from the tunnel, she went back to work and completed *Forced Conclusions*. However, the experience caused her to take a long look at her life; she didn't come out publicly, but decided not to hide any longer. Lauren fired me, fired Star Shield Security Group. Other clients followed suit, citing a number of innocuous reasons, or not even bothering with an excuse.

Then a strange thing happened. Eventually, as the facts were whispered, from one friend to another around both the entertainment and the security industries, it became understood that Lauren had been targeted, not because of a failure in security - Dale had given his life trying to save his client - but because of a failure to fund enough security. Dale Irvin's name was murmured with the respect due a true folk hero, because every operative in the business knew the same could have happened to him or her. When our clients sought new contractors, they found our competition, instead of circling like sharks, using the rumor of Lauren's kidnapping as a cautionary tale to increase the protection orders for their established customers, and stating that they weren't willing to guarantee a different outcome under the same circumstances, unless they were given a bigger budget. Eventually a number of our old clients came slinking back. All of the studios boosted their star security orders, and now everyone was busier than we'd ever been.

Lauren hired us back also. Once she got over her anger at me for leaving her alone in the tunnels, and she learned that my wife had also been kidnapped – the two women were kept separated when they were in captivity - Lauren came to visit me in the hospital, informing me that she and Mika were going down to Brazil where they were going to be married. She asked me if The Bull would be available to lead a team that could provide for their safety and privacy - but only the privacy that any public couple desired. That good news arrived on the same day that Victoria's divorce attorney had me served with the official papers, so it was with bittersweet gratitude that I told Lauren Star Shield would be happy to provide her with whatever services she required.

After the plates from my lunch with Holiday were bussed and double espressos were placed before us, we shared a mango and loquat sorbet. Holiday said, "I also heard that there might be a new woman in your life?"

I looked her in the eyes, and said sadly, "No. No, I don't think I'm ready to go there yet."

"Really?" she said, scrutinizing me. "Well, people sometimes talk about what they wish were the truth, instead of reality."

She let me off the hook after that. While we finished our coffee, she dished the dirt on some people we mutually disliked, and she shared some sad news about other people who we had regard for.

After a while we just sat, watching the beautiful people posing around the pool, and then I tossed my napkin on the table, and said, "I've got to get to physical therapy."

"My apartment's just up the elevator," she said. "I could work you out, and ease your tension?"

"I've been playing for the same team for so long," I said, pushing myself up with my cane, "that a trade this late in the season would be bad for the fan base."

"Well," she said, in mock disdain, "If I get turned down with a sports metaphor, I know I have a crush on someone who's irreparably straight."

She stood also, and I limped around the table, where I took her in my arms and hugged her tightly with all the affection I had for my unique friend.

"You're the best," I said.

She pushed me away, "Go do your physical therapy, before I get an erection and embarrass us both." Then she turned and slinked back to her chaise by the pool, signaling to the waiter for another cocktail.

I'd lied to Holiday, and she knew it, but I didn't want to confirm anything that might hurt Victoria more than she'd already been set back in her life.

I headed west on Sunset at a leisurely pace. I called the office to check in and then spent the rest of the trip wending my way into Bel Aire, working the phone, addressing the immediate problems of the day: I had to explain to a new client that it was not the responsibility of his personal protection to walk the star's one-hundred-twenty-pound Mastiff, nor was it the guard's job to clean up after it. However, I assured him that it was no trouble for me to retain someone who would care for the dog. Another call was spent listening to an irate music producer expressing his anger because our employees hadn't prevented his artist from scoring or taking mescaline, which prompted the musician to take all of his clothes off, hug everyone in the studio, and spend the rest of the time he was supposed be laying down tracks humping the dimpled acoustical foam on the wall of the recording space.

When I parked at the UCLA Medical Center campus, I excused myself from the call, after explaining for the third time the parameters of Star Shield Group's responsibility to its clients, and then spent the next several hours in the pool, the weight room, and on the massage table, rehabilitating my legs.

Then I traveled to my divorce digs, an efficiency suite in the Shangri-La hotel overlooking the Santa Monica beach.

I showered and cracked a cold Corona, slicing a couple of lime wedges and drizzling their juice into the neck of the bottle. Then I went out onto the balcony and watched the waves slide over the sand.

When I was in the hospital and our clients were leaving the firm like rats from a sinking ship, The Bull gathered together the team, putting them to work on a project of his own. They hunted down Joe Banning, who was hiding in Chang-Mai, Thailand, where he'd planned with Pemberton to build a sex-tourism resort with their combined share of the ransom.

Though The Bull was able to persuade Banning to provide access to the account where Banning's three million dollars were stashed, he still had to recruit Kaminoff to unlock the four and a half million that was sequestered in the account Pemberton had set up for himself… for which Kaminoff charged thirty percent of the take. As the sun disappeared over the horizon, I contemplated the ethical ramifications of the decision we'd made regarding the use of the rest of our salvage. It was thirsty work.

My hearing had returned, but it would never be what it once was, so my ears didn't register the lock turning on the front door to my apartment, but I did feel the door shut when the sea breeze pouring in from the balcony helped close it with a bang. I left the view of the ocean to see something even more beautiful. The giggling smile emanating from the Director of Investigations for Star Shield Security Group, Marianna Ruiz, as her curvaceous brown skinned figure hopped out of her Givenchy ankle boots. When she was barefoot, she let out a little sigh of relief, then skipped a little on her way across the carpet and into my arms. Her mouth tasted salty, spicy. Her body was warm smooth and soft.

When I'd ordered Natalie Williams to call 911, she stayed on the phone with the emergency dispatcher, who directed an LAPD helicopter to the Mission Road location. The Police pilot ordered all private aircraft, including the helo that Marianna was flying in, out of the immediate airspace. Therefore, it was two officers from the Air Support Division of the police department who lost their lives when Pemberton shot them down with the Russian manufactured missile.

Marianna was instrumental in The Bull's operation hunting the remaining kidnapper, she posed as a prospective sex worker interviewing for a job to gain access to Banning. Once our business started picking up, and I was still incapacitated, she shouldered some of the client relations and other duties I usually performed that The Bull had no stomach for.

One night, after I'd moved to Santa Monica and was starting to get around on my own, Marianna brought over some checks that needed my signature. I offered her a glass of wine, and she made fun of me as I tried to navigate my way out onto the small terrace, which created a serious obstacle for someone just learning to use his legs again.

Marianna is such a good investigator because she has no shame about broaching uncomfortable subjects. Soon we were talking about the ways in which I let Victoria down.

"I can't have children," she said eventually, looking off at the moon's reflection on the Pacific Ocean. "I had an abortion when I was seventeen, …in Chile, and the doctor wasn't very careful."

She re-filled our glasses. "Besides, I'd have to give up this work, and I think I would resent the child, because I really love what I do."

We clinked glasses. A warm evening wind encircled us with the fragrance of Night-blooming Jasmine. Marianna smiled, the moonlight made her teeth seem iridescent, and then she kissed me.

"Did you just sexually assault your boss?" I said, when we finally separated from each other for a moment.

"Yes," she smiled that radiant smile again, "and you're a cripple, so there is not much you can do about it, so relax and enjoy…"

It may not be happily-ever-after, but it'll do - for real life.

READ THE BEGINNING OF THE NEXT RICHARD BRADDOCK ADVENTURE:

The Grammy Awards presents my company Star Shield Security Group our greatest celebrity protection challenge of the year.

Musicians are the wildest, meanest, most petulant, erratic, loudest, and destructive type of client. They become even more irreverent and outrageous when they get together. And they are also the most likely to leave unpleasant bodily expulsions in a Star Shield Security Group vehicle.

What also distinguishes music events from other operations is the broad spectrum of other security providers we must interact with. Even among the other professional organizations that provide highly trained, skilled celebrity protection agents to the industry, friction erupts as we jockey to provide the best experience for our individual clients. We are constantly moving them in and out of mandatory weapons screenings, to and from vehicles, into lines for photos, interviews, cocktails, or the ladies room - always at the same time everyone else wants to be expedited. At these events headliners from every musical discipline who are used to being the *Most Important Person,* are downgraded to being just another VIP. This affects the egos of their elite protection staff as well.

Added to the mix are the yearly one hit wonder-overnight millionaires, who will often select the toughest thug they grew up with as their personal bodyguard, so that invariably a number of gangsta homies, redneck country bikers, and boyfriends who took some karate lessons or played linebacker, are swaggering around with their attitudes and chests puffed out attempting to muscle their way past protocol. This pisses off law enforcement and venue administration, causing them to clamp down restrictions on everyone.

As the evening wears on, every winner in each category creates four artists or group of artists, who suddenly feel like a loser. And it is rare that this feeling is expressed with grace or dignity. The security organizations that are able to protect their clients not only from the outside threats, but also the hazard they pose to themselves and others, are the companies who are given priority and leeway by the events promoters, producers, LAPD, and venue security supervisors.

On Grammy night more than any other, even the Oscars, the protection agent's skills as a psychologist-friend-confessor-cheerleader and diplomat are usually more important than their physical ability, tactical acumen, or combat experience. This year Star Shield Security Group provided personal security for fifteen of the nominees. The televised presentation is the culmination of Grammy week's narcotic and alcohol fueled parties, dinners, non-televised ceremonies, after-parties, orgies, and early morning raids on diners across Los Angeles. By the time it is over everyone is functioning on little sleep, a lot of caffeine or varied pharmaceuticals.

For me, Richard Braddock, this was the longest period of time I'd been on my feet without rest since being shot several times in the legs while trying to rescue my ex-wife from a kidnapper. My back, knees, quads and calves were screaming at me in protest. I resorted to leaning on my stylish hickory cane that otherwise I hadn't needed in a while.

"Number 3 is no joy and on the move to limo," crackled in my earpiece over the radio. The voice belonged to Natalie "Willie" Williams, the twenty-year veteran of the Los Angeles Police Department who was now the Star Shield Major Event Coordinator. She was advising me that our client, who hadn't received the gramophone for Best Pop Vocal Album, was ready to leave.

My company had been working the Grammys for a little under eight years, but in that time we'd earned a reputation with the promoters and police as a company that 'played well with others…'"

"Mike, I need to get number 396 up here pronto," I said to Mike Delancey, the off-duty LAPD Captain I stood beside, who was in charge of transportation coordination in and out of the Staples Center.

"You're going to have to wait a minute Braddock, one of the old guard is finishing her performance and she wants to get away before the mayhem starts."

"Age before beauty?"

Mike Delancey smiled and spoke into his handheld radio, commanding his people to herd the limo drivers in his prescribed order.

We were standing in the Talent Exit Coral - TEC, a waiting area in the bowels of the Staples Center furnished with black leatherette couches, plastic chairs, cocktail tables and an open bar. Red velour curtains were hung around the area to hide the loading dock and giant trash compactor behind them. Stained red carpet, no doubt retread from last year's entry area, was duct-taped together covering the smooth concrete floor. A number of the CEO's from the entertainment industry's exclusive protection firms huddled around Captain Delancey with me: Yuri Herzog from Blackthorn, Cavin DeVecker of CDE, Robert Steele from Steele Curtain, and several others who had earned priority with Delancey. We stood on a little platform a short way up the drive to the street where we had a vantage point of the whole area. Anyone not escorted by an agent working for one of the companies represented on the platform had to present their assigned vehicle ticket to a valet captain in a red jacket, who would then radio the limos to descend into the cavernous receiving area on a first-come - first-served basis, subject to the interventions of Delancey and his officers on our behalf.

The night's winners were still in the backstage and press areas getting their photos taken with the highly coveted trophies and vamping for anyone with a camera or microphone. The TEC was populated by a diverse group of losing artists and their entourages waiting for their limos so they could get to a party or club where they could drink, snort, or shoot their sorrow away, and then decide who they were going to blame for their failure.

True stars, the men and women who are iconic, radiate a charisma that is equivalent to natural phenomena such as heat or wind that you can sense ethereally. Most of the throng assembled in the TEC became moved by just such a power as incredibly strong clear heart wrenching notes began emanating their way up the tunnel connected to the arena. Char, one of the industry's groundbreaking Divas, was winding up the medley she was performing with one of her pop hits from the '80s, sung a cappella. The lyrics from the dance tune, now wailed as a soulful torch song, held the entire Staples Center enthralled for a moment that seemed to step out of time. Almost everyone in the TEC stopped talking completely and turned their attention back down the tunnel leading to the arena, as they were magnetized by the undeniable purity of the music.

Everyone that is, except for two rappers and their entourage who were arguing with each other, unable to hear Char's beautiful melody because of the hip-hop tracks they had pumping into their iPod ear-buds at full volume.

From the tunnel we could see the drop of the stage lights after the Diva's final crescendo, then the Staples Center rumbled with such intense applause it felt like an earthquake. After the superstar took her bows, and the event host began introducing the next presenters, the waiting musicians in our area remained turned expectantly towards the tunnel.

Yet the two oblivious rappers, and their four tank-sized, blinged-out body guards were still in a heated debate over whether or not screwing a second cousin was incest.

As Char glided down the tunnel, resplendent in an ivory Bob Mackie gown and headdress, she was preceded by her longtime bodyguard, John Geuylas, who was rarely called anything other than

Johnny G. The artists assembled in the TEC parted and respectfully applauded the woman whose career spanned four decades in which she'd garnered not only a trunk-load of Grammys, but also a number of Emmys, Tonys, Golden Globes, and an Oscar.

In my peripheral vision I caught Char's inbound silver limo descending the ramp to the pick-up area. At the same time I noted that the rappers spotted the limo and seemed to think it was theirs. A spike of warning adrenaline sent a tingle into my back and arms, and as I propelled myself forward I checked my nearby colleagues to see if any of them registered the same concern, but each man held his hand to his earpiece, attempting to listen to a transmission from one of their teams over the continued applause that echoed in the cavernous loading area.

I watched the rapper's behemoths push their way through the crowd towards the arriving limo on a collision course for Char's retinue. I cut across the area where the limos made a wide loop so that they could be facing straight up the driveway when they picked up their charges. Just before I descended to the level of the crowd I spied The Bull, my second in command at Star Shield, emerging from the tunnel - well behind Char's people. He was escorting Kalina, the beautiful Afro-Indonesian singer who'd just lost the Best Pop Vocal contest.

"Bull head's up," I said into the radio mike. "I may need backup at the pick up area."

"On my way," The Bull's baritone resonated in my earpiece, but already I could see we were too late.

Though the valet captain was imploring them to wait, the rapper's men didn't seem to hear him over the tunes in their headsets and the first of the meaty gangsters, wearing a gray LA Kings hat turned sideways, shrugged past the valet captain. He arrived at the rear door to the limo simultaneously with Char's lone protection, Johnny G.

"What do you think you're doing old man?" the big man in the Kings hat said when Johnny reached for the door handle.

"Excuse me?" Johnny said.

"Don't be trying to poach our limo, this here silver one's ours."

"Cool your jets kid, there's more than one silver limo at this event tonight."

Two more of the rapper's guards crowded in on Johnny, having pulled out their ear buds to hear what was going on. They each wore leather jackets and LA Lakers hats turned backwards.

"That's right and this one's ours, cracker. We been waiting for thirty minutes. You just got here."

Johnny G. looked to his client apologetically and said, "Yeah, and when you've put in the miles she has, they'll bump some shit-bird's limo for yours, but in the mean time, step back and let the lady get her ride home."

I was just coming around the trunk of the limo and I could feel some of the other pros in the room moving towards the confrontation when the clown with the Kings hat said something that ended in, "… your white bitch," and tried to shove Johnny out of the way.

Johnny had been guarding his client since the early seventies, and the big gangbanger was right, he was an old man. But Johnny was still sharp and strong. He rolled his shoulder under the weight of the bigger man's movement and using a seoi-nage judo move, pitched the rapper's guard onto his back in a direction that was careful not to collide with his fragile client.

Unfortunately the effort left Johnny with his back to the two in the Lakers hats and one of them grabbed Johnny in a half-nelson while the other moved to his left and wound up to punch. The gangster was so intent on mayhem he didn't even notice the sixty-four-year-old woman in the white gown that he knocked into.

I dropped my cane, leapt and caught Char just as she was toppling off of her high heals, scooped her into my arms and carried her away from the fray. When I was certain she was safely in the hands of her manager, I turned back to the fight. Another artist's security person had attempted to intervene, but the fourth of the rapper's gargantuan bodyguards had engaged him and they were grappling near the front of the limo.

The instigator had lost his Kings hat but regained his feet, and he was taking turns with his partner in the Lakers hat punching Johnny, while their cohort maintained the older man in a headlock.

This was the first real confrontation I'd encountered since being shot. I'd started sparring with The Bull every day as soon as I'd been able, but it was with a twinge of trepidation that I launched a roundhouse kick with all my weight behind it into the kidneys of the large African-American man who had been wearing the Kings hat. All my sewn-together parts held together on impact and delivered the satisfying sensation of a well-placed strike hitting its target. The big man let out an involuntary below and his knees gave way. My leg thankfully whipped back quickly without the pain I'd expected and I stepped in to land two hooking punches into the man's fleshy head, feeling his skin tear as my knuckles pinched it against the bones of his face.

The thug who'd been punching Johnny G. turned to face me, but before he could engage, a blur rushed out of the crowd and the two hundred-fifty pounds of muscle that is my partner The Bull, slammed into the big gangbanger, propelling him into the side of the limo with such force that you could hear ribs cracking. The Bull then stepped back and rained punches and kicks to the head and body of the gangbanger that left him crumpled in the fetal position.

As soon as I saw that The Bull eliminated my immediate threat I focused on the remaining thug holding Johnny G. clenched in the double shoulder lock. He looked panicked seeing his posse crippled so quickly, and swiveled to keep Johnny's body between us. Johnny's face had taken some crushing blows from the two men who'd beaten on him. I heard the shouting and could sense the arrival of uniformed police officers running down the driveway from the street where they'd been stationed for crowd control. I was content to just keep up our little dance until the cops arrived, but the panicked attacker probably knew that wasn't going to work out so well for him, so he thrust Johnny at me.

Here too I would have preferred to aid my comrade and let my adversary try to escape, but once he was free of Johnny's encumbrance I saw him reach into his leather jacket for what I could only assume would be a weapon. So instead of catching Johnny, I stepped sideways, placed my hand on the handle of my ASP expandable baton, and drew it from its holster in the fluid snapping motion that extended it to the full length while arcing towards my opponent's right ear. The cracking sound of steel impacting skull and tissue stunned him and slowed the hand pulling the weapon out of his jacket but didn't stop it. My second slash of the baton came down mercilessly on the wrist of his gun hand, sending the weapon clattering to the pavement. Then the police arrived with their fire-arms drawn commanding us to disengage.

When I checked on Johnny all he would say was, "Get her out of here," over and over, so I made my way to the frightened enter-tainer and her companions, secured a path for them to the limo and made sure that they were safely away. By that time paramedics were seeing to Johnny and the police had the four idiots who started the trouble cuffed. The belligerent rappers were complaining to the po-lice that their security had been provoked, which only encouraged the cops to put them in bracelets too. I went looking for The Bull and checked in on the radio to see if any of our other clients were impacted by the disturbance.

Thankfully the rest of the night only contained my usual work of facilitating our team in whatever way necessary. I filled in while one of our people changed clothes after being vomited on, fished out Neosporin and Band-Aids from the first aid kit in our Escalade when a singer broke her wine glass and refused to leave the EMI after party. I then drove to Griffith Park to explain to a client, who was blazing on acid with his two ragged looking groupies, why their Star Shield protection agent wasn't allowed to help them break into the LA Zoo so they could pet the animals.

At ten o'clock the next morning, when I finally arrived at the Shangri-La hotel in Santa Monica, and drew the blackout curtains against the bright sunlight flowing into my apartment and climbed into bed, I'd forgotten the fight that was going to open the door to a world I'd never traveled in before.

ABOUT THE AUTHOR

David Elliott started his artistic career as an actor, playing leading roles in the feature films *Jaws 2*, *The Possession of Joel Delaney*, *Phantom of the Open Hearth*, and *A Rumor of War*. Except he found that playing "let's pretend" was an unreliable way for a man to make a living. So he's also worked in Hollywood as a professional boxer, set builder, private investigator, and building contractor. He serves on the Executive Board of a major entertainment labor union, and as a PI, was elected president of the California Association of Judgment Enforcement Professionals.

Mr. Elliott is happily married to artist Gabrielle D. McKenna-Elliott. In addition to raising their son, the couple enjoys playing hockey and exploring the world with skis, bicycles, kayaks, or on foot.

www.ingramcontent.com/pod-product-compliance
Lightning Source LLC
Chambersburg PA
CBHW071246170626
46809CB00001B/87